HOUSES *HAVE* SECRETS

HOUSES HAVE SECRETS

HOLLY KNIGHTLEY

ISBN: 978-1-958761-70-0

Cover design: Marshmallow Designs

*For my husband,
for this story came as a dream on his
birthday*

CONTENTS

CHAPTER ONE
The Same Dream

All was blood. All was red. All was death. From a tumultuous sleep, my eyes flashed open, my lashes fluttering like bird wings braving a storm. I dreamed of blood last night—like the night before—like I had every night since my adoptive father, Franklin Fielding, went missing.

The warm, viscous liquid painted my small hands in violence. The rusty smell of blood formed a tincture mixing with the red wine on Mr. Fielding's breath. Blood was not thicker than water. I was blood and he went to hurt me. He was blood and I killed him. Who was I kidding, I was adopted. I was water. I was expendable.

I lay in the center of the bed with my arms and legs tucked under the stiff hotel linen as if being blanketed in starch could protect me from all of the blood. This dream had haunted me since childhood. There were so many unanswered questions when Mr. Fielding went missing. So much so that they manifested in my nightmares every night like a cruel joke. I wasn't surprised that Hilton's luxury suites didn't prevent the dream from creeping into my sleep like some unwanted visitor, like a vampire. But in my nightmare, it wasn't a creature of the night who spilled blood, it was me—Trinity Dunn Fielding, spiller of blood, dreamer of blood, bringer of death.

It was always the same. In my dream I killed Frank Fielding. How—I don't know. My dream didn't show me that, I just knew that I did it. Why—that I knew. I felt it. It was self-defense. It was him or me and I chose me. But that wasn't right. Mr. Fielding would never hurt me. I came to live with the Fieldings after my father died—after Mrs. Fielding died. My father and Mr. Fielding were business partners and in both of our moments of grief Mr. Fielding took me in without a second's hesitation. Mr. Fielding, Franky Fields as my father used to call him, was a great man. He proved it, becoming a second father to me at thirteen years old. It was at this tender age that I joined the Fielding family business of scaring people.

The Elenore Fielding House, for which my sister Elenore was named, needs no introduction. The ancestral home built by Emmit Fielding for his wife Elenore hits every top ten list of America's most haunted houses. The Elenore Fielding House is an old brownstone located on one of the busiest streets in downtown Brooklyn, New York.

The Fieldings were sitting on a gold mine but refused to sell the property for development, leaving them a house and no money.

Mr. Fielding refused my father's generous offer to buy the property, but from their first meeting they became close friends. A prosperous friendship and partnership flourished, transforming the Elenore Fielding House into a tourist trap. My father's entrepreneurial spirit saw the value in a *real* haunted house. He invited mediums, psychics, and paranormal investigators from all around the world to the house. Their testimonials put the Elenore Fielding House on the map and since then the house has been a favorite haunt of ghost hunters, thrill seekers, occultists, and a bunch of people who wore black and liked spiky things—hair, bracelets, belts—and anything you could put a spike on or through.

Four years ago, Mr. Fielding disappeared. He was presumed dead, but for all I knew he was alive and living it up on some tropical island. After all, his body was never found. There was no body to lay to rest in his casket, but nevertheless, we interred it—interred an empty casket to give us peace. A peace I still have yet to find.

Staring at the ceiling, my eyes homed in on a small watermark on an otherwise blank canvas. Ruddy as the stain was, it wasn't one of those tiny droplets of spilt life that enveloped me in a sea of red every time my eyelids closed. No—there was no blood. The sight of it, the smell of it, it was gone.

I was being silly again. A dream is a dream, and nothing more. Blood wasn't lurking under my bed like some monster ready to eat me or do whatever monsters do. My parents, both sets of them, are dead. I had no one to check under the bed for me. If I was scared, I had to do it myself. I was fine with that. I was raised to be tough. My father wouldn't have it any other way. A monster I could handle. A monster can be killed. But how do you kill something that's already dead? How do you dispel blood?

I shook my head at myself. I didn't need protection, and I didn't need a mop and bleach. I needed a strong cup of coffee with a shot of espresso. Make that four shots. I was about to become a living part of the Fielding quilt work again. It had been nearly four years since I'd seen my adoptive family. My oldest sister Elenore sent me plenty of emails and texts keeping me abreast of their general going-ons. But seeing my adoptive family in the flesh, well, that was something entirely different from reading about their lives as if they were just characters in a book.

I could have spent the night at home, but I feared seeing the Fieldings. There was a time, not that long ago, when I couldn't bear to be apart from Chamberlin and his sisters, Elenore and Madelin, and Mr. Fielding too. But after Mr. Fielding's funeral, I left the Fieldings and the place I once called home and went to college abroad. In London, I was far from the scene of the supposed crime, far away from guilt, and far away from Chamberlin Fielding.

The Elenore Fielding House was no stranger to death. Emmit Fielding, his wife, and daughters were among the first to die there. My father died in the house. Mrs. Fielding died in the house. The last death was *believed* to be Frank Fielding's, that was until

HOUSES *HAVE* SECRETS

yesterday when I got the call my little sister Madelin was dead.

CHAPTER TWO
The Same Goth Kids

I stood on the other side of the street from the Elenore Fielding House, surveying the home I had spent so much time in as a child and had lived in for four years as a Fielding. It was exactly how I remembered it. The over two century old brick home was painted a matte black that was somewhere between the color black, as desired, and an ashen gray. The shutters were black as well as the keystones, but they were glossy and shone in the sunlight as if they were metallic. The front door was also black. In short, the Elenore Fielding House was one big, black blight on an otherwise charming street, which was precisely what the Fieldings wanted. They wanted spooky. They wanted haunted. They wanted people to stop and stare and feel the pull of the old house daring them to enter.

The Elenore Fielding House was a particularly bewitching sight to behold with its new hipster neighbor. When I lived in Brooklyn, the house to the left of the Elenore Fielding House used to be a private residence but was now Plant Haven. It looked to sell exclusively air plants in all sorts of upcycled containers including what looked like soup cans and seashells. The store to the right was

Mikey Loves Brooklyn. Mikey's, as the locals called it, was a staple in the neighborhood. It was a thing before the Elenore Fielding House started giving ghost tours and is the best novelty shop this side of the bridge, selling everything from 'I Love New York' shirts to condoms. Admittedly, I had regularly shopped in Mikey's when I lived next door. Not for condoms, but for T-shirts and hats, not that I ever wore them while at home, but they were great to sport on the few ventures out of the borough. And then there were the stickers. My 'Brooklyn Does It Better' sticker from Mikey's ended up on my laptop. Every time I saw that sticker I thought of home.

It was weird to think of the haunted house across the street as my home, but it was. I felt it. Just like I felt that Mr. Fielding was dead. Before I officially moved in, I felt much as my father had—I belonged there. As a silly girl, I took it as a sign that Chamberlin Fielding and I were going to get married one day and I would become Trinity Dunn Fielding, the lucky wife of the most beautiful boy in the world. Well, my prediction did come true, I was Trinity Dunn Fielding now, just not in the way I thought I'd be.

At that moment, as a cool spring breeze rustled my hair, I thought of my father. He always said, as he patted the top of my head like I was The Grand Duke Wiskerton, my Great Aunt Girty's Persian cat, "Redheads have the ability to see into the future. There's something special about you my li'l Trinity Dunn. Redhaired women from the Dunn line all have it. Great Aunt Girty has it and you have it too."

At this point he would rattle off a bunch of names I only ever heard in this proclamation. He always told me to trust my gut, which was a saying that never failed to gross me out. I'd imagine the insides taken out of a turkey at Thanksgiving and set aside for The Grand Duke every time he said it and that was quite a bit. My father was very big on repeating himself. I think he did it for emphasis or maybe he just liked to hear himself talk. Either way, he had said to me time and time again, his Irish accent always sounding extra thick, "My li'l Trinity Dunn, trust your gut. It's more than just a feeling, it's a fact."

These days, I couldn't make out the difference between

hunger pangs or an upset stomach. If I did have some special ability passed down to me from all of the redheads on my father's side, I outgrew it, leaving my sixth sense or second sight in the past when I moved to London.

I had felt it in all of my heart, and in truth my gut, that one day I would be a Fielding. My adolescent prophecy had come to pass, but it happened at such a terrible cost. I no longer wanted to have these sorts of gut feelings. It was like I willed the universe to bring about my desired result, but things got messy. The universe didn't understand how I was supposed to become a Fielding and in this cosmic confusion took the lives of my father and Mrs. Fielding.

As silly as it seems, I have always harbored guilt for their deaths. I was just a thirteen-year-old little girl with a huge crush when they died, but someone had to be blamed. I never spoke a word about this 'gut feeling' to Chamberlin. I was worried he too would blame me for his mother's death and that would change things between us. Things changed anyway. There was nothing I could have done about that.

As I was crossing the street, I watched, with great curiosity, a young man who had been standing at the front door of my old home for some time. I could tell he was reading the sign posted on the door, and from how long he was standing there he either reread it several times or the Declaration of Independence was nailed to the front door. Being that cursive was no longer taught in the public school system, the poor guy would have to go about deciphering it like it was hieroglyphics. I couldn't read the sign on the door from my vantage point. I could only make out the white square on the otherwise black horizon, but I knew the gist of it. 'Sorry we are closed due to a death in the family.' I knew the Elenore Fielding House ran on scheduled tours but also allowed for walk-ins. My sister Elenore would never turn away a customer. She was the kind of person that had cash signs flashing in her eyes like Alvin the Chipmunk. If a tour was full, and maximum occupancy met, she could always fit you in for an additional fee. It would kill her to even turn away this one guy.

As I stood at the foot of the stairs to my old home, I noticed the young man was not a man but rather a teenager or maybe a college student. It was hard to tell his true age with the amount of makeup he wore. His eyeliner was drawn on in a thick smear. The combination of the chalk-like eyeliner and the shadow cast on his face by his spiky hair that resembled Sonic the Hedgehog made him look like he had two black eyes. He was one of those goth kids that were as common as rats in downtown Brooklyn. I felt cheated. He didn't have on a matching spike choker to go with his hair. In place of this tried-and-true rite of passage was, from what I could tell, a dog collar. The collar was beyond conspicuous, made of a red leathery material meant to look like alligator skin. From it hung a silver heart-shaped locket with the letter X engraved on it.

The goth approached me so suddenly, I found myself taking a step back. He was a lot taller than he looked from across the street.

"You think it's true?" he asked.

"What?" I said, still taken aback by his abrupt manner. Brooklynites were aggressive when provoked, maybe the most aggressive in the country as the New York hello is the middle finger; however, for the most part, Brooklynites keep to themselves. The sacred dogma of 'Mind-your-own-business' is instilled in us since toddlerhood.

"The sign says the house is closed due to a mysterious death in the family," he said, pointing to the front door.

"Oh, uh, well yeah," I stammered. I was also surprised by his very deep voice. It was so deep it almost had an echo to it. It seemed too manly a voice for its owner.

He smirked, with a grin of black lips that matched his black jeans and T-shirt. "You think a ghost did it?"

I should have thought of the family business and fed into his delusion like a true Fielding would have and answered: 'I'm sure a ghost killed whoever died', but I was too tired to think on my feet and answered with something near the truth. "We're not sure what killed my sister, but Maddy was found dead."

I knew that part was true. Maddy was found dead. Elenore didn't say more than that. She said it wasn't the type of thing to talk about on the phone and she'd fill me in when I got there.

His coal-colored eyes seemed to come to life, like the response kindled a fire in him. "You're Maddy's sister?"

"Um," I said, surprised he seemed to know Maddy, although evidently not well. News of her unexpected death didn't seem to upset him. Collecting myself, I answered his question as if this was a formal interview. "Yes. I'm Trinity Dunn Fielding. I'm adopt—"

Before I could finish my sentence, he had his phone out. "Can I get my picture with you?"

My eyebrows pinched together in surprise. "Um . . . yeah, sure, I guess," I said awkwardly as he pulled me closer to him and snapped a picture.

"Thanks," he said, looking at the picture pleased. "Sorry to hear about Maddy." He scrolled through his text messages. "I'm friends with your brother. I guess he hasn't told anyone yet. I'd be the first he'd tell. I should've said I'm his *best* friend. I'm sure he's mentioned me."

"Uh . . ." He pointed to his choker. "Uh, X," I said, as if that sorted everything out. X—Chamberlin's best friend.

"Short for Xavier," he went on to say, "but everyone calls me X."

"Yeah of course. Chamberlin mentions you all the time."

"You're a terrible liar," he said flatly, sliding his phone back into his jeans pocket.

I flushed. I could feel the heat rush to my cheeks. That's what I got for trying to be nice.

"Chamberlin isn't much of a talker, but nice of you to say. I know if he was more talkative, he would have mentioned me. That's just how we are. We can just hang out without talking and it's all good. That's when you know you're really close with someone. Chain and I transcend words. It's like we read each other's minds and communicate on this otherworldly plane of existence."

Wow, this kid was out there. But he was right about Chamberlin being quiet. After his mother's death he became taciturn, barely speaking to anyone, even me, and at the time I *was* his best friend. After his father went missing, he went silent for a year.

"You must be his sister who lives in London," X ventured.

"I am," I said, happy that with the few words Chamberlin did say, he had mentioned me.

X extended his hand to me now, as if a handshake made our meeting somehow official in his eyes. "Stoked to meet you, Trinity."

After we thoroughly shook hands, he opened the locket on his collar. It housed a black and white picture of my brother on one side and a picture of himself on the other. It was altogether the creepiest thing I'd ever seen. I was starting to think X was a stalker.

"I'm the founder and president of the I Love Chamberlin Fielding Fan Club."

I swallowed my laugh, seeing how very serious he was. Again, stalker popped into my mind.

"Yeah, it's an honor to work so closely with your brother. Like I said, he may not say much but he's a real enigma. My sister and I can't stay away from him."

Stalker. I smiled. What else could I do?

"I have to ask," he said thoughtfully as he closed the locket. "Is Chamberlin a vampire?"

"Huh . . . what?—No."

"I know he walks in the daylight, but that doesn't rule out vampirism. Everyone knows there're workarounds for that."

I'm the worst Fielding ever. I should have confirmed his suspicion. I'm sure Chamberlin being a vampire was good for business, but there was something about the way X looked at me that made me pity him. X may have been unsure if my brother was a vampire and turned into a bat, but I was sure he believed he walked on water.

"He's not a vampire."

X shook his head as if my denunciation confirmed it. "I wouldn't expect a member of his coven to rat him out." Taking my hand, that moments ago he'd shook, he flipped it over and examined it like he'd never seen a hand before. "You're really pale."

"Goes with the territory of being a redhead. I basically glow in the dark."

He scrutinized me. "Maybe," he said, seemingly ascertaining if I too was a vampire.

His phone dinged. Releasing my hand, he pulled out his phone. He beamed a smile of all teeth, and for the first time I noticed he had braces on. The black bands on each of his teeth made him look like he was missing a few pearly whites.

He flashed his phone in my direction and said, "It's from your brother."

I couldn't read the message, but I saw Chamberlin's name and picture pop up. Another ding. This text seemed to satisfy his Chamberlin Fielding fix, X was quick to leave. After taking a few steps towards Plant Haven, he turned around as though he just remembered we'd been talking. "Maddy really is dead," he said in a low voice. "I thought it was a publicity hoax, but it's not. Chamberlin just confirmed it."

I nodded.

With that, he turned about like he had experience in a marching band, his turn one of calculation and stiffness, as if he held a great trombone on his shoulders. In the blink of an eye, he disappeared into Plant Haven, the airy store darkened by his presence.

CHAPTER THREE

The Same House

I pulled the old iron house key from my wristlet and walked up the granite stairs that had been tread upon by thousands of visitors. I couldn't help but feel a little special. I was amongst the few to call the Elenore Fielding House home. Before inserting my skeleton key, one of a set that opened all the doors in the house, into the old brass lock, I read the sign that had engrossed X. 'The Elenore Fielding House is closed until Tuesday due to a mysterious death in the family.'

I rolled my eyes, turning the clunky iron key. Yep, nothing like a mysterious death to drum up business. I wasn't surprised Elenore had posted something like that. It was typical of her mindset, but still I thought it was crass to use our sister's death as marketing. 'House closed for renovation'. 'House closed for a family emergency', or just 'House closed' would have sufficed. This was Brooklyn after all. You didn't have to write a plot for a novel. Closed is closed.

I glanced up at the looming black door, at the trim arched above my head in several flourishes, before putting my shoulder to it with a shove.

I entered the house, passing through the portico and opening a pair of stained-glass doors with golden torches that led into the house's foyer. Red ribbon foiled around the torches like musical notes where they formed a bow over a laurel wreath.

The house was dark, much darker than the sunny street I just left. And quiet. That was the one thing about the house that unnerved me. Not that it was supposedly haunted. I never saw concrete proof of that. The house, despite having the old-fashioned 1700's sashes with single pane glass as thin as a sheet of ice, somehow blocked out the noise from the busy street. I'm sure the dark paisley curtains helped with that. Nevertheless, the silence in the Elenore Fielding House always astonished me. It was as though the house wasn't in Brooklyn but on a hill in the sprawling countryside by itself, far away from people, places, and chirping birds.

I took in the house, sweeping it over in a panoramic view. Things appeared the same, which wasn't a surprise. The Elenore Fielding House had looked that way for centuries. The Fieldings went through great pains not to change anything in the common rooms of the house, with the exception of updating the kitchen. The gray floral wallpaper was the same as it had been in Emmit Fielding's time. The hand painted keystone border, in greens and grays, below the crown molding was the same. The pictures adorning the walls were the same. Sure, new pictures were added over time, but an old one was never taken down to make room for a new one. And once up, it was up. Not to be moved under any circumstances on pain of death—so I was told. The house was a living time capsule, and the Fieldings—caretakers of their ancestral home—were slaves to the past.

My eyes surveyed the newel post of the heavy staircase. It was a skyscraper of walnut with an angel steepled on its peak. The angel's outstretched hands held a torch. The stained-glass doors and the angel were said to light the way for lost spirits—or so the guided tour went.

The angel, though beautiful with a pensive face and long

curls of ebony, was always a source of tension for me. That was because her wings were cut off. All that remained were jagged stumps where wings used to be. Chamberlin had told me, when I got up the courage to ask about the wingless angel, that Emmit Fielding, the builder of the house and his great-great-great-grandfather, had cut the wings off himself when his daughter Ivette died. Something about God taking one of his and he would return the cruelty. You could still make out the different shade of wood from where the crude cuts were made. This contrast between the stained and unstained wood gave the impression that you saw the fleshy part of the wing—saw the raw wound through the raw wood.

There had been no attempts to cover it up. It was part of the tour as well. Little Ivette Fielding died at six months old under mysterious circumstances, as all deaths in the Elenore Fielding House were said to be. The story goes, you can still hear the cries of Baby Ivette when you walk past the angel. Or, as the tour guide is supposed to muse: Is that the cry of Baby Ivette or the angel?

Chamberlin confided in me that he thought Emmit Fielding cursed the family when he cut off the angel's wings. We were eight years old then, and I was sure he was trying to scare me. It was his lot in life to scare people, after all. Nonetheless, that day he'd told me, as we stood next to the newel post that was taller than us, that the Fielding women always died young as atonement for the angel's wings. In a whisper, as if the angel and other things were listening, he went on to explain it was a little more involved than that. He said the angel of death would claim a Fielding girl every so many years until it could take their wings in heaven as its own. He mentioned finding a suitable pair of wings to replace the ones taken was a very hard thing to find. Wings were like fingerprints and that made the angels quest burdened with Fielding blood. He had relayed this as though he knew a lot about the subject matter, and I held my breath at his every word. It was a memory I replayed in my mind every time I saw an angel with their white wings and golden halo and wondered if angels were pious or if they were cruel as Chamberlin had me believe. I wondered then, as I looked into the sad eyes of the angel, if Maddy went to Heaven when she died and if cutting off her newly begotten wings would satisfy its bloodlust.

CHAPTER FOUR
The Same Boy

I had enough of the angel. I would saw off its head if I thought it really played a part in Maddy's death. Those were meditations of children, and I was twenty-one now. I made my way to the kitchen that was located in the back of the house. I decided to take the long way, cutting through the dining room versus walking past the stairs to the kitchen's other entry point. I was surprised, so much so, I found myself clutching my chest in shock. If the old rule of moving something or anything came with the pain of death, maybe this was the thing that did Madelin Fielding in.

The bay window to the right of the stairs, which used to function as a seating nook for visitors needing a break from a tour, was transformed into a gift shop. Some small partitions were put up to better showcase the wears. I understood and even saw the practicality in the Elenore Fielding calendars, stickers, and tarot cards, but then there was the 'I Love Chamberlin Fielding' merch. *That* was cringe worthy. My brother's face was on stickers, shirts, notebooks, and a whole lot of other kitschy things, from socks to hand sanitizer. I picked up a sticker with my brother's face on it, one of a few choices. This particular one was heart-shaped and featured him wearing vampire fangs denoting him as The Vampire Chamberlin.

"Trinity?" a voice said from behind me.

I turned around, shoving the sticker in my overnight bag's front pocket. I knew that voice. It was Chamberlin. I had seen pictures of him thanks to the Elenore Fielding House social media pages, but to see him—to really see him—stopped my heart. I resisted hitting myself in the chest to restart it.

None of the photos captured the real Chamberlin Fielding—captured those heavens that lived in his blue eyes. He looked down at me from his bowed head, a side effect of his youth. He was relentlessly teased as a child about his long, dark eyelashes. So much so, that the first time I met Chamberlin, he stood before me as he did now with his head bowed—his sandy colored hair shadowing his eyes, when his sisters informed me that their brother wore makeup.

"It's true," Elenore, the oldest, had said. "He sneaks into Mother's makeup every morning and puts on her eyeliner."

"I've seen it," Maddy told me. Maddy, being the youngest, was quick to collaborate with anything her older sister said.

I couldn't see Chamberlin's face to judge for myself. He kept his head down supposedly in reverence to his sister's tyranny. I was no stranger to being picked on. Though I was an only child, my red hair and freckles were often the subject of ridicule at school.

"Do you?" I'd asked Chamberlin. "Do you wear your mother's makeup?"

He shook his golden head.

"He says he doesn't," I had said to his sisters with the most scathing look my eight-year-old self could muster. "And I believe him."

It was then he lifted his head to me, and I saw those eyes. Never had I seen eyes like his. They were as light as tropical waters, and his thick, dark lashes covered them like the plumes of some exotic bird. I had never seen a boy as handsome as Chamberlin Fielding. He may have been teased as a boy, but no one was teasing him now. He was more beautiful in his manhood than ever he was as a child. And he was a child god.

His light eyes looked at me from their downcast position, his lashes dusting over his high cheekbones. I could see why X thought he was a vampire. It seemed inhuman to be that beautiful and still be mortal. He had to be something more, something not from this earth, something divine, as his younger years had hinted at. Or, maybe something evil. But that didn't matter. He held the kind of beauty that made you weak in the knees.

"What are you doing here?" Chamberlin asked, his voice trailing off like he lost his conviction to speak to me. His head lifted; conversely, his eyes remained downcast, avoiding my face like he was afraid that looking directly at me might turn him into stone.

"I flew in for Maddy's funeral. You didn't think I'd miss it, did you?"

His humbled head was bowed again, leaving his face in shadows. "I don't know what I thought," he admitted. A hot flush bloomed on his cheeks like rose petals painted on fine china. "You shouldn't have come," he added in a tone that was hard to read. Did he want me there or didn't he? His words would indicate the negative, but his tone had a pleading quality to it, like he didn't quite say what he meant.

"She was my sister," I said, running my hands down my black dress. It was a simple and elegant dress and didn't need to be fussed over. It required no straightening, or flattening, or adjusting; however, I needed to keep my hands busy, so I did all of the above to it and more in the name of anxiety.

"Your sister is dead. You should have come before that if you cared about her or Elenore—or me." Like before, he didn't say this unkindly but more as a reflection as if he wished I had come sooner but couldn't say the words.

It was astonishing he'd said as much as he did. After Mr. Fielding's disappearance, the Fielding family was turned upside down. We all dealt with it differently. Elenore, then twenty-one, took charge, becoming the matriarch of the family. She took legal custody of me and Chamberlin, who were sixteen at the time, and Maddy, who was fourteen. She had acted as the mother to her younger siblings after the death of their mother. It was natural for her to step into the role as mother and father.

Chamberlin, who had already changed so much after his mother's death, retreated further into himself after his father's disappearance, not saying a word. It was like his father's disappearance was the final blow to his already shaken constitution. Chamberlin was always a sensitive boy, not at all what you would expect from someone with looks like his. He could've been a jerk, a bully, but he wasn't. He didn't have an ounce of viciousness in him. He was kind and thoughtful and when his father disappeared, he wilted like a flower bud hit by frost. He was still there clinging to life, but the flower of his life had died off and only a shadow remained of what could have bloomed.

We spent a year looking for Mr. Fielding before Elenore decided to inter an empty casket. At the time, I thought, like X had thought upon hearing the news of Maddy's death—it was a publicity stunt. The Elenore Fielding House had a boom in business when the news broke that Frank Fielding went missing without a trace. Interring an empty casket was sure to get the newspapers circulating the Elenore Fielding House name again and bring about another whirlwind of tours, but Elenore said it was for Chamberlin. That he needed peace. And it did give him a little. I guess Elenore did know best—she always claimed she did. Chamberlin, who had not said a word since his father went missing, sobbed at his funeral. He sobbed so long and so hard, it was like his tears spoke a language only he and the departed understood. After that, he seemed to wake up from the burden of his father's disappearance. He'd say a few words here or there, no longer relying on head nods and hand gestures, though he was permanently changed. Maddy was changed too. And so was I. I can't deny that. After the funeral, I couldn't bear to be there and sought my peace at college abroad.

The day before my flight was to take off, Chamberlin had asked me not to go. It was the first words he had spoken to me the entire year we looked for his father. And it was the last words between us until today.

His voice was so familiar to me, I could never have forgotten it, though it had a coarseness to it that had not been there before. It was like a scent that brings you back to your childhood, magically transforming you into the person you used to be. That's how it felt the moment I recognized his voice from behind me. All of my girlish feelings came rushing back to me just as they did that day he asked me not to leave. I ran from them. He was my brother now, no good could or would come from my feelings. But as I stood across from Chamberlin in the gift shop, surrounded by his likeness on novelty trinkets, I knew there was no running away from this. The feeling was deep inside of me, buried so deep it seemed attached to my soul, lodged in my gut—a gut feeling. My father's words rang in my ears, 'My li'l Trinity Dunn, trust your gut. It's more than just a feeling, it's a fact.' I wasn't wearing a collar with a locket to denote my undying love and attachment to Chamberlin like X, but I might as well have been. My love for Chamberlin Fielding hung around my neck, choking me.

CHAPTER FIVE
The Same Elenore

The silence between Chamberlin and me grew into tension. It killed me to be so close to him and not have the honor of seeing Heaven on Earth. I wished he would look at me.

"Sister!" cut through the silence like a knife.

We both turned our heads toward the stairs. Elenore was trotting down them, her arms already outstretched before her like Frankenstein's creature. In a moment, I was in her arms, and she was swinging me to and fro like I was still a child. In truth, I hadn't grown very much since I left. I, like my father, was petite. It was one of a few traits I shared with him along with my red hair and auburn eyes. I just hit five feet tall, and my figure was more child-like than any woman would desire. I overcompensated with a water-bra, platform shoes, and wore a cosmetic store's worth of makeup. I felt exceedingly small in Elenore's hands, not that she was much taller than me, but it was the way she jostled me about like I was a wrapped present, and she was trying to figure out what was inside. "So glad you came, Sister."

'Sister' was the name given to me by Elenore when I was

officially adopted, and I hated it. She insisted everyone should call me Sister as a way to welcome me into the family. This was met with zero obstinacy, even on my part. I already knew what Elenore said went. The struggle would have been futile. So, from that point on, I was stripped of my birth-name and was known as Sister. I thought of Sister Bear from Berenstain Bears every time I heard it, resulting in a feeling somewhere between disgust and dismay, and it always produced a headache. I had more headaches in the name of *Sister* than any other sister in the world. It didn't help that Chamberlin embraced my new name. If I was his sister, I was his sister—and couldn't be anything more. Chamberlin calling me Trinity upon seeing me was just as surprising as the new gift shop. More things had changed than I thought.

Elenore finally released me, only to clasp my waist between her hands. "Sister, I tell you, you never looked so pretty," she said, as if my beauty radiated from my waistline. Elenore struggled with her weight. She always seemed to marvel at my smallness, so maybe she did think beauty came with thinness, but most people besides Elenore would agree I was too thin.

"Ain't that right Linnie?" she asked. "Doesn't she look pretty?" Elenore didn't wait for Chamberlin to respond. Her attention was back on me. "Black is your color, Sister."

I glanced at Chamberlin, a warm blush already on my face. He hated his nickname from his sister as much as I hated mine, even though Linnie was more of a generic name. Linnie was the name Elenore used for both Madelin and him. If she called for Linnie, Chamberlin and Madelin would both come running like puppy dogs. I guess there would be no confusion now.

As if he read my mind, Chamberlin said, "We should retire that name."

"Don't be stupid, I still have a Linnie," Elenore said, taking my overnight bag from my shoulder. "Here," she said, handing Chamberlin my bag, "make yourself useful and bring Sister's things to Dad's room." Her eyes rested on me. "That's all you brought?"

Chamberlin took my bag from Elenore and slung it over his shoulder.

"Yeah, that's it," I said. I wasn't staying long. I was there for the funeral, then back to London. "Did you say Dad's room?"

"Yeah, I spruced it up for you this morning," Elenore said in a chipper tone. "Clean sheets—the works." For a moment, her eyes darted to the floor before finding their way back to me. "I hope you don't mind we turned your room into an office?"

"*You* turned her room into an office," Chamberlin mumbled under his breath as he passed us on the way to the stairs. He was no longer slouching, apparently his frustration with Elenore gave him purpose of mind and body.

"It's not a big deal. You didn't know if I'd ever come home," I said, more for his sake than Elenore's, as she was clearly not bothered by the change.

Elenore took my hand, leading me into the kitchen as she spoke. "We started this new thing on the weekends where you can rent out the place to look for ghosts and ghouls. We call them Night-ins. It's bringing in big money and has been very successful. But I didn't like the idea that guests could go through my desk in the kitchen, so I moved everything into your room."

"I understand," I said. I'd feel the same. But letting guests roam freely around the house seemed reckless. "You rent the whole house out for the night? Isn't that . . . um . . . risky? What if someone gets hurt?" I had seen something about Night-ins posted on Facebook but didn't give it any thought.

Elenore had me sit down next to her at the kitchen table. I noticed the ceiling fan over the table was hanging cockeyed in such a way that it made it look like the plaster around it had crumbled. There had been an attempt to duct tape it to the ceiling. It was done with great care, the duct tape having been painted to match the ceiling, but it left the fan visibly askew. "Sister, always the practical one of the bunch," Elenore said. It sounded like she was chastising me. "Don't worry your pretty head about it. We had a lawyer draft up a whole packet of papers for guests to sign before they stay the night. It's all encompassing. Guests sign away their right to sue us, and there's a bit about the need to disclose any and all medical conditions. And in the event of an unforeseen medical emergency, we're not responsible. We're protected, too. We have the right to sue if any of our family heirlooms get broken. It cost a fortune to have it drawn up, but it was worth it for the peace of mind. But never mind that," she said patting my hand. "It's perfect. Guests arrive for midnight, we lock them in, and we head up to the attic."

The attic was the space in the house reserved for the family. It was always that way. From the first day I visited the Elenore Fielding House with my father, the common rooms were for the business, the attic was for the family. The attic was like its own house inside the house. It was a huge space with high pitched ceilings following the many steep angles of the roofline. We each had our own room and en suite bathroom. There was a small common space we called the rec room that served as a living room where we would play games. There was nothing cold and spooky about the attic rooms. To the contrary, the attic space was modern and warm and very bright, mind the furniture that was like the rest of the house— Fielding hand-me-downs.

"There's a big downside to the overnight guests," Chamberlin said, rejoining us in the kitchen but opting to stand rather than sit.

"What's that?" Elenore asked thoughtfully.

"The screaming."

She waved her hand dismissively at him like he was being silly. "It's no different from the screaming that comes from your room. Use ear plugs like the rest of us."

The thought of screaming coming from Chamberlin's room reddened my cheeks. The heat—unbearable. I cursed myself for having a fair complexion.

"It's not that bad," Elenore went on to say. I assumed she guessed my change in countenance was over the fear of loss of sleep. "I have extra earplugs, don't you worry Sister."

"It *is* that bad," Chamberlin protested. "Tuesday, we have a bachelorette party booked, so prepare for no sleep."

"You didn't cancel it?" I asked, wondering when we were going to talk about Maddy.

"Can't," Elenore said. "It was booked over six months ago,

and they already paid."

"I think they'd understand," I said. I knew Elenore was not one to turn away a paying guest, but Maddy just died. It seemed wrong to have people spend the night the day of her funeral.

"We already spent the money," Chamberlin said.

Elenore shot him a glare that made him bow his head. "Maddy wouldn't want us to cancel it. So, we're not." A silence filled the room. I was waiting for her to tell me what happened to Maddy. Instead, she asked me what I thought about the gift shop.

"The 'I Love Chamberlin Fielding' stuff is a nice touch," I said, the corners of my mouth turning up in a playful smile.

It was Chamberlin who blushed now, not the bold red I knew my cheeks turned but softly, like he was cold. "It wasn't my idea."

"It was X's," Elenore said, throwing her hands up in the air excitedly. "Oh, you haven't met X yet! He's great."

"Actually, I have," I said. "Outside of the house."

"Shoot, I hope you texted him," Elenore said, looking to Chamberlin who now leaned against the wall with his arms crossed over his chest, his head slightly stooped to avoid her eyes.

"I did."

"Good," she said, returning the conversation to me. "Usually X comes by in the morning to see Chamberlin and has breakfast with us." At this, she pushed a plate of homemade blueberry muffins in my direction. I took one to be polite. I wasn't hungry. "X lives next door. His parents own Plant Haven."

"Oh," I said, more than a little surprised. He didn't look like Plant Haven material. Mikey's—yes; Plant Haven—no.

She laughed, getting more from my 'oh' than I intended. "Yeah," Elenore tittered, "his parents are not happy about his friendship with Chamberlin." There was another laugh, this one sounding more like a wheezing sneeze. Collecting herself, she took on a snooty air overemphasizing her words. "His father asked me to discourage the friendship between his son and our brother. And that was over three years ago. Today, they're inseparable." Now she was imitating Darth Vader with his heavy breathing. "Chamberlin has turned him to the Darkside."

"So, uh, before Chamberlin, X wasn't wearing black?" I asked curiously.

"No," she laughed, shifting in her chair. She sounded like a piglet now, stringing her laugh together in oinks. "The first time I met him he had on a white polo and khakis with his hair parted down the middle. He was a sight. But Linnie—or Chain, as X calls him—cured him of that by the end of the week."

"I didn't tell him to change how he dressed," Chamberlin said.

She gave him another dismissive wave of her hand. "Of course not sweetie. He idolizes you. And imitation is the sincerest form of flattery."

"I don't dress like X," he said, with a rolling shake of his head, sending his long bangs flying about like a shampoo commercial. They fell along the cut of his cheekbones, like wisps of sunshine.

Elenore tapped on her chin in thought while I carefully peeled the paper shell from my muffin. "Well, you do wear a lot of black," she pointed out.

"That's because I'm paid to wear black."

"As you should," she said, wiping her hands on the tops of her thighs like they were dirty. "X worked hard to get you those sponsors, and the image is great for business." Her eyes were back on me. "Can you believe our brother almost has a million Instagram followers?"

"Uh, no," I said, covering my mouth as I chewed. "I didn't know he had Insta."

"I don't," he said.

"X runs it for him," Elenore said delightedly.

"X must be busy between Instagram and the fan club," I said.

"He is," Elenore nodded. "They both are. It's good for Chamberlin. Gets him out doing things."

"I hate it when you talk about me like I'm not here," Chamberlin said, his tone spiking.

"Well Linnie, be more active in the conversation, and I wouldn't."

Chamberlin breathed heavily through his nose. "What are you going to do when I'm forty and no one believes I'm a vampire and my sponsors drop me? You can't rely on this gimmick to last forever. We should be utilizing our efforts elsewhere."

Elenore grew serious for a moment before regaining her sanguine nature. "When that happens, we will hide you away, so no one knows you're an old man. X will run your pictures through as many filters as it takes to keep you young and beautiful. And please," she said, with a shake of her head, "don't act like you don't like the attention you're getting. I know you do. You can still plug away at your college classes online. I let you do that, don't I? This is the right thing for the business."

He rolled his eyes and muttered, "You know best."

She mused, "I do, don't I? I got us this far."

I acknowledge Elenore made sacrifices to raise us, and so did Chamberlin. We both nodded, falling back into our roles as complacent children.

"Speaking of business . . ." Elenore said, getting up. She rummaged through what we called the junk drawer. It was an infamous drawer in the kitchen, next to the sink, that held anything and everything you could possibly need to avert disaster. Elenore triumphantly held up two rolls of white duct tape. "You're about Maddy's size," she said to me with a twinkle in her dark brown eyes, "be a dear and lay down at the foot of the stairs while Linnie and I mark out your body."

"You're not," Chamberlin said, his eyes becoming stormy with what had to be frustration. "It's too soon."

"I am," Elenore said hurt. "It's my duty to make Maddy part of the tour." She gestured to me in the direction we came from. I got up from the table and followed her to the staircase. Chamberlin lagged a few paces behind. I turned to look at him. Our eyes locked and for a moment I saw Heaven.

The wingless angel's eyes were not filled with the soft blue of Heaven like Chamberlin's. They were dark—black. I laid down at the foot of the stairs. The wood floor was cold and hard beneath me. Elenore positioned my body, moving my right arm behind my head and folding my left leg. "Perfect, don't move," she said proudly, handing Chamberlin a roll of duct tape. From the corner of my eye, I watched him—watched his blue eyes web over in red—watched tears bead in the corners of his eyes—watched as one silently hit the floor.

Elenore, perhaps noticing her brother was crying, perhaps not, went about tearing and taping around my splayed limbs. "When I die," she said to him, "I hope you will add me to the body count in the house. Remember the Fielding's golden rule Chamberlin, you're not dead until everyone forgets you."

CHAPTER SIX

The Same Kind of Dead

I sat in the front row of Christie's Funeral Home, my vision aligned with Maddy's resting face. The news of her death didn't seem real until I was looking at her. It was true; she really was dead. Death—the dark art of decomposition—all looked the same to me. It dawned upon my consciousness that it didn't matter when or who you were when you died, death's mask was constant. We would all wear it, all look like that at our funerals. It's true, isn't it? The one certain thing in life is that we *will* die. It's the same inevitable truth in my life as it is for every single thing that was ever born.

I saw it now, clear as day. Maddy had the same blank countenance my father and Mrs. Fielding had. The soul was gone, if you believe in that sort of thing, and all that was left was the shell, like a hermit crab moving on to bigger and better oceans in the vast blue heavens. But if that was so, and things were better elsewhere— better far away from the people who care about you—why did they all wear that face? Why was it that no matter how hard the mortician toiled, they couldn't erase the traces of something darker? The cheeks, regardless of the cheekbones or age of the deceased, were always flaccid, like gravity affected them more than anything. They gave the impression of invisible fingers tugging on them from both sides. There was a restlessness to Maddy's stillness that made me doubt she, or any of the dead that came before her, was in a better place.

I couldn't look at Maddy any longer. My melancholy thoughts were compressing on my shoulders like boulders, and we were no longer alone. The room was filling up now. Today's viewing was the only chance for people to pay their respects. The funeral was directly after and for family only. Most people I didn't know, which was fine. I didn't feel like playing greeter like Elenore. She made it her duty to go up to everyone who entered versus letting them come to her. Chamberlin was his usual withdrawn self, hovering in a corner of the room like a spider. A beautiful spider, like one you see in a magazine and are dazzled by its fierce beauty—but a spider nevertheless. He was watching everything, his eyes spinning webs as he observed Elenore. There was something going on between them.

X entered with a small group of guys wearing top hats, and suit jackets with coattails, all sporting walking canes like they were part of a Charles Dickens reenactment. They must've been the elite of the I Love Chamberlin Fielding Fan Club who paid a premium to be near him. It was always business with the Fieldings. It should've been no surprise to me that Maddy's funeral was looked at as a cash cow. Chamberlin was as guilty of this crime as Elenore. The black suit jacket he had on was from one of his sponsors. They sent it to him to wear explicitly for his sister's funeral and expected a picture posted. It was a nice jacket that was a modern style, being slim fit and without tails, but I think it would have looked better without the embroidered skull on the breast pocket and the skull pocket square sewn into it. I wondered what he was getting paid to wear it and if it was worth it to whore himself out at his little sister's funeral for a couple of bucks.

Chamberlin wasted no time approaching X, a distinction that seemed to make X happy. He was smiling; his teeth looked black from where I was sitting. In a wave, X and the rest of his entourage took off their hats in a display of respect. It was like watching a bizarre dance. It concluded with the Vampire Chamberlin shaking their hands. I was impressed X's spiked hair was somehow still spiked after taking off his hat, not a hair or point out of place.

A tall young man I had mistaken as part of Chamberlin's fan club approached Maddy's casket. As he got closer, I wasn't sure why I'd originally thought he was with X. In place of Victorian garb, he had on a rather simple black suit jacket that was too small for him. His long arms poked out of the sleeves uncomfortably. He wore thick coke bottle glasses that he kept pawing at. In place of a top hat was a mop of dark, curly hair. He was sobbing in low hiccups that fogged his glasses until they were eye patches.

I saw it coming before it happened. Then it happened in front of me in slow motion. He tripped, tumbling to the ground in a reverberating thud, just missing Maddy's casket. Silence spread over the room. I'm sure for a split second everyone thought he knocked the casket over.

I helped him up as quickly as I could. He was easily over a foot taller than me, and I didn't do much in the way of helping besides directing him to a seat.

I had him sit down next to me in the front row.

"Thank you," he slurred through hiccups, his face as red as a strawberry and just as dimpled. I rubbed his back, not sure if that helped or not. It seemed to make his hiccups grow louder as though he was a cat purring under my caresses, but the noise coming from him was anything but pleasant.

"Did you know Maddy well?" I asked, still rubbing his back. That was a stupid question, and I regretted asking it as soon as the words flew from my mouth. He wouldn't be falling over sobbing if he didn't. He nodded, taking out a small cloth he had in his pocket, and wiped his glasses. He did this with great difficulty, as if without his glasses on, he couldn't see to clean them, and there was no way around this conundrum.

"Maddy was my sister," I volunteered, not sure why I told the stranger that. I guess I did it to fill the silence between the growling hiccups.

He donned his glasses, squinting at me from behind their thick rims. "You're Sister?"

I gave a soft smile followed by a nod. "My nickname precedes me."

"She talked about you every once in a while. She missed you. She always said she hoped you would come home one day and be friends again."

Chamberlin's earlier words about me coming home before Maddy died stung with a new life. My eyes instinctively went to him. He and Elenore were busy accepting condolences. I noticed Elenore take a man by the arm and lead him into the corner Chamberlin had been lurking in when we first got to the funeral home. The man looked very familiar. I had seen him somewhere. He was older. Not old, but probably in his mid-thirties. I knew I was an adult, but I still viewed myself as a child and thirty seemed far off. The man had closely cropped black hair and tan skin. He was dressed all in black like most people, but in place of a suit jacket was a leather one. He must've been hot. Even with the air on, it was warm in Christie's Funeral Home, thanks to the heat wave.

Elenore appeared flustered—something Elenore Fielding seldom was. This whole time she had been so composed. It was as if it wasn't her little sister lying in the casket. But now, I could see the strain on her face from across the room. Her cheeks were flushed, the redness traveling down her neck onto her chest. She wiped at tears that I couldn't see but knew were falling.

Elenore, as though she knew I was watching, excused herself and took the seat on the other side of me. No sooner had she sat down, did the tall man with glasses stand up and stagger off like he was drunk. My eyes followed him, afraid he would topple over again. It wasn't alcohol that altered his equilibrium—I would have smelled it. It was crippling grief. As he passed, he gave X, or maybe it was Chamberlin, the middle finger. Both X and Chamberlin seemed to be holding each other back, so it was hard to discern who the New York hello was directed at.

I was about to get up and see what that was about when

Elenore seized my hand and squeezed it. "I'm glad you came. I didn't think you would. It may not show, but I know Linnie is glad, too."

My eyes went to my sister's coffin, to her blonde hair that was the same shade as Chamberlin's and Elenore's—it was a trait they got from their late mother, Dorothy Fielding.

"I mean Chamberlin," she said. "He's right, the nickname should be retired."

My eyes darted to my stepbrother where he was surrounded by his little group. "He seems well," I said. "I'm glad he has lots of friends."

Elenore wiped a tear with her index finger as if she was cleaning dust from a window ledge. "Please, you know him. Besides X, I don't think he knows any of their names."

"But you do?" I asked, lifting an eyebrow.

"Of course I do, it's my business. So, trust me when I say he's happy you came home."

"I'm not home for long. My flight leaves tomorrow morning." Yesterday had been a wash. Elenore was so busy with funeral preparations that we hadn't had time to sit down and talk— really talk. Which meant we still hadn't discussed Maddy, and she didn't know my travel plans.

Elenore was wiping tears from both eyes now. "Wow, you really made your first trip home the pimple of your existence."

"It's not like that. I have people waiting on me in London."

"I'm sure you do," she said, moving a curl off my shoulder to better see my face. "How could little Trinity Dunn not have people waiting on her? But just so you know, you have people here who need you."

My face wrinkled. I felt like I was almost baring teeth. 'Little Trinity Dunn'. What happened to Sister? I could part with 'Sister', but I didn't think Elenore could. And what happened to Fielding? By stripping my name, I felt like she stripped me naked in front of everyone there. I glanced at Chamberlin to see if he noticed, then to Maddy's placid face. "Trinity Dunn," I mumbled under my breath, pulling my sweater on despite being hot.

"I want to tell you something," Elenore said in a whisper, most likely unaware how her words had affected me. "You have to promise me not to say anything to anyone."

I nodded. I could tell she was battling something. She nibbled on her bottom lip while her eyes darted side to side in agitation like a caged animal.

"I need to hear you say it," she said, taking both of my hands.

"I promise," I intoned with sincerity, my heart galloping. This was not like Elenore.

"Swear on Chamberlin's life," she commanded.

I didn't like swearing on lives, especially not his and especially not at our sister's viewing—but I gave my promise. "I swear on Chamberlin Fielding's life."

Elenore leaned in. Resting her head on my shoulder, she tilted her mouth to my ear and whispered, "Chamberlin tried to kill himself the night Maddy died."

"What?! What are you talking about?!" I asked, sitting straight up and forcing her to do the same.

She shushed me, looking in Chamberlin's direction to make sure he wasn't watching. "He found Maddy in her car in front of the house. It was too late; she was already dead."

"Car?" I mused. "I thought she fell down the stairs?"

"No," Elenore said, keeping her hawk eyes on Chamberlin. "That was just for the tour. I didn't want to talk about it in front of him, you understand?" She was back to pushing my hair away from my face.

"No, I don't understand. What happened?" I asked.

She looked at me with sad eyes and I realized for the first time the years that separated us. Elenore had been my age when she took custody of the three of us. I couldn't imagine doing that, being that selfless.

"Maddy . . . well," Elenore said, gripping my hands harder. "I can't bring myself to say suicide, but that's what it looks like."

"Why?" I asked.

She swallowed a sob. "Why does anyone kill themselves?"

"I don't know . . . Did she leave a note?"

"Not that I found."

"What about Chamberlin? Did he find anything?" I asked, trying to make sense of everything—my sister supposedly committing suicide and my brother attempting to do the same.

"If he did, he didn't say."

I leaned toward Elenore, keeping my voice low and my eyes on Chamberlin. "And Chamberlin, you're sure he . . ."

I knew the answer already. My mind linked it together in a quick, vivid movie in my head. I saw the kitchen fan pulled from the ceiling. I'd noticed his coarse voice. I knew what he had attempted. I closed my eyes, covering my face with my hands, trying to get the image out of my head. "The kitchen fan," I said breathlessly.

Elenore cried softly as she spoke. "I heard the noise. It reminded me so much of the noise I heard when Mom . . ." She trailed off. "I heard the fan drop out of the plaster. The idiot. I slid the table under him and cut him down. Oh, the idiot." She was drawing attention, but not so much as she would have if it were under different circumstances. "He was sorry. But the damage was done, you know?" she asked, looking at me as if my eyes held the answers to the universe. She wiped my mascara for me. "The damage was done. He cried but he never said he was sorry. I think he wanted to die, but seeing what it did to me he thought better of it."

"I'll stay," I said, attempting to find my voice. "I'll stay for him. For you. For the family. You're right Elenore, I'm needed here."

* * *

The Fielding Mausoleum was at the end of a snaking path backing up to a grassy knoll. The grass was so green it looked fake. I had never seen grass anywhere else like it. It was always cut to just the right height and never seemed to be blighted with weeds or moss. It was nature's perfect carpet, giving way to a mature cherry tree. The tree had to be over a century old. It blanketed the east side of Brooklyn Keeps Cemetery in a rich shade, as its branches swayed under the breeze perfuming the air. A few cherry blossoms still clung to some of the branches, although most of the tear-shaped petals had fallen, hinting at a vibrant spring that had passed.

I was grateful for the shade. Little beads of perspiration dripped from my forehead. Funerals are not for late spring. We also entombed Mr. Fielding's casket in the Brooklyn heat while the same tear-shaped petals lay on the ground.

The Fielding Mausoleum, like the Elenore Fielding House, was designed by Emmit Fielding. It was constructed when his daughter Ivette died. Flanking the decorative iron door were wingless angels. They were not young maidens as what may have been assumed upon seeing them. I knew better. I knew what to look for. There were two little humps protruding from each of their backs. They, like the angel that adorned the house's newel post, held a torch in their outstretched arms, their hands clasping the base of the torch like a hilt of a sword. Emmit Fielding was making a statement when he commissioned the mausoleum. I wondered what he meant by the gargoyle seated on the top of it. It was humanoid for the most part. But in its claws and eyes I saw a beast. It clutched the top of the mausoleum with what had to be the talons of an eagle, while its dark eyes berated all those who passed.

Elenore taking center, we three stood with our hands interlocked, facing the mausoleum. Madelin had been placed in the vault set aside for her and it was time for us to say our final farewell and head home. I couldn't help but notice X waiting on the other side of the cemetery fence. I was pretty sure he was filming us. At this point, nothing would surprise me. The kid was obsessed.

A young girl next to X came into view. She appeared to have stepped out of his shadow into existence. I hadn't noticed her at the funeral home. She was so thin it withered her youth, making her look sickly. I wondered if she was X's sister, the one he had mentioned. 'My sister and I can't stay away from him.'

Chamberlin didn't seem to care or notice X or the girl. His head resumed its usual posture—bowed. Tears ran down his face in torrents, however not as much as a whimper escaped his well-formed lips. I was sure if he tried to move, he would stumble about like the bespectacled young man at the funeral home, who had also followed us to the cemetery. He stared at the mausoleum from the opposite end of the fence from where X was as if he was hoping for one last glimpse at Maddy.

Elenore's hand became clammy in mine. The burning desire to let go of it overcame me. I faked a sneeze to free my hand. I couldn't wait to leave the cemetery. I felt trapped in there like the fence kept me locked in like a criminal. Where I felt trapped in the iron confines of the old cemetery, the young man in the glasses clung to the bars of the fence, pressing his face to it as if being made to wait outside was the greater punishment. Every few moments, as though his grief was set by clockwork, one of his sobs broke free seducing me to look his way.

It was after one of these sobs that I noticed there was one more person waiting outside of the cemetery—the tan man in the leather jacket. He was much more discreet than X and the guy in the thick rimmed glasses. He casually leaned against a tree on the other side of the fence, but he was watching.

As we approached the gate to leave, the man in the leather jacket abandoned his position by the tree. Crossing the street, he got into a black sedan with government plates. He was a cop. Something clicked in my brain. I recollected who he was now—Vincet Mallory—Vinney, the Irish-Italian detective assigned to Mr. Fielding's missing person case. I remembered Elenore and he had come to be very close during the investigation. So close, he had attended Mr. Fielding's funeral service with Elenore. Now that I realized who he was, I was surprised it took me so long to put his name to his face. I blamed it on his haircut. The last time I saw him, he had shaggy hair that went to his shoulders. Four years and a decent hair cut could really change a man.

Coming through the gate, X and the girl approached us. The girl wasn't as young as she'd seemed from across the way and was much taller. Probably taller still, but her posture was stooped and her stance awkward as if she was deliberately trying to make herself look shorter by tucking her limbs and head into her body like a turtle without a shell.

She was, however, just as thin up close. Her black dress that was meant to be formfitting was loose and shapeless on her boyish figure. She had brown hair that was nondistinctive. It was neither thin or thick, dull or shiny, straight or curly, long or short. She was dappled with so many freckles it made her look tan. If she was X's sister, she looked nothing like him, besides them both having brown eyes.

The girl hugged Chamberlin, stopping him in his tracks. He said nothing, in a silent exchange between the two of them. Chamberlin and X also exchanged a silent greeting that left the impression of a secret meaning.

CHAPTER SEVEN
A Different Kind of Dream

After getting a bite to eat at Maddy's favorite Italian restaurant, we returned to the house together. Chamberlin and Elenore had a few things to do before the bachelorette party arrived for midnight. Refusing my help, I decided to go upstairs and go to sleep. I was drained, just as though the house *did* have a real-life vampire, and it had sunk its fangs into me the moment I arrived.

Taking the stairs slowly, I avoided looking at the wingless angel. I had enough of them at the cemetery. I was halfway up the first flight of stairs when I heard a strange noise. I thought it was the wind. It had been particularly windy since I arrived, but it came out of nowhere producing a rattle that was too acute to be wind. The sound itself was low, but the pitch was high like the pitiful cry of a lost kitten. I stopped my ascent, turning around to survey the downstairs. Chamberlin was still talking with Elenore. He stood with his arms crossed as Elenore spoke with her usual excitement, her hands moving about her like she was swatting at gnats. The first few buttons of Chamberlin's dress shirt were undone, and I could see the rope burn on his neck. It looked like it was still sore.

I heard the strange noise again. I glanced at the angel on the newel post. From my place on the stairs, I could only see the back of her head and the stubs of her cut wings. "Is it Ivette or the cry of the angel?" I mused, repeating the line from the tour.

The thought of Maddy dying because of the angel's quest for new wings kindled a burning rage in my soul. I came down the stairs like lightning, my anger culminating with a kick to the angel's head. A loud pop filled the air as its head sputtered to the floor.

Elenore and Chamberlin glanced upward at the sound. Having seen me, there was no escaping what I'd done. The angel's head teetered on the floor by Chamberlin's feet like a dreidel. He picked it up, examining it for a long while before he clenched it in his fist. With eyes that seemed gray and cloudy, he fixated on me and spoke in a tone that was a marriage between anger and anxiety. "What did you do?"

I descended the stairs on the verge of tears. They burned the back of my throat as I fought to hold them back. "I didn't mean to," I said, filled with the bitterest remorse. "I hit it accidentally." They didn't have to know it was my high heel that beheaded the angel.

Elenore rubbed my arm. "It's not a big deal, we'll just glue it." She took the head from Chamberlin and attempted to put it back on. It slid off. It wasn't a clean break. The break forked through the angel's face on an angle, going through her lips. My eyes welled with tears. "Still not a big deal," Elenore said, trying to make me feel better. "It'll be fixed by tomorrow. Why don't you head upstairs and get some rest."

I glanced at Chamberlin. His face was stony, but his eyes were agitated as if they were two hurricanes building momentum.

Elenore's hand moved to my back, where she attempted to rub out my tension. "Seriously, don't worry about it, Sister. You sure you don't want ear plugs?"

"I'm sure," I said, turning toward the staircase again. This time, I made quick work of them, bounding up the stairs to the clicking of my heels. When I reached the banister of the second story, I looked down. Elenore and Chamberlin stood over where they would tell guests Madelin Fielding died. But it wasn't her body they were standing on, it was mine. At the sight of the decapitated angel, a sense of mortality washed over me in a shiver. Or maybe it was Chamberlin's intense stare that made me tremble.

As I rounded the second staircase, it struck me how so many things had stayed the same and yet so many things were different. It was a welcome sight to see the familiar cracks in the plaster as I continued my way to the attic. Long ago, the Fielding family decided not to make repairs to the plaster when it cracked or fell off the wall exposing lath and horsehair, but to leave it in a state of decay to ramp up the creepy factor.

I wasn't sure if this was an attempt to keep things authentic or if it had originally been the byproduct of money problems. Before my father infused cash into the house, I knew the family was bankrupt. After our first visit, my father had told me how dire the Fieldings' situation was. He had said it was a shame a nice family like the Fieldings was going to lose their home and he wished he could help. I had loved Chamberlin since our first meeting and cried when he told me. My father had patted the top of my head. "Come now child what's wrong?" he'd asked.

I thought of Chamberlin, the most beautiful boy in the world, with his handsome face and his bright eyes, homeless and wept. "Oh father," I'd said, "please give them money." And he did. The Fieldings would rather have been evicted than sell their ancestral home. Yet a partnership—that Franky Fields accepted with a ready heart.

The Fielding family's money troubles started before Frank Fielding. In fact, Mr. Fielding inherited debt. After the death of Emmit and Elenore Fielding's son Elias, his son Wiliam was forced to sell parts of the estate to make ends meet. A neat fact that's part of the Elenore Fielding House tour is that the buildings on each side of her, the now Plant Haven and Mikey's, used to be part of the house. These buildings were not part of the original dwelling, but additions Emmit added on as his fortune grew. As though he had foreseen there would be money problems in the future, the renovations were added on as wings that you entered through corridors. With the sale of the flanking properties, the corridors were deconstructed, making way for two single-family homes to be sold off. The only hint that the three structures used to be one could be seen from the back of the properties, where a stone archway connecting the three homes still stood.

I took the final stairway to the attic. The space was separated by pocket doors. I pulled the small brass handle and slid the door into the wall. I entered the familiar rotunda, my eyes going to my adoptive father's bedroom door. His room had always been the space I was least familiar with in the entire house. I could close my eyes and imagine every nook and cranny in the place, but his room always had a mysterious air about it. In fact, I had only been in it once before it became my temporary bedroom and that was with Chamberlin. It was on one of my very first visits to the Elenore Fielding House. Chamberlin had given me a private tour of things typically off-limits. Our time spent in his parents' room was brief and he'd talked in a hushed whisper as if we would be in big trouble if we were caught there.

My childhood memory of this forbidden place spurred my imagination over the years as I tried to recall the details of his bedroom. But his bedroom was like any other room, comprised of four walls. It did have the bonus of having pitched ceilings, akin to the other rooms in the attic.

My nose tingled in such a way that I thought I was going to sneeze. Elenore overdid it with the sprucing up. The smell of citrus potpourri was nauseating.

The room was dark. The darkness somehow seemed to sharpen my sense of smell. The meager light filtering in from the dormer cast the room in shadows. The corners seemed to melt into the walls around them. I flipped on the light. In the center of the room, a brass chandelier with shard-shaped glass prisms lit. Even with the lights on, the room was still dark thanks to the black wallpaper with its variegated green leaves that ran up and down it in a loosely striped pattern.

Pushed against the farthest wall from the entry was a massive four-poster bed. The spires of the bed twisted around like the horns of unicorns. From the canopy hung dark burgundy curtains that were drawn shut. I hadn't remembered closing them in the morning, but there they were, a wall of red. I opened them, a feeling of mystery pervading my fingertips at the touch of the soft velvet.

Above the headboard, hanging on the wall, was a painting of the Elenore Fielding House the way it had looked during Emmit Fielding's life. I admired the watercolor rendering. It was done with so much detail my eyes hungered to take it all in. I stared at it yesterday for some time, committing to memory each little black stone of the house. I decided I would sleep facing the painting tonight.

I went to my overnight bag that was sitting on the chair in the corner. I quickly undressed as if death clung to my clothes and slipped on my pajamas. I had to brush my teeth. I felt like a garlic clove. I got that feeling every time I ate Italian food, like garlic was leaking out of every pore of my body. Unfortunately for Chamberlin, we debunked his vampirism tonight and unfortunately for X, he wasn't there to film it. Chamberlin ate enough garlic to kill himself and all the vampire covens on the East Coast.

I noticed the sticker from the gift shop that I had shoved in my overnight bag was on the floor. I picked it up, my finger tracing Chamberlin's lips and his pointy vampire teeth. On the back was his social media handle.

I sat down on the bed and went to his Instagram. X may have stalker tendencies, but he did take good pictures. And then there were the sponsor videos. They were my favorites. They usually consisted of Chamberlin stripping down to his boxer briefs followed by him putting on his gifted clothes. I had watched the same video of him in his underwear nearly ten times before I shut my phone off. He made one hell of a brand ambassador. Any more of that and I would never get to sleep.

Hopping up from the bed, I went back to my overnight bag and took out a bottle of sleeping pills. Shaking it, I realized I didn't have a lot left, but with how truly exhausted I felt, I didn't think I would need them tonight. After tossing the pills back into the bag and placing my phone on its charger, I shut off the lights. The room was once again cast in warring streaks of shadows and silver from the moonlight. Pushing the extra pillows to the foot of the bed, I crawled in, keeping my eyes on the painting of the Elenore Fielding House until the darkness crept in and my eyelids closed.

* * *

The rich aroma of wine permeated my nostrils. I knew this smell well. Mr. Fielding always drank a tall glass of red wine at night to help him get to sleep. I always liked the smell and found it intoxicating without actually having a sip. Perhaps it was because I wanted to taste it—wanted to enjoy what the adults seemed to enjoy— wanted to be an adult. But my dream didn't stop with the wine, it never did. An acute scent mingled with it, turning it into something not so pleasant. Metal—metallic. Oh, how very metallic it smelled. I always smelled the blood before I saw it, tasted the rusty metal of it in my mouth. But I always ended up seeing it, seeing the bright red stain of it on my hands and on Mr. Fielding's chest. The blood flowed freely as if it sprang from a geyser. The smell of wine on his lips struck me like a slap with each of his forced exhales. I didn't want to be an adult anymore. I didn't want to know death and blood and dying.

My small, blood-soaked hands trembled. I looked up to see the painting of the Elenore Fielding House in all of its grandeur hanging on the wall before me and realized for the first time my perpetual nightmare took place in Mr. Fielding's room. I had always known I was in a dark room, hovering over a bed with my bloody hands as Mr. Fielding took his last breath. But Mr. Fielding's room . . . why? Before my trip home, I had only been in his room that one time with Chamberlin and it was a quick pop in and pop out. Why would my mind place me here with him like this? How could my nightmare remember things I'd forgotten?

I pulled back the bed curtains to get a better look at my surroundings. I wanted confirmation that I was right, and I was in Mr. Fielding's room. I left red fingerprints on the dark fabric, but I didn't care. I was aware I was in a dream. Nothing that happened here mattered. Soon, I would wake up.

Cognizant as I was that I was in fact dreaming, it didn't stop my breath from catching in my throat at the sight of Madelin and Chamberlin. My dream had always been of me and Mr. Fielding, they were never in it.

But there they were, huddled in the corner like specters of the past. Chamberlin looked how he did the day I left for London. He was a teenager and so was Maddy. Maddy was pale. All of the color had been drained from her face. Chamberlin was in distinct contrast. His face was red, bright red. His hair was damp and clung to the sides of his cheeks. He was crying. It was the only sound in the dream. Every time a sob broke free from his perfect mouth my heart ached for him. He was in so much pain.

I glanced behind me to see Mr. Fielding lying motionless on the bed. He had drawn his last breath. He was dead.

On shaky legs, I approached Chamberlin. He didn't seem to notice that I was in the room. His eyes and his sister's eyes were glued on their dead father. I was too upset to speak, to tell him, despite how it looked, I didn't kill his father. As I drew nearer, I noticed a thin scratch ran across Chamberlin's face and lips on an angle. The scratch grew and blood trickled from it. At first, only a few tear-shaped drops of blood rolled down his cheek, but then the blood came in torrents and wouldn't stop. It happened so slowly and yet so fast. The top part of his face began to slide off like snow off a mountain's peak. I ran to him and sandwiched his head between my hands to stop the top of his face from falling off.

"What did you do?" Chamberlin garbled as blood spilt from his torn lips, the heavens in his eyes clouded over in death.

My words had no voice. I locked eyes with him. I saw myself, my auburn eyes, reflected in the blue skies of his. They were rimmed in bright red, encircled in blood.

CHAPTER EIGHT

A Different Way to Communicate

I shot out of bed, my hands outstretched like I was still holding Chamberlin's face between them. The painting of the Elenore Fielding House was before me, thanks to deciding to rest my head at the footboard. The painting took on the moon's silvery luminosity. The image seemed to move in and out of focus as if the moonlight filtering in through the attic dormer was being obstructed by something or someone. Behind me a floorboard groaned. Was it Elenore? Was it Chamberlin? Could it be Maddy? I twisted around, peering into the darkness, straining my eyes to examine every shadow. My heartbeat pitter pattered in my ears. I was alone.

I smiled at myself, feeling silly, when the mattress moaned. It was as if someone sat down on the bed near my feet. I could just feel the impression of something near me. My neck jerked forward, my eyes landing on the painting of the house again. I *was* alone. There was nothing there. It was just me and my galloping heart. "Old houses make odd noises," I muttered to myself in a half-baked attempt to make myself feel safe. That's what it was; I didn't feel scared. I felt unsafe like I was in danger. Mr. Fielding had said, "Old houses make odd noises," every day I lived with them. But I had never felt unsafe. I had never once woken up from a nightmare like I did tonight, or slept with a nightlight like Maddy. Maybe Mr. Fielding could see the future and knew I would need to hear that at this very moment. Maybe he had some of what Aunt Girty and I had. Maybe the Fieldings had their own sort of magic. X seemed to think it of Chamberlin.

I let my hands freefall to my sides. They had still been outstretched, still in the act of holding Chamberlin's beautiful face after I had been frozen by the uneasy feeling that crept up from my toes all the way to my fingertips.

I rubbed my fingers together to see if I could feel blood on them. I couldn't tell. My hands were so cold, too cold for May in the attic. Slowly, afraid of what I may discover, I moved my trembling hands to my lap, my breathing still strained. My breath came out in gasps as though I had just finished a sprint. Tonight's nightmare was like nothing I'd ever had. The rules had changed. Anything was possible. I felt that deep in my core as I sat in Mr. Fielding's bed. Anything could happen. I could look down and find blood on my hands.

I counted to three and glanced down. My hands looked very white in the dark room. The freckles going up and down them made me think of blood—little drops of blood. Holding my breath, I turned my hands over. Nothing—no blood. That was good. I was almost convinced there would be. There was something about Chamberlin and Maddy being in the dream with me that made it seem more real, even if they were young again. That, and now I knew my nightmare took place in Frank Fielding's room. My dream had a location. Before, it was just Mr. Fielding and me, and the blood, in some unknown place. Not knowing where I was always gave my nightmare a fantastical quality, but now I knew I had been in the Elenore Fielding House the whole time.

I didn't put a lot of stock in dreams telling you things your subconscious mind couldn't puzzle out for itself. But why, after all these years, did my dream change? With a shrug, I chalked it up to coming home and staying in Mr. Fielding's room. Those were some pretty big changes. And then there was Maddy's death. It was obvious Maddy's funeral got to me. But then again, last night my dream went as it always did. The change had come tonight.

Something gnawed at me from the inside out, a gut feeling I wanted to go away. The cut on Chamberlin's face mirrored the fractured head of the wingless angel on the newel post. The gash on Chamberlin's face sliced through his lips, cutting his face in an uneven half in precisely the way the wingless angel's wooden head fractured when I kicked it.

Chamberlin's warning about a curse and the wingless angel's search for new wings made me tense. I wasn't afraid for myself, that was never it. I was afraid for Chamberlin, afraid he was in danger. That's what my dream showed me. It took Chamberlin's fear of the curse and inflicted him, turning my nightmare into my worst nightmare.

I got out of bed and tiptoed to my phone, as I was not in the mood for more odd noises. It was just past midnight. The bachelorette party should be here, and that meant Chamberlin should be in his room, unless they hired him as a vampire stripper. With Elenore, nothing was out of the realm of possibility. She'd make him jump out of a coffin in his underwear to *The Rocky Horror Picture Show* soundtrack if it meant cold hard cash.

I would crash the bachelorette party and face the wrath of Elenore in the morning, if I had to. I needed to see Chamberlin. Just for a second, just to make sure my nightmare was only a dream and stayed that way. I was still shaken from seeing his face do a landslide, and then there was the way he had looked at me when I decapitated the tour's shining star at the foot of the stairs. I was sure it was all just my nerves getting the better of me. I had lived in the Elenore Fielding House as a Fielding for four years and nothing supernatural ever happened and I doubted it would start tonight with the beheading of Chamberlin Fielding, but I needed to make sure.

In the small possibility he did need help, I wanted him to know I was there for him. It was, after all, my high heel that had broken off the stupid wooden angel's head and sent it skittering on the floor. It was Emmit Fielding who started the war with God, but I'll be damned if I didn't just fire a shot.

I resorted to tiptoeing again and made my way down the hall without so much as one floorboard groaning. I lightly knocked on Chamberlin's closed bedroom door. I didn't want to alert Elenore that I was up or that I was going to Chamberlin's room.

Chamberlin opened his door so quickly it was like he had been expecting me. "Oh hey, is everything okay?" he asked in a low voice that was just an octave above a whisper.

I examined his face to the best of my ability. Most of it was cast in shadows from the unlit hallway. Even his eyes seemed black, like the night shut out the blue sky forever. I had to move closer. The top of my head grazed his chin as I looked up. "Is everything okay?" Chamberlin asked again, his slitted eyes scrutinizing me as I continued my examination.

Satisfied his face was as perfect as it was when we got home from dinner, I took a step back.

Chamberlin closed the distance, taking a step forward and entering the hall. "Trinity, what's going on?" he asked, his voice well above a whisper now.

I played it off, pointing into his room. I saw X and the wiry girl from the cemetery sitting on his bedroom floor. "That's precisely what I was going to ask you."

He glanced behind him before returning his focus to me. "X and Tilly are spending the night, we're going to—"

"Commune with the dead," X said, cutting Chamberlin off. "Wanna join?"

Chamberlin pushed his bedroom door wide open. "Yeah, come in," he said. He gestured to Tilly. "Trinity, this is Tilly; and Tilly, this is my sister, Trinity, from London."

"Nice to finally meet you. My father has a habit of whisking us off to the city on the weekends and any time he senses danger," Tilly said. "We weren't home the night it happened and as soon as my dear old dad found out it was back to the Big Apple to see some show he just had to see and insisted the entire family went. He's not very good at covering up his motives. X and I are lucky we were able to get back for the viewing." Without getting up, Tilly stretched her hand to me. I shook it. "X has been blabbing on about you for what feels like years," Tilly told me before shooting a smile in X's direction. "I feel like I know you already, but it's nice to see your face in real time. X's picture of you on his phone didn't do you justice."

Tilly's demeanor was very much changed from the withered girl in the ill-fitting dress at the cemetery. She was confident in her Care Bear crop top and black cargo shorts. She had a prettiness to her I hadn't noticed earlier. Maybe it was the girl next door look, which I found humorous as she was literally the girl next door.

As politeness dictates, I should have responded to Tilly immediately, but I was off my game. My nerves were still raw. Her word choice to describe her father's sudden need to take a trip to New York City with his family brought me right back to the uneasiness of my nightmare. Danger. I could feel the blood rush to my head in what I knew would later become a headache. On top of that, I found myself distracted by Chamberlin's room. It had changed very little, if at all. He had the same bed, down to the same navy comforter. The desk that was too small for him then was still next to his bed and the same Elvira poster, which I always found obnoxious, glared at me from the other side of the room.

I was grateful for the birdsong melody of Tilly's bangle bracelets rubbing together as she rummaged through her purse for her ChapStick. Recalled to the present, I smiled at her and said, "And you must be X's sister he was telling me about."

She smiled back. Her beauty vanished as if by a magic wand. Her mouth was too small for her teeth. They all fought for space in a battle that would never be won. I wondered why X had braces and she didn't. I felt bad for her.

"Places," X said. "We want to do this as close to midnight as possible."

Chamberlin closed the door behind him and took his seat between X and Tilly, leaving me to sit across from him on the blanket on the floor.

I felt a little too old to be sitting like this or to hang out with friends for a sleepover. I was surprised Chamberlin didn't feel the same. Maybe X and his sister were younger than they looked. Height could do that, and they were both very tall. There was less than a year between Chamberlin and myself, me being his senior by four months. Maybe I felt silly because I was the only one in pajamas. I was glad I packed a solid yellow top and bottom set, but there was a small pink bow on the collar of my shirt exposing it as sleepwear. X, like Chamberlin, was wearing what he wore to the funeral, ditching the jacket and all of the little extras, but he still had on his dog collar and Chamberlin locket.

As silly as I felt, admittedly, there was something novel about the idea of a sleepover and it made my inner child happy. It was nice to spend time with Chamberlin and his friends even if they were a little weird. Chamberlin's state of mind seemed to have mellowed and that helped me return to my zen state. It pushed the nightmare far away. It already felt like it happened days ago. Soon it would seem like years and soon I would completely forget about it—poof, gone.

From his satchel, X pulled out what appeared to be a piece of black cloth. He unfolded it with a reverence that almost made me laugh. He acted like it was the cloth Jesus of Nazareth was wrapped in when he died. It wasn't—it was a piece of material with a Ouija board printed on it. After closer inspection, I could see it was hand painted.

My eyebrows arched instantaneously. Mr. Fielding didn't allow Ouija boards in the house. Sure, it was assumed Mr. Fielding was dead—we had buried his empty casket and held a funeral for him, after all—but it still seemed unlike Chamberlin not to honor his father's wishes whether he was alive, dead, or missing.

Ouija boards were always a big no, no for Mr. Fielding. He considered it one of his golden rules, right up there with you're not dead until everyone forgets you. The Ouija board ban always seemed bizarre because they were all about ghosts and anything most typical families would be against. Mr. Fielding always said, "You never truly know what or who you're talking to through a spirit board. It's best to avoid the whole thing on the principle of safety."

This lends itself to another Fielding golden rule, the number one rule really: family first. As a Fielding, we were to do right by the family and for the family, protecting the family from everything including the Hasbro board game.

"What happened to no Ouija boards in the house?" I asked Chamberlin, resisting reminding him his father would be pissed.

"It's not a board," X said, answering for Chamberlin. "It's my *Yu-Gi-Oh!* mat." He flipped the homemade Ouija board over. "See, one side *Yu-Gi-Oh!* mat, one side spirit mat. No board. No rules being broken here."

"One of your work arounds," I said, disapprovingly. Elenore may like X, but Mr. Fielding wouldn't have. He clearly knew about Mr. Fielding's 'no Ouija boards in the house' rule and was breaking it. He was a manipulative little goth.

X turned to Chamberlin. "Your sister's hot, too bad she's a nark. She's going to tell Elenore."

I took a jab at him. It was only fair; he threw the first punch. " *Yu-Gi-Oh!?* How old are you, ten?" I knew *Yu-Gi-Oh!* was a card game for little kids, it was around when I was in grade school. I assumed the mat was used to keep the cards in place as you played the game.

"I'm legal, if that's what you're worried about," X said with a wink. "And what's wrong with *Yu-Gi-Oh!? Yu-Gi-Oh!* is an anime classic from the golden age of anime. All the cool kids still play it. Chamberlin plays."

I glanced at my adoptive brother, who was grinning. "I'll give it to X, it's actually fun," Chamberlin said in his friend's defense.

Tilly leaned back on her elbows and laughed, "The only fun part is watching how upset X gets when he loses."

"I seldom lose," X said exulted.

Under my breath, just loud enough for X to hear, I mumbled, "I bet."

X took out one of his earrings from his ear. It was surprisingly not a spike but a hoop. He jabbed the tip of his finger with the sharp part and squeezed a drop of blood onto the Ouija mat. Tilly wasn't far behind, taking a *Ziggy Stardust* pin off her purse and piercing her finger. She added her drop of blood to her brother's. The mat sucked it up like a blackhole. I looked at Chamberlin like they had ten heads. I couldn't believe he was going along with this. He ignored my glances and grabbed a box cutter from his desk drawer. He, like his friends, pricked his finger. Blood welled from it. Ceremoniously, he flipped his hand upside down and let the drop hit the mat. The sight of blood—his blood—made me queasy. I kept waiting for the scratch to appear across his face and for half of his face to slide off.

Chamberlin handed me the box cutter.

"Yeah . . . I don't feel comfortable with that," I said.

He shrugged before leaning to the side to place the box cutter on the top of his desk.

"I have an idea," X said. "Why don't we try something new tonight?"

"Uh, what's the old?" I asked, trying to get up to speed with what Chamberlin and his friends usually did at sleepovers.

"Old is we try to commune with Chain's dad," X told me.

My eyes darted to Chamberlin. Elenore had said their father was dead and believed that, but I was always under the impression Chamberlin thought his dad was still alive and would show up one day with an explanation for it all.

He noticed my glance. He answered it with a bow of his head, his eyes hooded with his thick lashes.

"Okay," I said, drawing it out. "So, what's the new?"

"Why don't we try to commune with Maddy tonight?" X suggested.

"No," Chamberlin said without a second's hesitation. His voice was deeper than his usual tenor.

"Hear me out," X, pleaded. "She just died. It might be easier to reach her. Think about it Chain, you don't want to miss the opportunity."

Chamberlin's cheeks flushed as he nibbled on his bottom lip. I could tell he was holding back tears. He shook his head, clearly not able to say no again without crying.

With her teeth like fangs, Tilly glowered at her brother as if to tell him to drop it.

"I get it. I'm sorry," X apologized. He sounded sincere. "Well, either way, I'm psyched we have a quatrefoil," he said, changing the subject. "This should shake things up."

Tilly made a cross with her fingers, presumably denoting the importance of four. "See, I said we'd get a fourth person. I confess, I thought it was going to be Allison, but hey they both have red hair—close enough."

"Allison?" I asked. "Is that Chamberlin's girlfriend?" I thought of Kris back home. Well, back in London. I left so abruptly; I owed him a call. I'd dodged a few since I've been back. But Kris with a 'K', not to be confused with his friend Chris with a 'C', had golden blond hair like Chamberlin. It wouldn't be so strange to think Chamberlin ended up with a girl with red hair like me.

"Not mine," Chamberlin said, his complexion almost back to normal. "Allison is X's dream girl."

"Oh . . ." I intoned thoughtfully.

"Oh?" X said, sharply turning his head to me. "What does that mean?"

I had to be more careful about how I said 'oh'. I cowered a little. "Oh, means oh," I said.

Tilly laughed, throwing her head back. "Let me guess, you think my goofy brother is in love with yours," she said.

"Well yeah . . ." I mused. I looked to X. "Aren't you? I mean—the locket . . ."

Tilly and Chamberlin filled the room with a roar of laughter. I couldn't help but laugh too. Chamberlin stretched out his foot and touched X's thigh. I noticed a hole in his sock.

"Gross! Get your stinky feet off of me," X said annoyed. He took on a snooty air, locking eyes with me, and said in as firm a voice as possible, "I am not *in love* with your brother."

I glanced to Tilly for confirmation. She wore a big smile that caused her two canine teeth to poke out from under her top lip.

"We have a platonic bromance," X clarified. At that, X and Chamberlin pounded fists to seal the affection of their brotherly romance.

Still giggling, I said, "You're gonna have to explain the choker thing to me."

"He wears that stupid thing to get noticed," Tilly told me with a shake of her head. "And he gets noticed. Just not in the way he wants to be. I keep telling him he tries way too hard. But he thinks the more gothy he makes himself the more likely Allison Heart will notice him. She hasn't noticed him yet and we've hung out with her several times courtesy of The Vampire Chamberlin."

"I hate it when you call me that," Chamberlin said to Tilly without malice.

She patted Chamberlin's knee like he was a child. "No you don't," she said with a smile.

X shoved his phone in my face. "Here's Allison."

Allison Heart was very pretty. I had seen her pictures on Chamberlin's Instagram. "Pretty," I said. She wasn't a natural redhead. She had the shade of red you could only get from a bottle.

"Gorgeous," X corrected, as if pretty meant hideous creature that no one could love.

"She is both pretty and gorgeous," Tilly admitted, "but she only has eyes for Chamberlin. It figures, he finally meets a girl Elenore will let him date and he can't date her because X has made him promise in the name of all that is bromance not to."

"That's what brothers do. They don't get with each other's girls," X said to his sister.

"Wait a minute," I said, making sure I heard Tilly correctly. My eyes settled on Chamberlin. I wanted him to answer for himself. "Elenore has to approve who you date? Like actually approve?" I imagined girls lining up around the block while Elenore conducted interviews.

"Yeah, something like that," Chamberlin said. "They have to be good for business."

Tilly flipped her hair off her shoulders as she spoke. "Allison being an alternative model with her own following is perfect. Elenore was literally drooling when she met her. That's in comparison to. . ." She tapped her chin in thought, and I noticed she bit her nails. Her black nail polish was chipped on almost every finger, her nails very, very short. "I forgot her name," Tilly finally said, "but once your brother brought this girl home for Elenore to meet and, well, in Chain's defense, she was really nice." Tilly again patted Chamberlin's knee. "Nice and boring," she said. "The girl had blonde hair and was dressed all in white. She looked like a virgin sacrifice if I ever saw one. Elenore thumbed her down the second the girl walked in the door. And that was the end of whatever her name was."

"Jill," Chamberlin mumbled.

Tilly repeated herself, taking on a dramatized tone. "And that was the end of Jill."

"Wow," I said, not sure if I believed Tilly's full account, but I trusted there was some truth to it. "I didn't realize Elenore was so . . ."

"So Elenore," Chamberlin said, finishing my sentence.

"Well yeah." I said.

With his fingers, he combed his hair away from his eyes. His celestial orbs were in full view, and they were divine. Lazily, he blinked, letting his lashes rise and fall like the veil of night. "It's always about business. I'm just glad as I'm being tortured by Allison, X has something to look at."

"As if hanging out with the smart, sexy Allison is torture," Tilly mumbled under her breath.

"You don't have to do it," I said.

"Yes he does," X countered.

"I do," Chamberlin said. "She's gotten me a few modeling gigs with her, and we need the money." He inclined his head in X's direction. "And I owe X."

"Yeah Trinity, not everyone is independently wealthy like you are," X said with sass.

My cheeks flushed, I could feel the heat rush to them and knew I looked like a tomato. I wondered how much Chamberlin told X and Tilly about me.

"We heard all about it," X said like he'd just read my mind. "About how you took your money and left after Chain's father's funeral, and how you didn't give a shit the family who had taken you in was struggling to make ends meet."

Chamberlin kicked X hard. "Hey, knock it off."

It was true my father was very wealthy and when he died, I inherited his fortune. I didn't think about the financial repercussions of me moving to London. I just assumed Elenore would take care of everything as she always had. She never asked me for money or said they were in want of it. I thought the Elenore Fielding House was self-sustaining. I could never forget that it was my father's money and intervention who had saved it, so the most beautiful boy in the world wouldn't lose his home, but I thought since then the business ran in the black. I had no idea that may not be the case.

I thought about my adoption with new eyes. My adoption may not have been solely out of compassion for an orphan. It's true, I chose to stay with the Fieldings over my only living relative, my Great Aunt Girty who lived in London. Despite her dislike of children, she was willing to take me in. But I wanted to be near Chamberlin, near people I was fond of. London seemed so different, so far away. I didn't want to run away from my problems then.

It's true that after I was adopted, Mr. Fielding and I went to my father's accountant several times withdrawing large amounts of money for what he always called 'Trifles for Trinity'. I can't recall the money being spent on me specifically, but rather for the family or unseen necessities. I had no idea leaving would put Elenore, Chamberlin, and Maddy under financial stress. Unbeknownst to me, I had ended the partnership with the Fieldings my father had started. When I left, my father's fortune went with me.

In a moment of clarity, I realized what I had done to people I love. The tiny hole in the bottom of his sock, the same bedroom décor, the sponsors, the ploys for new business options, renting out the house for bachelorette parties and who knows what else, all made sense now. It was all because of me. I pulled my father's money out of the house. I was the vampire.

"I'm sorry Chamberlin, I didn't realize," I said barely audible, fighting to keep my emotions in check.

Chamberlin leaned back, his eyes in shadows.

"He didn't say it like that," Tilly said in a sympathetic tone. "X is always dramatic." She glanced at Chamberlin. "He's doing fine now. They're all fine now."

"Not Maddy," Chamberlin said softly, his voice deep in his throat. "She's dead. She wanted out and now she'll never get away."

Tilly placed her hand on his knee. "Maddy's in a better place. I believe that. What happened is not your fault," she told him.

I puzzled at Tilly's words. 'What happened is not your fault.' What would make Chamberlin think Maddy's suicide *was* his fault? The kitchen fan came into view. I shivered. The idea of Chamberlin hanging from it chilled my blood. Whatever did happen, he felt responsible enough to try to take his own life.

"I'm sorry, Chamberlin," I said again. "I wasn't there for you in the past, but I'll be there for you from now on. I'm not returning to London. I'm staying here."

"Awesome! We just increased our friends circle by fifty percent!" Tilly said, high fiving her brother.

Chamberlin said nothing but mouthed to me while Tilly and X were enraptured over having a new friend, "You should leave while you still can."

I'd let Chamberlin be sulky, Maddy did just die after all.

"I have a good feeling about this," Tilly said, her excitement still waxing. She pulled four candles already in holders from her purse, which was like a bookbag, and placed one in front of each of us. Pulling out a lighter from her shorts, she lit them. "Someone get the lights."

"I'll get it," I volunteered, as I was the closest. I flipped the switch down. The room was dark even with four lit candles. Everyone's faces seemed distorted—mean—cruel, none crueler than Chamberlin's. From my vantage point, the small flames seemed to hover above the candles as if they were no longer tethered to the wick but free to float away. I eagerly sat back down. It was lighter closer to the flame and that was comforting.

"Almost forgot," Tilly said, taking the heart-shape planchette out of her purse and placing it in the center of the mat. "Without that we wouldn't be communing with the spirits." The planchette didn't look handmade. I was sure they borrowed it from their board game at home.

"Hold hands," X instructed, and we did. I had always thought the participants put their fingertips on the planchette and let the spirit guide them to the letters, spelling out their ghostly message. But Chamberlin and his friends played differently. I should have figured when they all drew blood.

"It is I, Xavier Deedle, we would—"

"Deedle," I repeated, laughing. "Your last name is Deedle?" The dark didn't seem so scary now.

"Yeah," Tilly said, "I'm Deedle Dee and he's Deedle Dum.

I laughed and so did Chamberlin. I could definitely see them as some strange gothic version of Wonderland's most famous twins.

"I like that a lot better than X," Chamberlin confessed.

"Me too," Tilly said, with a haughty chuckle.

X cleared his throat. "Shall I continue?" he asked.

"Sorry. Yes, please continue," I said for all of us, swallowing my giggle.

"It is I, Xavier Deedle. We would like to make contact with the spirit of Franklin Fielding. I am here with my kin, Tilly Deedle, friend to your only son Chamberlin Fielding, and your daughter Trinity Dunn Fielding."

At my name the candles flickered. It was for only a split second, but I was sure of it. I wondered if anyone else noticed it. If they did, they didn't say.

"Franklin are you there?" X asked. "By the name you preferred in life, Frank Fielding—are you there? Franky do you hear us? Frank?"

The planchette shook on the mat. "Whose doing that?" I asked fearfully.

"Not me," Chamberlin said, glancing to X like he was known to have a trick or two up his sleeve.

"Not me," X attested. "We have a real spirit." He focused on the Ouija mat. "Frank is that you?" he asked.

The guide slid across the mat so fast I thought it was going to shoot across the room. It abruptly landed on the word 'No'.

"Ask who it is," Tilly said in a rushed voice, as if our visitor could leave at any moment. Her grip tightened on my hand, or maybe it was the other way around and I squeezed hers.

"Do it," Chamberlin ordered, in the same anxious tone of Tilly.

"Spirit, what was your name in life?" X asked.

Nothing—no answer.

"Spirit, tell us your name, I implore you!" X said, sounding very official.

The guide moved slowly. I could hear my heart beat in my ear, each beat a distinct thud as it glided across the mat and landed on the letter 'M'.

"Maddy," I said in a low voice.

"Maddy?" Chamberlin echoed.

The planchette moved to the letter 'I'.

"M—I," Tilly said as it moved to the letter 'T'. "M—I—T."

We waited for the guide to make its next move, but it remained on the letter 'T'.

"Mit?" X said. "Whose Mit?"

My voice shook as I spoke. "It's backwards. It's Tim—Tim was my father. He died in the house with Chamberlin's mom." I never spoke about my father's death and Chamberlin never spoke of his mother's. It was just something no one talked about.

"Should I continue?" X asked in a tender tone I hadn't heard him use until now. I was surprised he was being so courteous after pushing the idea of trying to contact Maddy.

"Yeah," I said, "continue."

"Tim," X said, "do you have a message for your daughter, Trinity?"

The candlelight flickered again. This time it was as though a vagrant wind raced through the room attacking only the flames. Everyone noticed it. Everyone's eyes looked like golf balls. "Don't break the circle," Tilly warned.

X would have, if I hadn't dug my nails into his hand. "Don't break the circle," I hissed at him.

"If we break the circle, we lose connection," Tilly said, speaking specifically to her brother. "Stay holding hands no matter what."

"Okay," X said, taking a deep breath. "Tim, Trinity would like to have your message."

The guide spun around like a broken compass until it zoomed over to the letter 'D'. Then to 'O'. Then back to 'O'. Next to the letter 'L', and finally the letter 'B'.

"It spells blood backwards," Tilly said, no doubt following the logic of Mit spelling Tim in reverse.

My chest heaved. Blood. It all came back to that. "What does it mean?" I asked X.

He shook his head. "I don't know."

"Ask him what he means," I said, desperately.

"Tim Dunn—whose blood? What do you mean?" X asked.

A loud scream sounded. It came from underneath us. We all screamed, all jumping to our feet and breaking the circle. Breathing heavily, Chamberlin was the first to speak. "The bachelorette party. It was just the bachelorette party downstairs."

"Shoot you're right," Tilly said as we heard another shriek.

I sat back down with my hands outstretched, not wasting a second. "Come on guys, hurry. We need to get my dad's answer."

They rejoined me on the floor, and we all held hands, once again forming a circle, or a quatrefoil depending on how you looked at it. But no matter how many times and different ways X asked my father to answer us, the planchette didn't budge from the letter 'B'. My father was gone.

"Maybe your dad said blood because you're the only one who didn't put blood on the mat," Tilly mused.

"You have a point," I said, breaking the circle to take one of many pins off of Tilly's purse. The Munster pin was dull, but I was still able to draw blood. I let it drip onto the mat. My task accomplished, I took Tilly's and X's hands again.

"Tim are you there?" X asked. "We have given you blood. The blood of Trinity Dunn Fielding," he said like they just sacrificed me.

The candle flames grew. We all looked at each other in marvel, our teeth and eyes sparkling in the glow of the flames like stars. My pulse surged.

"Bingo," Tilly said.

X, for a spirit guide, was very nervous. I wished Tilly was guiding this spiritual conquest, but figured it was X's mat, so it was his honor. X's hand trembled so much it was hard to hold on to it. His hand was cold and clammy. It was like trying to hold on to a fish out of water. "Tim, do you have another message for your daughter?" X asked.

The flames died down to their original height. There was nothing extraordinary about them now.

"Maybe it's not Mr. Dunn," Chamberlin said. "The circle was broken. Ask who we're talking to."

"You're right," X acknowledged. His focus was back on the mat. "Spirit, what was your name in life? Were you Tim Dunn?" he asked. The flame shrank again as if to tell us we were getting colder.

"Timothy," I told X. In his nervousness, I wasn't sure he would figure out Tim was an abbreviation of Timothy.

"Were you Timothy Dunn?" X asked. The candles were scarcely lit now. The guide still hadn't moved. "Frank Fielding?" The candles burned a little brighter. "Were you Madelin Fielding?" he asked.

Flames like sparklers shot up from the candles, casting the room in an amber glow as though we were burning in Hell. We all gasped, sucking in the air in a hideous hiss like it was our last breath.

"Don't break the circle," Tilly said, her conviction wavering as if she wasn't sure we shouldn't let go. I almost lost X's hand. He fought against my grip. I didn't think it was intentional. I was positive he was scared. He eventually relaxed when the candle flames stabilized. They were burning brighter than before but there was nothing otherworldly about them now.

Chamberlin was breathing loudly. I was worried he was going to hyperventilate. His words came out in gasps. "Tell her I'm sorry. Tell her I'm sorry, X!"

X didn't sound much better than Chamberlin, despite the

reduction in his trembling. I think he was crying. It was too dark to tell for sure. "Maddy, your brother is sorry," he said. "I'm sorry. We are all sorry." The flames died down, they were close to being extinguished now. Only the base of the wicks held onto an orange glow. "Maddy," X said, pleadingly. "If that's you, let yourself be known. Talk to us."

The flames shot up again as if to say yes, it's me, here I am. X squeezed my hand so tightly, I thought if he squeezed any harder, he would break it.

The orangey red glow of the flames made Chamberlin's face look like it was covered in blood. They were all covered in blood. In the center of the mat, a figure began to materialize. It started off as a dark spot in the center of the flames and grew into a towering shadow, taking on a humanoid form. My body was covered in goose flesh. I held my breath. I was trembling. I was freezing. Transformed into a broken compass again, the guide spun around and around on X's homemade Ouija mat.

We all heard it—we must have all heard it. It wavered like the sound came from underwater. "Sister."

I jumped to my feet, breaking the circle. The flames went out. I groped for the light switch. Finding it, I flicked the switch up, grateful for the lights.

My face was wet with tears and so were the faces of Chamberlin and his friends. Behind Chamberlin, a shadow rushed across the room, disappearing through the wall.

CHAPTER NINE

A Different Name for the Angel

"I'm sorry," I said to everyone, wiping my tears on my pajama's sleeve. "When I heard the voice say my name. When I heard it say Sister, I just . . . I just freaked and went for the lights."

Hearing my Fielding-given name scared me—really scared me. I wasn't sure if the voice we heard was Maddy's or not. It sounded like hers, but it was different as if in death it took on a new life—a darker one. That was more than enough reason to break the circle. She was gone, nothing could change that. No good could or would come from using a spirit board or a spirit mat that doubled as a *Yu-Gi-Oh!* card game mat. Madelin Fielding was dead.

Tilly rubbed my back. I tensed, almost screaming. I hadn't noticed she'd gotten up to comfort me. "It's okay," she said, seeming not to have noticed my aversion to her touch. "I don't blame you, that was pretty scary stuff." Tilly made another circuit of my back. "We've had the guide move twice but we've never had an interaction with the dead like we did tonight."

"Never?" I asked, trying to keep my voice steady.

Tilly shook her head. "It's like you're a supernatural conductor," she said.

I didn't like the sound of that, and I was sure my face showed it. She responded with a kind smile, taking my hand and leading me back to the broken circle. We took our places on the blanket. "Do you have a lot of interactions in the house?" Tilly asked. She rambled on, not giving me a chance to respond. I was okay with that. I found her voice soothing, and I was too shaken to formulate coherent sentences. "Chamberlin says he never does. I have. They don't believe me," she said, her eyes darting to X and then to Chamberlin, "but I've heard Baby Ivette's cry."

I, too, had heard it. Heard it for the first time that very night—the pitiful cry that sounded like a kitten. But I wasn't going to share that. I didn't want any more attention on me. It was my turn to glance at Chamberlin and X. They hadn't moved or spoken since I turned on the light. Their silence made me feel uncomfortable. X was in his own world, his head bowed, his eyes on his homemade Ouija mat. Chamberlin, on the other hand, watched me, his eyes taking on a piercing quality.

I was grateful for Tilly. I liked her even more. "I heard Ivette twice," Tilly went on to say. "Once at twilight and once in the middle of the night. Her cry was the loudest in the middle of the night. I think that's because that's when it happened."

"What happened?" I asked, giving her my full attention. There was no point in getting into a one-sided staring match with Chamberlin.

Tilly smiled, showing her top row of crooked teeth. Again, I felt sorry for her. "The most interesting thing about the Elenore Fielding House is the Fieldings," she said. "They die in the house or because of it, and when they do, everyone acts like it's an honor to be added to the death toll. Their names are forever to be spoken in some campy tour. But they never tell you the true story. They don't talk about it. Like how Chain never talks about his mother's death or your father's. Over time the truth gets lost and the Fieldings rewrite history, making it whatever suits their little tour. But you can't hide the truth. The Fieldings, though they try, can't hide from it. It finds them, like a bad rash."

I was on the edge of my seat, so to speak. I didn't need a lecture on Fielding Wonderland logic. I had firsthand insight into the twisted way their minds operate, especially when I let Chamberlin and Elenore use me as Maddy's body double at the foot of the stairs.

"What happened to Baby Ivette?" I asked. "What's the real story?" In truth, I didn't know what the Fieldings said was Baby Ivette's cause of death, just that she died mysteriously. I assumed she succumbed to an early childhood disease, like most children of the 1800's, and hadn't given further thought to it.

Tilly was all teeth. "Her big brother Elias murdered her."

I couldn't help it, my eyes darted to Chamberlin where he remained as still as a statue. X also remained in the same posture, fixated on the Ouija mat.

"How do you know that?" I asked. Chamberlin never said Baby Ivette's mysterious death was in fact a murder. I was sure of that. That would be something I think I would remember.

Tilly spoke hurriedly now, full of excitement. "Chamberlin is in possession of his great-great-grandfather's journal," she told me, her eyes widening until I thought they would pop out of her head and roll onto the floor. "Elias Fielding wrote all about it. He said it was an accident, but I don't think it was. Before he smothered her with a pillow, he had made several entries on how much he hated his little sister and how jealous he was of her. Until Ivette was born, he was the baby." Tilly nodded, apparently agreeing with what she was about to say. "I believe he murdered Baby Ivette in cold blood."

Chamberlin smacked the floor with a mighty thud. Tilly and I jerked our heads in his direction. X was still in his own world. Chamberlin's face was bright red, verging on purplish. I didn't think he could blush that deeply, or at least I had never seen him look like that before. The vein in his forehead was pulsing. I instinctively held my breath.

"That's enough Tilly!" he said in a burst of emotion. "This is not some campfire story. This is my family you're talking about. I shared things with you because you're my friend, not so you have something to gossip about."

I had never heard Chamberlin talk like that. All traces of the sensitive boy were gone. His voice was like a whip. From the look on Tilly's face, this was also a first for her and she felt the sting of it. Her limbs folded into her body like they had done at the cemetery. They seemed too long, curling in on her frail core until she resembled a mutated insect. That was it, she resembled an insect not a shell-less tortoise. Her limbs were too long to be compared to a turtle and then there was her last name Deedle—Deedle rhymes with Beetle.

Tears coated her brown eyes. "I'm sorry Chamberlin," she said, avoiding looking at him. "That was insensitive of me. I love your family. I didn't mean to say it like that, like it was gossip. I wouldn't have said it to anyone but Trinity. I'm sorry."

In saying, 'I love your family', I knew she meant him. If X wasn't in love with Chamberlin, Tilly was. His biting remark robbed her of all of her confidence. She regressed to a child. She seemed so small and weak. And very distraught. It's hard to explain it. It was as if Tilly couldn't physically handle Chamberlin being mad at her and the only thing left to do was to implode. Her arms and legs retracted further into her body while her eyes seemed to grow larger and larger again. It wasn't her eyeballs that were going to roll but tears. I could see she was trying very hard to stop the tears from spilling over.

"I'm sorry, too," Chamberlin said in such a low voice I could scarcely hear him. "I lost my temper. It's not you I'm mad at. Forgive me?"

Tilly nodded. A solitary tear fell from her eye. She turned her face away from Chamberlin so he couldn't see she was on the brink of a meltdown. She focused her attention on her brother, who was still staring at the Ouija mat.

"You okay, X?" Tilly asked, her voice hitching as she swallowed tears.

"Do you think that was really Maddy?" X asked.

Chamberlin answered for Tilly. "Yes. Maddy always wanted Trinity to come home."

"She could have been talking about Elenore," X posed.

"Maybe," Chamberlin said, "but *Sister* is what we always called Trinity."

We were all quiet for some time after that. X and Chamberlin seemed to be in thought. Tilly was attempting to regain control of her emotions. She kept her face turned slightly from Chamberlin. Her lips quivered as tears beaded on her lashes. She used her insect-like arms as a shield, covering her heart, which from the looks of it Chamberlin broke. She was not able to rebound as quickly as her offender, who looked as beautiful and at peace as ever as he sat across from me. But Chamberlin was not ignorant of the effect his words had had on Tilly. He kept glancing at her, although only a little portion of her face was visible to him.

"Tilly?" Chamberlin said.

"Hmm," she answered. I assumed she didn't want to risk speaking and risk the potential rain shower that was so close to touching down.

"Why don't you give me a reading?"

Bowing her head and letting her hair fall in her face, she opened her purse. Tilly discreetly wiped her eyes under the cover of her hair. "Um . . . I can't," she said. "I took my decks out of my purse to fit the candles."

"You do tarot readings?" I asked, hoping talking about herself would take her mind off Chamberlin.

"I dabble in it," she said humbly.

"She's in psychic school," Chamberlin told me, keeping his eyes on Tilly.

"There's a school for that?" I asked.

She wiped her tears again before lifting her face to me and smiling. It wasn't a smile of teeth, but it looked genuine. "You sound like my dad," she said. "But yeah, there's a school for it. I always thought I had a sensitivity to the unseen world and have been trying to nurture it."

"It's why she doesn't get her teeth fixed," X said, seemingly fully recovered from shock.

"That helps somehow?" I asked, curious what teeth had to

do with a spirit world.

"No, not really," Tilly said, her smile brightening, "but I think you can't trust someone who is too pretty."

"Like Chamberlin?" X asked. There was no jest to his tone. It was as if he really wanted to know.

"I trust Chamberlin more than anyone," Tilly said, still not looking at him. "But you wouldn't want someone who looked like Chain to give you a reading, it would seem less real. Less authentic. Like he was some Hollywood actor playing a part. But someone like me, with teeth like me, will give the impression of a *real* reader. I mean—I *am* a real reader. I just want to come off sincere. Honest. Genuine. Like the world is ugly and so should be your—"

Chamberlin didn't let her finish her sentence. "You're not ugly," he said, in a sterner voice than his usual.

She accepted this with a nod and nothing more.

Tilly made sense in a strange way. She did have a genuine look to her. If I had to pick someone to give me a reading it would be someone who looked like her.

"I do all sorts of readings. Palm, tarot, astrological readings, and I'm working on becoming a reiki master," Tilly continued.

"She's really good," Chamberlin said.

"She is," X agreed. "So she doesn't need to have shark teeth. Tell her she should fix them. Maybe she'll listen to you."

"I like her teeth," Chamberlin objected. I wasn't sure if he was overcompensating to get Tilly out of her slump or if in some strange way he did like her teeth. He was a Fielding, and that meant he wasn't exactly normal.

"That's nice of you to say Chain," Tilly said, "but not even the Tooth Fairy likes my teeth."

Chamberlin and X laughed and so did I. Even Tilly let out a chuckle. She seemed to relax a little after that. Her limbs were less contorted, like she was unfolding in front of us.

"Well, I for one," I said, "am glad you don't have your deck. I don't know how much more communing with spirits I can handle. I don't think I'm going to be able to sleep tonight."

"You can stay in here if you like," Chamberlin offered. "I let

X and Tilly have my bed when they stay over, and I lay down your old mattress for myself. You can have your old mattress, and I can take Dad's room, or we can share if that's not too awkward for you."

"I have a better idea," X said. "Why don't I share the mattress with Trinity, and you take Tilly. I know in the past I was against you sharing a bed with my sister, but that was before I knew what a stand-up guy you are. I, Xavier Deedle, offer you my only sister's virginity for the privilege of sharing the same mattress with Trinity."

Tilly laughed, hopping onto Chamberlin's bed. All traces of the insect were gone. She grabbed her chest. "Oh Chamberlin Fielding, deflower me."

He laughed, a deep bellowing laugh. "That's quite an offer, X."

"Too bad I'm not a virgin," Tilly said with a sigh. "Would you still call it deflowering?"

"You're not a what?!" X said, his face flushing.

"Heck no," Tilly said, outwardly offended he thought she was. "No way am I going to be used as a virgin sacrifice. I watch too many scary movies. As soon as I found a guy that was willing, I was willing."

X looked me up and down like he was eyeing a cut of meat. "Trinity's too hot to be a virgin. I guess only Chain and I are going to end up virgin sacrifices."

Chamberlin shot X a glare that could have killed.

"What?!" Tilly said, beating her hands on the bed like a drum. "Chain, you're not?!"

He didn't have to respond. His crimson face told us what we needed to know.

"Wow," Tilly said evidently shocked. Honestly, so was I. If anyone was too hot to be a virgin it was Chamberlin. "I knew Elenore is a guard dog, but I didn't know she was a chastity belt too. Oh, Chamberlin Fielding," Tilly said in mock sympathy, "don't die a virgin. It will be my honor to deflower you." She put her finger to her chin in thought and asked, "Is that what you call it when the guy is the virgin?"

I smiled. I really liked Tilly.

* * *

We talked about everything and nothing until Tilly called bedtime. She had her Goddess Divinity class at 8 a.m. and needed to get a little sleep to be able to function. With that, we all took our spots. It felt wrong to kick Chamberlin out of his room to have my old mattress to myself and there was no way I was going back into Mr. Fielding's room tonight, so, to X's disappointment, I shared a bed with Chamberlin.

I lay there next to Chamberlin wide awake while everyone else slept. It looked like I did need my sleeping pills after all. I wasn't sure who the snorer was, X or Tilly, but I found myself listening to every exhale with wonder. Some sounded like snorts, others like the famous images of sawing logs.

All of a sudden, I felt eyes on me—Chamberlin's. He was watching me out of the corner of his eye.

"You can't sleep?" he asked.

"Not really. You?"

"No, not really."

"I like your friends," I said, meaning it.

"Thanks. I was lucky when they moved in next door. I don't have a lot of free time to go out and meet people."

"The family business," I said.

"Yep, the family business."

"I hope I can help a little."

"About that Trinity, you don't have to stay here. It's probably better if you go."

"You don't want me here?" I asked while I held my breath.

Chamberlin exhaled loudly, turning to his side to face me. His light eyes shone in the dark like stars. "I didn't say that," he retorted in a soft whisper. "It's just that if you stay, you may not get a chance to leave. I'd leave, if I could."

I mirrored him, lying on my side. "No, you wouldn't," I said. "You would never leave Elenore. And think about how much you would miss X and Tilly."

"Do you think Tilly's still mad at me?"

"Um . . . I don't think she was ever mad at you," I said, adjusting my hands under my head.

"It's not her I was upset with. It's not Maddy. It's not Elenore. It's not you. It's me. It's what was in Elias's journal."

"Yeah, about that," I said. "Where did you find it?"

He brushed back a golden strand of hair that fell into his face. "I didn't, Tilly did. She found it in her house in one of the walls that used to attach her house to ours."

"That seems a little too fortuitous. You sure it's real?" I asked. I didn't want to come straight out and say Tilly made the journal, but her finding it seemed fishy to me.

"It's real Trinity. It's how Tilly and I became friends."

"Oh, you were friends with Tilly first?" I asked, surprised. I had just assumed X had been the glue between them all.

"Yeah. She knocked on the door one day, not long after they moved in. While renovating her room, she found a journal in her wall. She didn't know her house was once attached to ours or who we were, just that she lived next to the Elenore Fielding House and the journal belonged to Elias Fielding. She thought maybe our ancestor hid it in their neighbor's house for safekeeping. When she came to the house to return the journal, Elenore made her buy a ticket to the tour I was just about to start. At the end of the tour, she gave me the journal."

"That's nuts."

He finger-combed his hair back again, tucking the long strands behind his ears. "Yeah, it was all in the journal. How he did it. How Elias held the pillow over his sister's face to stop her from crying."

"That's horrible," I said, a sinking feeling pervading my chest. "How could anyone do that to their baby sister?"

Chamberlin's exhale sounded loud in the room, louder than the snoring. "I couldn't believe it at first. I think I read it four times before it sunk in. I asked Tilly if she read it, and she said she had. But she hadn't told anyone about it besides her brother. I asked her if she could keep a secret and if her brother could. She said yes and we have been best friends ever since. It's funny how secrets can make or break a relationship."

I agreed, secrets can be a double-edged sword.

"I never told Elenore or Maddy about the journal and made Tilly and X swear not to mention it to them." Chamberlin rolled onto his back, his gaze on the many angles of the ceiling. "Earlier, I was just surprised how casually Tilly mentioned it to you. I didn't make her swear not to tell you, and she does know how much I trust you, but still it caught me off guard."

"I trust you, too, Chamberlin," I said, meaning so much more than that.

He pulled his eyes from the ceiling, propping his head up with his elbow. "Do you really?" he asked. "I wonder if that trust isn't misplaced."

I resisted moving his bangs out of his eyes. "Why would you say that?"

"There's so much more to the story Trin, so much more. When Emmit and Elenore found Ivette dead, the blame was put on a servant named Angeles Hillings."

"Angeles," I repeated.

"Yeah, that's right. Angeles, angel in Spanish. Angeles was an immigrant from Spain and spoke poor English. It was her word against Elias's. The end result was that she was hung for the murder of Ivette Fielding."

"Oh my gosh!" My hands moved to stifle my voice.

"That was the start of the Fielding curse. The day after her hanging, Elias's older sister Bethany died."

My pulse quickened. The decapitated wooden angel popped into my mind's eye. I kept my eyes fixated on Chamberlin's face, making sure a scratch didn't appear. "How? How did Bethany die? What's the real story?"

"She hung herself. Who knows why? Maybe it was guilt. Maybe she knew the servant Angeles was innocent," he whispered. I avoided asking about his recent brush with death, although I burned to. "After that," Chamberlin said, leaning closer to me, "Emmit cut off the wings of the angel on the newel post and the war officially began. I'm sure Emmit thought Angeles was still in the house, somehow embodying the angel at the foot of the stairs. It was as if he knew Angeles was innocent and thought that her hanging somehow caused Bethany's suicide. Claiming the wings of the angel was meant to hurt Angeles just as much as it was meant to hurt God."

"So, Emmit didn't just take any angels wings. He took Angeles's and she's the one who's out for Fielding blood," I mused.

He nodded. "And there's more," he said. "I could never tell Elenore or Maddy. And X doesn't know. Only Tilly knows. I told Tilly, well, because I trust her, like I trust you."

My pulse continued to quicken. I could hear my heart beat in my ears in a dull echo. I had no idea what he was going to say. I wasn't sure if I wanted to know, but figured not knowing was worse especially if it was something he could only trust Tilly with. "Tell me," I said, "I want to know everything."

Chamberlin took a deep breath, apparently contemplating if he should in fact tell me everything. "My father killed his baby sisters," he said as if he just pushed his words from the depths of his soul.

"What are you talking about?" I asked, my words coming out in a rattle. "I didn't know your father had sisters."

"*Had* being the key word. Lillian and Clementine Fielding were said to have died mysteriously as small children, but I know the truth. I was named for them as a reminder of what my father did. Chamberlin is a combination of both of their names. My father didn't add them to the tour. He couldn't because he was their killer."

"They died twice, having been forgotten. So much for the Fieldings' golden rules," I huffed.

"No, they're not dead, they're in the house," Chamberlin said. "I haven't forgotten them."

The way he said it, with so much conviction, like he knew it to be a fact, made the little hairs on the nape of my neck stand up. On impulse, I rubbed my neck until the feeling passed. "How did your father kill them?" I asked.

"He pushed them down the stairs. It was an accident, like Elias said of Ivette's death. As you know, Tilly thinks Elias killed his baby sister in cold blood, but Elias said it was an accident. According to his journal, he was playing peekaboo with a pillow in an attempt to stop her from crying. He'd cover his sister's face with it for a few moments before removing it to surprise her with a silly face. He left the pillow on too long and smothered her. I didn't know Elias, so I can't say for sure if his sister's death was an accident, but I knew my father, and I'm not sure if the deaths of his little sisters were truly accidental."

This confession shook me. Mr. Fielding was a kind man. He loved me and his children. I was sure of that. How could Chamberlin think he could kill someone, let alone his baby sisters? Yet, there was that feeling in my dream. The knowing that Mr. Fielding, as I always called him, even after I was adopted, had wanted to hurt me. Kill me even. But that was in my dream. In reality, though in fairness my dreams seemed real, Mr. Fielding had been a second father to me.

Chamberlin went on, his eyes on the ceiling again. "It was winter, and they weren't allowed to play in the snow, so my father pulled his sisters around the house on a blanket pretending it was a sleigh. They were having lots of fun until they hit the stairs and fell to their deaths, their skulls cracking open like eggs."

I covered my mouth with my hand, my words hardly distinguishable as English. "Oh my God."

"Elenore doesn't know about our aunts. If she did, I don't think she would have added Maddy's body to the foot of the stairs. I only know about it because my dad told me. He warned me Trinity—warned me of Angeles's curse. It's like Tilly said, we pass our family history on by mouth, reshaping it, rewriting it. With Tilly's help, I fact checked everything, from Angeles being hung for murder, to my father's sisters dying as children. It's all true. I have no choice but to believe my father's warning."

I studied him, my eyes dancing around his face for a hint. "What warning?" I asked. "What are you talking about?"

His long lashes fluttered, shadowing his eyes in darkness. "My father told me one day, by intent or by accident, Angeles the angel would make it so I killed one or both of my sisters. And that it's my duty to make sure I never do. He told me I have to look out for them always."

That was it—why Chamberlin attempted to take his life. He believed in the curse—believed he somehow had something to do with Maddy's death and didn't want to risk Elenore's life.

His voice grew raspy. "Maddy is dead, and I can't help but feel responsible. She wanted to leave. She wanted to go out on her own and make her own life. Elenore said no, and I supported Elenore. I didn't want Maddy to leave; I was being selfish," he said in a sob. "I told Maddy it was her duty as a Fielding to stay, like the rest of us. If I had given her my blessing, she would still be alive. She felt trapped because of Elenore—because of me. She saw no other way out."

I held his face to my chest, his tears hot as they penetrated my pajama top, my hands in his soft hair. I hadn't been this close to him since before my father's death. To hold him again felt like a dream come true even if it was over a nightmare situation.

"Tilly's right, it's not your fault," I said gently.

"What if the angel isn't done with me?" Chamberlin asked, being dead serious. "What if it kills Elenore? What if it kills you?"

A sob broke free. I held him closer to my chest. I didn't want Tilly and X to wake up. I wanted this moment to be just for us.

CHAPTER TEN

A Different Noise

I woke up to find I was the last one left in Chamberlin's bedroom. Everything had been cleaned up, aside from the mattress I was on. There was no sign of the blanket on the floor or the Ouija mat. No sign of the Deedles. Chamberlin's bed was made, and everything was put away, the box cutter included. It was so spick and span in there I wondered if Elenore performed morning checks of his room.

Doing my best, I made the mattress on the floor look presentable and returned to Mr. Fielding's bedroom to take a shower and get dressed.

I slept later than I thought possible given my dream last night and spiritual communing. I'm sure having Chamberlin in my arms had something to do with that. His being pressed against me seemed more like a dream than my actual dream, as if it was more plausible to time travel to the past and watch Chamberlin's face slide off in a bloody heap than it was to share a bed with him. It already seemed blurry in my head, like with waking it was destined to disappear.

The first tour started at 9:30 a.m. and it was almost 9 a.m. I hurriedly took to the stairs. As I was coming down the attic steps, I heard a noise that sounded like a rocking chair. Old houses make odd noises, but my curiosity got the best of me. I must have been a cat in another life, although The Grand Duke Wiskerton never seemed too curious about noises. He'd perk up his ears, lick his paws, ignore whatever it was he thought he heard, and go back to bed.

I thought the sound came from Baby Ivette's room, which was a staple on the tour, and one of the first rooms passed on the way downstairs. Her door was open. I walked in. Like most of the house, it was the same as I remembered it.

The room was large, no doubt she was meant to grow into it. In the corner sat a hand carved rocking horse with a mane and tail of real horsehair that she never got to use. Several other antique baby toys were lined up on a bureau including rattles and a stuffed rabbit that I was convinced was made from real fur. In the center of the room was a bassinet. The once white silk fabric was now yellowed with age. A large painting of Baby Ivette hung on the wall. The painting practically went from the floor to the ceiling. The background, her nursery, as I assumed it looked the day she was born, comprised the bulk of the painting. Ivette was drawn to scale. It was as if she had crawled into the painting and could make her escape at any moment. She was painted in a white gown with a delicate lace collar, the gown covering her feet. The same lace trimmed her bonnet. She had dark eyes like Mr. Fielding, like Maddy and Elenore. I can't say she looked like a happy baby, or even a baby. Though her body was small and infantine, her face seemed older, despite the fullness of her cheeks. There was just something about her face that seemed off.

I made my way to the door. I was wasting time; the clock was ticking away while I searched for phantom noises that I knew were nothing more than an old house making an odd noise. Abruptly, I stopped and spun on my heels. There it was again, the rocking. It had, in fact, been rocking I heard. The bassinet in the center of the room was swaying back and forth in a slow rock as though I had accidentally bumped into it, but I hadn't. I kept my eyes glued to the bassinet waiting for it to be still as I retraced my steps in my head. Maybe . . . maybe I *had* elbowed it or grazed it when I went to leave.

The bassinet didn't stop rocking. In truth, it never slowed. It continued at the same slow, methodical pace, to-and-fro, as if a restless baby was being lulled to sleep by an invisible hand.

My chest felt tight. I knew my heart rate must be elevated. I noticed I was cold despite feeling little beads of sweat at my hairline. I could leave or I could check the bassinet. It was now or never. I really must have been a cat in another life because I approached the bassinet. It was empty and I laughed at myself, my stressed giggle filling the room. For a split second, I half expected Ivette to be in there. I placed my hand on the bassinet to stop the rocking, and it did so without a fuss.

The mobile, consisting of tiny handstitched angels, swayed softly from their strings like they were flying. Their eyes were made of tiny black glass beads. Their felt faces had no other defining features besides those beady eyes. Like the wingless angel on the newel post of the stairs, these angels held torches in their hands. The torches were hand-embroidered in reds and oranges recalling me to the flames on the stained-glass panels in the portico doors and their purpose as guiding lights for the Fieldings and all lost souls.

I noticed a small pillow, also yellowed by time, in the bassinet. I couldn't help but wonder if it was the pillow Elias used to smother his baby sister. I shook off a chill that traveled down my spine with icy precision. I'd had enough of this room.

Right before I made it to the door, I heard the same slow rocking of the bassinet. Frustrated, I turned around. I would make sure the stupid thing never rocked again. I approached it with heavy strides, stomping my feet like a petulant child. I outstretched my hand to stop the rocking, when the bassinet suddenly sped up. Faster. Faster. Too fast now, every rock threatened to send the antique bassinet topside. My eyes remained fixated on the ever-rocking bassinet as I took a step back, then another, before I darted for the door. I was in the hall now. I turned around to close Ivette's bedroom door. If I couldn't stop the rocking, I could, at the very least, muffle the sound behind a closed door. That I had the power to do. My hand was on the decorative brass doorknob, and I was about to yank the bedroom door closed when something ice-cold grabbed my wrist. I screamed. It came out as a burst of air, the sound getting trapped in my chest. There was nothing there. I was alone. I slammed the door closed and sprinted down the stairs.

I leaned against a wall in the entry way and took a deep breath to collect my thoughts. I had lived in the Elenore Fielding House for nearly four years and in all that time I had never heard anything strange except for the occasional groaning floorboard. But they—whoever they are—said the Elenore Fielding House was haunted. Ghosts have been seen, voices heard, cold spots felt. I hadn't had anything close to what I would call an encounter until last night with the Ouija mat. But I was under a lot of stress and was exhausted. And to be honest, we were asking for it. You call a ghost enough times, one's bound to show up. I couldn't let last night get to me. It was like Mr. Fielding always said, "You never truly know what or who you're talking to through a spirit board." I couldn't trust that it was my father or Maddy we made contact with. I couldn't jump at every little sound and make something from nothing. I was here to stay and couldn't be scared off.

It wasn't ghosts trying to chase me out the front door with phantom cries and rocking bassinets. I was doing it to myself. The house was haunted. If anything, I was overdue for some haunting. It takes a strong woman to face her past. Running back to London would be an easy out. But it wasn't an option this time. Chamberlin needed me. It was time for me to face the truth. I should have come home sooner, before Maddy died. No— I should never have left in the first place.

I found Chamberlin sitting at the dining room table in front of an amazing breakfast smorgasbord. His back was to me. Hearing me approach, he turned and smiled. It was one of his genuine smiles that made him look timeless, like he really was a vampire. "You're finally up," he said. "I was getting worried Elenore was going to send a search party."

I didn't smile back, I couldn't. I noticed a small scratch ran over his right cheekbone. It was a pink line, the color of the inside of a grapefruit. The skin didn't appear to be broken. I saw no blood, but my mind went to Chamberlin in my nightmare from last night, to the scratch on his otherwise perfect face—to it bleeding—to the sound his face made as it slid from its lower half.

My eyes naturally gravitated to the wingless angel crowning the newel post at the foot of the stairs. I had been careful not to look at it on my way to the dining room. Elenore had done a good job gluing her head back on. You could barely make out the seam that ran across her face in a fine line. It was just as faint as the scratch that I saw on Chamberlin's face last night in my dream. That was until it started to drip blood.

The new addition to my nightmare was easily explainable. I kicked the head off a stupid angel that was believed to be in the market for a new set of wings. Of course that would manifest itself in my nightmares. Now that I learned the wingless angel was thought to be the embodiment of a vengeful servant, I was bound to be a little freaked out. But could I ignore this coincidence and the knot twisting in my stomach?

"What happened to your face?!" I questioned too loudly.

"Oh, that," he said, running his hand over his cheekbone. "I think you accidentally scratched me in your sleep."

I looked at my nails like they were deadly weapons, harbingers of the future. I thought about what my father said about Dunn women having been blessed with insight given to us by our ancestors and somehow magically manifested in our red hair.

My father said a lot of things, and as much as I love him, a lot of the stuff he said was hot air. What was I to believe, that Chamberlin was going to lose half his face because I scratched him in his sleep? That didn't even coincide with Chamberlin's theory of the Fielding curse. According to Fielding lore, the women were afflicted, not the men. If I thought about it logically, taking into consideration that my father said Dunn women had insight into the *future*, I would see, as what seemed to be my new normal, that I was overreacting.

I always dreamed of my father's partner—dreamed of Franklin Fielding dying. That was the past. Chamberlin and Maddy being in my dream as children proved that. I didn't glimpse the future. No—what I saw or what I conjured up in my nightmare was a vision of the past. Not a vision—I don't think there was anything prophetic in it. It was just something I dreamed every night as a conclusion to Mr. Fielding's disappearance—answering questions there were no answers for. No, I didn't want to see the future, and I hadn't. Chamberlin was fine and was going to be fine.

Chamberlin turned his seat to get a better look at me. He was in black jeans with holes at the knees and a black T-shirt with a grim reaper on it. He didn't need to wear eyeliner like his friend X, his thick lashes outlined his light blue eyes in a dark veil. To complete his look, he wore black combat boots with bright red laces, the color of freshly spilt blood. "Hey Trin, don't worry about the scratch," he said with a dismissive wave of his hand. "It's not a big deal. I didn't even feel it and it'll be gone in a day or two."

I nodded, rubbing my right wrist. It still felt cold.

"Good, you're up," Elenore said, coming into the dining room. She appeared frazzled. She wasn't as put together as usual. Her long hair was tied back in a messy bun, and she didn't have her makeup on. She handed me a packet of papers. "Thanks so much for agreeing to stay and help."

"What's this?" I asked, thumbing through it.

"It's Maddy's schedule. Until I come up with a game plan, we're just going to have you work her shifts."

"Um okay, so uh, the tours run all day?" I asked.

"Yep," Elenore said in a chirp. "This is how it goes, Sister. We all eat breakfast as a family. The rest of the meals are on you. I usually have snacks in the kitchen. Last tour is at 6:30. Lights out is up to you, except when we have a Night-in like last night—then lights out at midnight."

"Any time off?" I asked, my eyes darting to Chamberlin who found this whole thing humorous.

He let out a laugh that sounded more like a roar. "She runs the house like a prison. I told you to book your flight. Get away when you still can Trin."

Elenore ignored him for the most part, but she made one

small correction. "It's Sister, not Trin, not Trinity. Just Sister. Do not pollute her name Chamberlin." Her focus was back on me. "And yes, Sister, to answer your question, we each get two days off a week. Chamberlin usually works weekends and holidays, so his scheduled days off are Tuesday and Wednesday. But Linnie is a team player."

"So much for retiring Linnie," Chamberlin mumbled under his breath, reading my mind.

Elenore went on as if she hadn't heard him. "Linnie's already agreed to do Maddy's tours today to give you the opportunity to shadow him as a way to refresh your memory. Then, tomorrow, you're on your own."

"Okay," I said, hoping it would all come back to me like riding a bike.

"Good, now eat up Sister," Elenore insisted. "The first tour starts in twenty minutes. And when you're done, help carry the food into the kitchen." She elbowed Chamberlin. "Help clear the dining room table."

"I'm still eating," he said with a whine, grabbing a slice of breakfast pizza as Elenore headed into the kitchen. Moments later, she came back into the dining room and handed me a plate.

"Wow, Elenore you out did yourself," I said, taking a cheese Danish and some fresh strawberries. This was a far cry from yesterday's muffin.

"Not her," Chamberlin said with his mouthful. "Leftovers from the bachelorette party breakfast."

"Oh," I said.

"Yeah, this is the one and only perk of Elenore's Night-ins," Chamberlin told me. "Sometimes they leave us leftovers."

Elenore was cleaning the dining room table at warp speed, but she still found a moment to comment. "Told you the Night-ins were a good idea," she piped over Chamberlin's shoulder.

"I didn't say that," Chamberlin called after her. "But I do like this breakfast pizza. I wonder where they got it from."

"Good," she said, moving the fruit bowl that sat in front of me, "because it's also your lunch and dinner."

"Fine with me," he said.

I put my Danish down and decided to help Elenore. "Why the rush?" I asked.

"We can't leave the food in the dining room during the tour. Some brat kid will eat a strawberry, have an allergic reaction, and sue us," she said.

"Oh, I didn't think about that," I admitted.

Chamberlin brought a box of donuts in from the dining room and placed them on the kitchen table along with his slice of pizza. "I was thinking Elenore . . ." he said.

She walked past him, heading into the dining room. "What's that Linnie?"

"The dining room is the dullest part of the tour. Nothing really happened in there and it's such a huge room. It's wasted potential."

"No," she said sharply.

He pouted, making himself look like a boy again. Elenore and Chamberlin seemed to have more of a mother-son relationship than a brother-sister one, even more so than I remembered.

"I'm curious. What's your idea?" I chimed in. I knew the conversation was between the two of them, but I was a part of this family again and thought my opinion should matter. Chamberlin was right about the dining room being the most boring part of the tour. It was also the quickest stop. It was used to talk more about Victorian customs rather than anything spooky.

"Be quick about it," Elenore said, "people are already lining up outside."

"Tilly is getting really good with her readings. Why don't we have her set up in the dining room at the table or in one of the corners offering tarot card readings or palm readings after the tour. The dining room is close enough to the gift shop that it could lead to spill over and more sales."

"No. Capital 'N', 'O'," Elenore said in her no-nonsense voice.

"Why not?" Chamberlin asked.

Elenore brought in the last of the platters from the dining

room and placed them on the kitchen table. I sat down to finish my Danish, trying hard not to look up at the kitchen fan.

Elenore kept busy. She was unloading the dishwasher now, placing the yellow handled knives, which always made me think of bananas, back into the knife block. "I know you want to help out your little friend but it's not good for business," she told Chamberlin.

He protested, "It will bring—"

She cut him off. "Think about it Linnie. Tilly has to get paid, right? She's not family, so that means she'll want money for her services. She can only charge so much for a reading. We can't ask her to hand over half of the little money she would make. It's not practical. Besides, readings can take a long time, and they may run into the next tour. Sorry Chamberlin, it's just not good for business."

"Forget it," he said, tossing his half-eaten piece of pizza on top of a platter of bite-size quiche before storming out of the kitchen.

Elenore grumbled, "He's so dramatic."

My eyes lifted to the kitchen fan. I thought Elenore should be a little more delicate with him. I knew he was only trying to help her and Tilly. I had a feeling he was still upset over how he spoke to Tilly last night and was hoping to give her some good news.

I saw the practicality in everything Elenore said, but I was sensing there was more to the story. "You're not a fan of Tilly?" I asked.

"It's not that," she said, taking a seat across from me.

I lifted an inquisitive eyebrow.

"Okay, it is like that. I don't like her."

"Why? She seems really nice."

"She is . . . she is, it's just, well . . ." Elenore folded her arms into herself like Tilly did last night after Chamberlin yelled at her and as I had first seen her at the cemetery—the living embodiment of a human-insect.

"Yeah, I noticed that," I said. "I think she does it when she's feeling uncomfortable. Anxiety, I guess."

I took another strawberry. They were really good. Elenore didn't have to worry about guests going into anaphylactic shock after eating a strawberry, I was going to eat all of them.

"And then there are her teeth," Elenore said, retracting her own lips for emphasis. "Good gracious, her family has enough money, you'd think they get her teeth fixed. I hear Plant Haven is doing very well." She shook her head in what could only be frustration. "I know the Fieldings have good genetics when it comes to the looks department, but I don't think they could cancel out the genetics behind teeth like those."

"What are you talking about?" I asked.

She picked up Chamberlin's half eaten slice of pizza and took a bite. "Chamberlin's at the age where any girl he's hanging out with could potentially . . ."

"Have his babies," I laughed, finishing her sentence. I was thinking of Tilly's comment about Elenore acting like a chastity belt. She had nothing to worry about. At this rate, Chamberlin really would die a virgin.

"You laugh Sister, but it's true. Fielding sperm are like Olympic swimmers. I don't want ugly nieces or nephews. And we can't afford braces."

"You know you're being ridiculous. Tilly and Chamberlin are just friends."

"Yes, I know that, but I worry about those sorts of things. I'm his sister, his mother, and his father all rolled into one, so that's three times the worrying. We owe X so much, so I tolerate Tilly following Chamberlin around, but I don't like it. If you don't think that girl is in love with him, you're blind."

I was about to agree with Elenore that I thought Tilly did like Chamberlin, but that it was Chamberlin who was blind to it, when the phone rang.

"You still have a landline?" I asked, surprised anyone did these days.

"Yep," she said, moving platters of food to get to the phone where it sat on the kitchen countertop. I noticed the Brooklyn Community Food Bank cardboard box on the counter. I put down my Danish. My appetite was gone.

"The Elenore Fielding House, Elenore Fielding speaking. I

can help you. —Oh, hi Allison," she said with a sickly-sweet voice that made me laugh. "—Yes, we did get the card. Thank you. —He's doing okay. He must've shut his phone off. —No, perfect timing, he's just about to start a tour." She covered the receiver with her hand and yelled for Chamberlin.

Chamberlin entered the kitchen with his arms crossed over his chest, shuffling his feet. Elenore was right, he was being dramatic, but did he have to look so adorable doing it? He took the phone from her, giving her stony eyes.

"Oh hey Allison. —Thank you. —Tonight . . . um . . . my sister's here from London. —Uh yeah, I guess that will be okay. I'll invite X and his sister. —Yes, that's them. —Bye. See you tonight."

"I'm glad you're hanging out with Allison. I like her." Elenore said, pleased, taking her seat at the kitchen table.

"I don't," Chamberlin said spitefully. He turned to me, tucking his bangs behind his ears. "I hope you're up for hanging out tonight? It will be less awful if you're there."

Before I could answer, Elenore asked Chamberlin, "Why don't you like Allison?"

"Elenore, I'm not doing this now. I told you, X likes her."

She poked him in his side. "But she likes *you.*"

"Allison's nice," he said. "There's just nothing else there." His eyes darted to me. "I just don't feel anything."

Elenore shook her head at him. "There's something wrong with you—something really wrong."

The phone rang again.

"Allison," Elenore said, "better get it."

"The Elenore Fielding House, Chamberlin Fielding speaking. I can help you." He handed the phone to Elenore. "For you."

Her eyebrows scrunched up. She got to her feet, taking the phone from him. "I thought I told you not to call here again," she said nastily before hanging up.

Before I could ask who that was, Elenore was hurrying us out of the kitchen. "You two better get a move on. You're past go time," she said, tapping on the face of her watch. "Sister, make sure you pay close attention and ask Chamberlin any questions that pop into your head. Remember, you're on your own tomorrow."

"Got it," I said.

Chamberlin and I made our way to the front door. The awkwardness between us when I'd first arrived was gone, but the closeness of last night was also gone. It was like a fleeting dream. I wanted it back.

"So, who was that on the phone?" I asked.

"Do you remember that young detective that was on my dad's case?"

"Yeah, I do, Vinney."

"That was him. Elenore dated him for a long time after we entombed my dad—years. They almost got married."

We made it into the foyer, standing side by side in front of the stained-glass doors of the portico. The tour could wait a few more minutes before we unlocked the front door.

"What happened?" I asked.

Chamberlin shrugged. "Not sure," he said. "All I know is she called it off and he didn't take it very well. I used to like him. I liked him a lot. But now, not so much. We've exchanged some words over him harassing Elenore. I think she should file a restraining order, but she won't."

I rubbed my wrist again. "I saw him at Maddy's funeral."

"Yeah, he was there. Low, if you ask me."

"Maybe he wanted to pay his respects," I said over the sound of the growing crowd. The house seemed so normal then, the magical stillness of the Elenore Fielding House stripped away. The house was just a house. I could hear the conversations taking place a few feet from us on the other side of the stained-glass doors. Elenore always unlocked the front door early in the morning, allowing people to huddle into the entryway in case there was bad weather. It wouldn't be long now before Elenore came running out of the kitchen to see what the hold-up was. People were basically pressed against the stained-glass doors. If a few more people squeezed into the entryway, I was sure the doors were going to give way and the tour would start without our say so.

"Vinney came to Maddy's funeral because he wants Elenore back," Chamberlin told me, his voice dropping as if he thought Vinney could be on the other side of the stained-glass doors. "It wasn't the time or place." He smiled at me. My eyes went to the scratch on his cheek. "But it is time to start the tour. Ready?" he asked.

"Ready as I'll ever be."

"Let the torch lights of the angels above guide lost spirits home to the Elenore Fielding House," he said ceremoniously, opening the stained-glass doors to our first tour.

CHAPTER ELEVEN
A Different Tour

We had a group of twenty-five, which, from what I gathered, was considered a sold-out tour. We had a nice mix of the young and old. I used to hate it when a large group of kids would come together, or a senior group. There must be something about hanging around your own age group that turns you into a raging jerk.

"Welcome to the Elenore Fielding House. My name is Chamberlin Fielding, and I will be your tour guide this morning," Chamberlin told the group as we huddled in the foyer under the brass gasolier chandelier. "The Elenore Fielding House, as you may have heard, is a real-life haunted house. The Elenore Fielding House has been featured on television in such shows as *True Hauntings* and *America's Ghosts*, in magazines and books, such as *Haunted New York* and *Brooklyn's Haunted Past*, and most recently on the *Real Haunted Houses of America* podcast. If you will follow me please, we will start the tour upstairs today."

Chamberlin led his group down the hall, taking the servant stairs to the second floor, avoiding the main stairs and the guests who would soon be waiting there for Elenore's tour. Things were not always so chaotic, but Elenore had a lot of rescheduled tours to fit in. I lagged behind so as not to obstruct a paying guest.

"The Elenore Fielding House was built in 1792 by Emmit Theodore Fielding for his wife, Elenore," Chamberlin told the tour group once we reached the second story landing. "Emmit and Elenore lived in the house until their deaths. They had three children: Bethany, Elias, and Ivette, who we will talk about in great lengths on the tour, but first I want to tell you a little bit more about Emmit Feilding. Emmit was one of the richest men in New York City, his business being the always lucrative gold. He also owned a copper plant. When the American government issued the penny in 1793, Emmit Fielding was one of the few people with copper refineries and became, by today's standard, a billionaire."

Chamberlin delivered his lines as he first had when I was a child visiting the house with my father and he conducted a tour just for me. It was all second nature to him now. Where he had tripped up on facts before, he now rattled off the names and dates like it was common knowledge.

He led the tour down the East Hall. It was too wide to be called a hall really, but I'm not sure what else to call it. It was almost four times the size of an American standard hallway, but everything in the Elenore Fielding House was on a large scale: the hallways were wider, the ceilings taller, the rooms larger, the fixtures grander.

"Emmit's wife, Elenore, wanted more space so they moved from New York City to Brooklyn," Chamberlin said as the group followed him. Everyone laughed at that and so did Chamberlin. "As hard as it is to believe, in the late 1700's Brooklyn *did* offer more space," Chamberlin said. "Brooklyn was a small shipping community then and had lots of land for development. The house you see now is only a glimpse into what she used to be."

It unnerved me to hear Chamberlin refer to the house as a *she*. Sure, the house had a woman's name, but it made me feel like the Elenore Fielding House was more than a house—more than a place for lost souls to come home to.

Chamberlin went on. "The house you see before you today

is the oldest and original part of the Elenore Fielding House. With the news of his wife's first of three pregnancies, Emmit decided to have a wing added onto the house. Mikey Loves Brooklyn was originally the Bethany Wing and where Plant Haven is now used to be the Elias Wing, duly named for his first two children. These wings were added to the house through corridors." He pointed to a photograph of the Elenore Fielding House that was blown up and framed in the hall. It lacked all of the beauty of the original daguerreotype and the painting in Frank Fielding's bedroom.

"The use of corridors proved to be an ingenious idea," Chamberlin went on to say after everyone had a chance to look at the picture on the wall. "As future generations of Fieldings fell upon hard times, they were able to sell parts of the house off. The corridors were simply deconstructed, and the doorways bordered up. But before we get ahead of ourselves, let me point out that it's believed that the murderer of Emmit and Elenore Fielding used one of these corridors to get to the unlucky couple in their sleep."

Chamberlin opened a door to a room on his right and gestured for the tour group to enter. "Which leads us to our first room on the tour, Emmit and Elenore Fielding's bedrooms."

I knew the rooms well. It was always one of my favorite stops on the tour. Probably because of the *mysterious* story of death and love that surrounded Emmit and Elenore and the way their rooms were attached to each other through a huge arched door that made me think of giant hobbits.

"The bedroom we are standing in now belonged to my great-great-great-grandfather Emmit Fielding," Chamberlin told the group. "It was customary through the 17 and 1800's for husbands and wives to have adjoining bedrooms, and through that door," he said, pointing to the door that made me think of hobbits, "was Elenore's room."

A little girl with pigtails raised her hand. I assumed she was around six or seven years old.

"You have a question, great! I encourage questions," Chamberlin said warmly. "Let's hear it?"

"If they had to sleep in separate rooms where did their

babies come from?" the little girl asked in a serious tone.

Chamberlin swallowed a laugh along with the rest of the group, me included. A rosy glow highlighted Chamberlin's high cheekbones and the scratch that cut across the side of his face. For the first time, I noticed he was wearing vampire fangs. "I'm not sure how detailed a response I should give that," Chamberlin mused.

The group laughed.

"Don't be stupid," the little girl's older brother said with a nudge. I marked him as a teenager. He had all of the moodiness of a high schooler.

"You don't have to answer that," the little girl's mother said, her cheeks flushed with what I knew had to be embarrassment as she stood behind her daughter, holding her two hands so she couldn't raise them again. "Sorry, please continue."

Chamberlin nodded. "Uh so, like I was saying, the room we are standing in was Emmit's," he said. "On the wall, you will see the only known painting of Elenore Fielding. She had it painted for her husband in 1809 for his birthday. In the adjoining room, you will see a painting of Emmit he had commissioned for his wife. In both rooms, you will notice numerous paintings of the same child. They are of Elias Fielding, Emmit's and Elenore's first and only son. You will see similar boyhood portraits of Elias throughout the home, so keep an eye out."

He encouraged the tour group to look around and view the paintings.

After everyone made their way around both rooms, Chamberlin spoke, standing near the door we'd entered from. "Emmit and Elenore were not the first to die in the house. But their deaths are the first deaths that pointed to murder. Though it was customary for husband and wife to sleep in their separate rooms, Emmit was found with his wife in this very bed," he said, pointing to the four-poster bed in the room. It was very similar to Mr. Fielding's bed—huge and ornate. It had the same spiraled posts that nearly hit the ceiling.

Chamberlin walked over to the bed and threw back the sheet to expose two bodies mapped out in duct tape on the mattress.

"Emmit and Elenore were found dead in this bed holding hands."

"Who killed them?" the little girl with pigtails blurted out, not having a hand to raise.

"That's a good question," Chamberlin said. "There are a few theories."

"You don't know?" the brother asked.

"Unfortunately, no one knows for sure," Chamberlin said. "What we *do* know is that both of their bedroom doors were locked from the inside." Chamberlin pointed to the door behind him. "The servants used an axe to get through the door. You can still see a cut in the trim where they missed the door trying to get it open." The group pressed forward to see the mark left by the axe.

"A suicide pact was highly popular for a while amongst neighbors," Chamberlin went on to say. "Why end their lives? No one knew. But a planned suicide did help to explain how they were found and why the doors were locked. It gave purpose to them holding hands. It was like they knew death was coming for them. It did seem like they weren't casually sleeping but waiting for death and locked their doors as not to be disturbed in their undertaking."

Chamberlin finger-combed his hair back. "There were those who thought suicide was too neat and thought the Fieldings were murdered. One of those being Head Inspector Mallory. It was his belief that the Fieldings were poisoned by one of their servants. Remember the corridors I mentioned earlier?" The group nodded their heads in unison. "Well, Mallory speculated that the murderer used the Elias Corridor to enter Emmitt's bedroom at night and poisoned his decanter." Chamberlin sauntered over to a decanter made of cut glass that sat with matching long-stemmed glasses on a small table. "This would have been the decanter and glasses Emmit and Elenore would have enjoyed their evening glass of wine from before bed. It was customary for the Fieldings to enjoy a glass of wine before they went to sleep and the maid, knowing this, poisoned them. Inspector Mallory pointed his finger at Angeles Hillings."

I sucked air, not because Mr. Fielding had carried on the tradition of drinking a glass of wine before bed, and that brought me back to my nightmare and all of the blood, but because of Angeles

Hillings. That was the name of the servant Elias framed for the murder of Baby Ivette. That couldn't be right. I knew that Emmit and his wife died a middle-aged couple in bed holding hands. But if Angeles was hung for the murder of Ivette, how could she have poisoned Emmit and Elenore?

Chamberlin ran his hand over a section of the wall near the bed. "This used to be an entrance into the Elias Wing. If you look closely, you can see where it was patched. This is most likely the corridor Angeles Hillings took."

"Why would the maid kill them?" a young man asked, from the back of the group.

"Love," Chamberlin said. "Emmit was not only a man of exceptional wealth but was a man of exceptional beauty."

"The apple didn't fall far from the tree," a middle-aged woman said with a good-natured laugh.

Chamberlin blushed, clearing his throat before he continued. "Emmit was known to get into trouble with the ladies. We have several letters he wrote to his wife apologizing for what he called digressions of the heart. Elenore often writes in her diary of her husband's handsome face and it being the source of their marital problems. You can read the letters and diary entries downstairs if you like before you leave, copies are hanging up in the downstairs hall. I will point them out as we pass them."

"You don't look like him," the little girl in pigtails called from Elenore's room as she stared at the painting of Emmit Fielding.

"No, not much," Chamberlin agreed. "I take after my mother, Dorothy Fielding or as she was better known, Dottie. We will see pictures of her soon. But I always thought my sister Elenore resembled him in the mouth area."

The Emmit Fielding painting could have been a painting of Franklin Fielding. Elenore did look the most like her father. Frank Fielding was a very attractive man. As handsome as his wife was beautiful, but where Chamberlin's mother had light hair and light eyes, Mr. Fielding was all dark.

Chamberlin continued. "Inspector Mallory speculated

Emmit's and Elenore's deaths were the result of a spurned lover, although Angeles Hillings was never convicted, leaving Emmit's and Elenore's deaths some of the most mysterious in the house. But before we move on with the tour, there is one more theory I should mention. Emmit's and Elenore's son Elias, their only child survived by them, was a suspect. No evidence was officially brought against Elias; however, half of the household thought he did it and abandoned their posts. The reason given—greed. Elias was said to have wanted control of his father's money. But Elias did not have the same head for business as his father, and after Emmitt's death the family fortune began to dwindle."

Chamberlin picked up an embroidered pillow off an antique chair next to the door. I knew what was coming. This was my favorite part of the tour. "Oh, I should mention another theory, if I can even call it that. It has something to do with this pillow. It reads: True love breathes death."

"That's creepy," the little girl in pigtails said, coming closer to get a better look at the pillow.

"Very, very creepy," Chamberlin agreed. "This pillow was embroidered by Elenore. Some think it's a cruel joke to her ever-cheating husband. Some think it's a prophecy. Some think it's a curse. The curse being when true love finds a Fielding, they die. Elenore, being a Fielding only by marriage, the curse didn't apply to her. But Emmit, on the other hand, was a Fielding. Some believe that Emmit finally found true love with the servant Angeles and that was what killed him. In this retelling, Emmit dies and Elenore, loving Emmit as she must have to put up with his behavior, poisons herself, taking her husband's hand in death."

"I like that ending the best," an elderly woman said.

Chamberlin nodded. "It's the one I like the best as well."

It was the same for me. I found something so romantic in Elenore's gesture of devotion. Her love for Emmit was so great, she couldn't abandon him. She followed him to the grave.

A teenage girl spoke now, twirling her dark hair around her finger. "Does that make you afraid to fall in love?"

Chamberlin glanced at me before he answered. "To be

honest, a little. But I don't think love is in my cards. Despite my many tarot readings that say otherwise."

"Trust in the cards," the girl said. "I'm single."

Everyone laughed.

"Well, with that," Chamberlin said, as red as a lobster, "let's head across the hall to Baby Ivette's nursery."

While everyone piled into Ivette's room, I grabbed Chamberlin's arm, keeping him in Emmit's bedroom with me. "What's that about Angeles? That can't be the same servant Elias framed for Ivette's death."

"No, I don't think it is," he said. "There was only one Angeles Hillings, and she was hung for the murder of Ivette Fielding. I think the name just got passed on through the generations and no one knew why until Tilly found Elias's journal. It's like a little truth helps tell a new lie."

"So, what *is* the truth?" I asked.

Chamberlin shrugged, his bangs falling over his blue eyes. "I have my own theory," he said.

"I'm all ears."

He glanced at the tour group; they were still busy exploring Ivette's bedroom. "I think history repeats itself," Chamberlin said in a low voice, ensuring the conversation stayed between us. "I think Elias killed Ivette and framed Angeles because Ivette was his half-sister. Tilly and I discovered that Angeles gave birth to a girl the same year Ivette was born. Her name was never written down. Just the letter 'I'."

"'I' for Ivette," I said.

He nodded. "I think Elias knew about his father's affair with the servant or maybe he guessed at it. Remember, he would have been eight at the time, so I'm not sure how much he understood, but I think he killed Ivette and framed Angeles to free the house of his father's lover and their love child. Maybe he did it for his mother. Maybe he did it for himself. We will never know. The only thing he says in his journal is that Ivette's death was an accident."

"What about Bethany?"

"Like I said last night, I think Bethany guessed at the truth or came to know it and felt guilty for not speaking up when they hung Angeles for Ivette's murder. I suppose it could have been her father's affair that drove her to it too."

"And Emmit and Elenore," I said in a whisper, "who killed them?"

"I think they learned the truth. Maybe from Elias himself. His last journal entry read: 'I have purged my soul to my parents'. I believe he told them he killed Ivette, and they decided to end their lives."

"Wow," I said, not able to say anything more.

"Yeah," Chamberlin said, "wow." He leaned against the wall, his head just missing a painting of Elias Fielding. "Each generation is more screwed up than the last."

I ran my finger across the back of his hand. "Hey, it's not that bad," I said, trying to sound cheerful.

He scoffed. "You only know the half of it."

"Then tell me the rest," I said, taking his hand. It was soft, trembling, or maybe that was my own. "Let me share the burden with you. I know you told Tilly."

His eyes lifted to mine. He held me in the frame of his thick lashes. I could have stayed like that forever, staring into his celestial globes and holding his hand. "I don't tell Tilly everything," Chamberlin said just above a whisper. "She likes to think I do, but I don't." He squeezed my hand, sending a pulse of electricity up my arm that traveled to my stomach, making me warm. "Well Trin, I better get on with the tour.

I reluctantly let go of his hand and watched him cross the hall. I wasn't going in Ivette's room. I'd wait for the group right where I stood, next to Elenore's embroidered pillow. I picked it up, holding it in my two hands like it was something precious. "*True love breathes death* . . . The love of a child," I mused. I thought about Elias playing peekaboo with his infant sister and put the pillow down.

* * *

After stopping in several rooms where unsolved murders were said to have been committed by servants, by ghosts, by curses, and even one about the house cat being the culprit, we took the servant staircase once again and headed down to the living room. There was no way I was going to remember all of this by tomorrow. I had forgotten more than I knew. After the group left Baby Ivette's nursery, I had given up hope and just enjoyed the tour.

Chamberlin encouraged everyone to gather around the fireplace in the living room. The brick fireplace always fascinated me because of its size. As children, we could stand in it without hitting our heads and I'd imagine witches gathering around a huge cauldron boiling over. Chamberlin wasn't drawing the group's attention to the gargantuan size of the hearth but rather to an odd curio cabinet that sat on top of the fireplace mantel. It had all of its glass panels blackened out.

"I would like to introduce everyone to my family's pet," Chamberlin said as he pinched the small brass knob between his fingers and opened the door to the mystery cabinet. Inside, perched on a branch, sat a taxidermied raven. It had luscious black plumes that were so dark they shined under the gasolier chandelier, making them look like they were dipped in purple velvet.

"Let me guess," the older brother of the little girl in pigtails said, "its name is Nevermore."

That got a chuckle from the tour group.

"That would have been a splendid name for her," Chamberlin said, petting the top of its head like it was still alive. "You see, my little sister really wanted a parrot, but my father thought that wasn't macabre enough. Instead, he brought home a fortune telling raven named Polly. Everyone meet Polly Fielding."

The boy laughed. "I like that name."

Chamberlin smiled proudly. He always did like that bird. When we were kids, it would sit on his shoulder and do tricks for marshmallows.

"Polly was a favorite amongst guests and our most vocal family member until her death," Chamberlin told the tour group. "But she's been known to let her presence be heard in the afterlife."

I wasn't surprised that he excluded from the tour the little fact that Polly died the day before his father went missing.

"Quiet please," Chamberlin said with a smile that melted every girl's heart in the room, including mine. I couldn't help myself from wondering if this group paid more to have Chamberlin as their tour guide or if they just lucked out Maddy died.

"If you listen, really listen, you can hear Polly talking," Chamberlin said in a hushed voice.

"What does she say?" the girl in pigtails asked.

"Polly wants a cracker," her brother teased.

"Sometimes," Chamberlin said. "But it's a good thing she didn't say that today. You see, if Polly says her name, and sometimes she did, someone always died. Being a narcissistic raven, she was quite fond of her name. Oh, how she would tease us. She'd say poll-mee-a-drink or poll-eese do this or that, or all different things that made us think she was going to say her name."

"Did you ever hear her say it?" asked the same little girl.

"Once, and only once."

"Did someone die?" her brother asked. "You know, when she said her name?"

"No," Chamberlin said.

The teenaged boy shook his head, as if to say this tour is stupid.

"Two people died," Chamberlin told him and the rest of the tour group. "My mother and my father's business partner."

"At the same time?" an older gentleman with a mustache asked.

"Yes, they were together. Let's move into the foyer and I'll elaborate," Chamberlin said.

I didn't know his mother was part of the tour now. She hadn't been while I lived there. It was an understood thing; we never spoke about her death or my father's. I never gave my consent to have my father be part of the sideshow.

The tour group followed Chamberlin into the foyer. He ushered them to the side of the main staircase, to the elevator. He stood in front of the elevator's filigree iron doors. They were in an art deco motif resembling two large tulips—wilting tulips—as their petals and stems seemed to droop. But now as I looked at the elevator doors, I realized what I had always thought were leaves pulling away from a center stem were actually wings—wings of angels.

"This elevator was put in by Elias Fielding for his son, William, who lost the use of his legs due to polio," Chamberlin told the group. "The elevator functioned into the modern era requiring very little maintenance." He knocked on the iron doors. The little hairs on my arms bristled as a rattling, that reminded me of a baby's rattle, filled the air. "They don't make things like they used to," he said with a smile.

The older people in the tour group chuckled.

"But all good things have to come to an end," Chamberlin said, keeping his face slightly turned away from the group. "One night, after the house was closed for tours, my mother and my father's business partner, Timothy Dunn, took the elevator to my father's office on the top floor. At the time, I was in the living room with Polly and Timothy Dunn's daughter Trinity. We were alone and things were quiet except for a few squawks from Polly, which was her custom when she wanted attention. Then—I heard it."

You could have heard a pin drop; everyone was hanging on Chamberlin's words.

"Polly said it," Chamberlin said dropping his voice. "She said her name. She said Poll-ee. I remember turning to Trinity and asking her what she thought Polly said. Before Trinity could answer, we heard the screeching of metal on metal. It was so loud it shook the house." Chamberlin was physically shaking as he recalled the story. I was certain I was too. It pained me to know he had to relive this moment every time he gave a tour. "And then there were the screams," Chamberlin said, his voice just above a whisper. The tour group pushed closer to him; they had to. "My mother's screams. I still hear them in my dreams," he said, seemingly talking to himself. "Trinity and I rushed out to the foyer. Black smoke from the elevator filled the air . . ." He bowed his head, hiding his eyes behind his hair. There was another push from the group, and they moved closer. "There was the smell of smoke, and burnt metal, and blood."

"Did they die?" the little girl in pigtails asked.

"Yes, they died on impact. But I didn't know it then. I . . . I couldn't get the doors to the elevator open so I got a fire poker from the living room," he said, pointing back from the way we came. "I pried the doors open, but there was nothing I could do. They were very much dead."

I covered my mouth with my hand. I felt lightheaded. If it wasn't for my surging pulse making my heart beat faster, I think I would have fainted. That night, before the tension wire to the elevator broke, was the best night of my life. Chamberlin and I were alone in the living room with Polly. He was showing me a new phrase she learned, which happened to be 'kiss me'. I'd laughed, telling him I wasn't going to kiss his raven. He asked me if he would be a suitable replacement. He was so different then—happier, so confident when we were alone.

I can still feel his soft lips against mine, it was perfectly perfect. My first kiss. My first love—my stomach filling with heat and butterflies. My heart filled with so much love that if I didn't kiss him again, I would die. Just as our lips touched for the second time, we heard Polly say her name—heard the sound of the tension wire breaking. It sounded like a clap of thunder. We heard the hideous screeching noise of the elevator crashing down to the first floor, heard the screams of his mother and then there was nothing. They were gone. Like Chamberlin said, they were killed on impact, and with their death came the death of my brief but passionate love affair with the most beautiful boy in the world.

"How old were you?" a gentleman that had been quiet the entire tour asked.

Chamberlin wiped a tear. "I was thirteen when my mother died."

Condolences were given to him by everyone. I couldn't believe he just lived through that in front of all those strangers. Making himself naked, bearing his soul for all of them and for what, a few bucks?

"Why do you stay in this house if everyone dies?" the inquisitive little girl asked.

"Now that's a very wise question," Chamberlin said, collecting himself, his eyes still cast in shadows. "And I think the only answer I can give is it's my duty to my family to stay here until the house claims me."

"You still want that date?" a woman asked the teenage girl.

"Well yeah," she said. "I'm not a Fielding. I have nothing to worry about."

"Neither were his mother and his father's business partner," the woman pointed out.

"Oh," the teenage girl said, looking at Chamberlin, presumably weighing out the pros and cons.

"More than Fieldings have died in the Elenore Fielding House," Chamberlin confirmed, "but the house does have a fondness for family. It's perhaps because our golden rule is family first."

While the teenage girl remained in apparent thought, Chamberlin went on with his tour. "I have had visitors to the house tell me they can feel a cold spot near the elevator. You can touch the doors, but no one is allowed inside."

"Have you ever felt a cold spot?" the brother of the little girl in pigtails asked.

"No," Chamberlin said. "It's one of the many Fielding curses. We never get to make contact with our dead loved ones. No hearing, seeing, feeling—zip." His face flushed anew, and I wondered if he was thinking about Maddy from last night. "But I hope I will get to see them again when I die," Chamberlin said, seemingly losing himself in the moment as if he didn't have a crowd. "Sometimes, I come to the elevator and look in," he said in a low voice. "I try to imagine what was going through my mother's mind when the tension wire to the elevator snapped. Was she thinking of me and my sisters, or Tim Dunn . . ." Chamberlin raked his golden locks away from his face; a sadness pervaded his beauty. He never looked so much like a real-life angel. "I guess I will have to wait until it's my turn before I can ask her."

With that, Chamberlin stepped aside to make room for the guests who wanted to feel for the cold spot near the elevator. One old woman claimed to feel something, and everyone rushed over.

"Chamberlin . . ." I said in a whisper as he came to stand

next to me.

His head was bowed as what seemed to be his usual. He wouldn't look at me. "Sorry," he said in such a soft voice that I had a hard time hearing him.

I inched in.

"I'm so sorry," he said. "Our parent's deaths were added to the tour after you left. You don't have to talk about it in your tour. I change up what I say to what group. I should have just cut it today, but I wanted you to know, and I didn't have the guts to tell you."

"Elenore," I said, fighting tears.

He lifted his eyes to mine. "Yeah, Elenore."

I assumed he saw the tears beaded on my lashes because his cheeks blushed bright red, his scratch becoming a scarlet line. "Oh geez Trin, I'm so sorry."

"It's okay, it was just unexpected."

He balled his fists at his sides. "I'm a coward. I should have told her no and I should've cut it today, but it just happened organically."

I placed my hand on his arm. "You don't have to explain yourself," I said. "It's okay. It's just like what Tilly said last night, Elenore thought she was doing me an honor adding my dad to the tour."

"She really does think it's an honor," he said. "But hey, the tour is wrapping up, next stop's Maddy's fall down the stairs, then Dad's mysterious disappearance into the ether, and then the final stop, the gift shop. You don't have to stick around for the next tour. Why don't you go clear your head?"

"Elenore won't be mad?"

"Who cares?" he said. "I think she's putting too much on you."

"What about you?" I asked, my mind going to the duct tape on the kitchen ceiling. I didn't like how he said he would ask his mother when his time came, as though his time was coming soon.

"I have no problem doing all of Maddy's tours. It's not like I have a life," he said with a mock smile.

Chamberlin's dark lashes fluttered, pulling me closer to him.

"Your duty to your family," I said in a whisper.

His lips twisted into a grin as he said, "Yeah, exactly."

"Okay," I said. "I'm going to take a walk around the block." I didn't want to tear myself away from Chamberlin but standing that close to him and not being able to be with him filled me with just as much anger as my father and Mrs. Fielding being added to the tour. I felt like I was going to explode or maybe spontaneously combust. Now that would be an addition to the tour Elenore couldn't pass up.

As I went to leave, I heard an old woman speaking to Chamberlin. "You look so much like your mother," she told him.

"Thank you. I never get tired of hearing that," he said. "I'm sure you noticed her pictures all through the house. I don't think we can ever have enough. She was renowned for her beauty. We sell my mother's head shot that was used for her New York performances in the gift shop. Before she married my father, she was an actress playing many of her best roles in theater, most notably Juliet in Shakespeare's *Romeo and Juliet* on Broadway. Over here is a newspaper clipping from the *Times* calling her performance purely haunting."

I walked over Maddy's so-called body and out the front door, sick to my stomach.

CHAPTER TWELVE
A Different Crack

I hit the sidewalk in a near jog. I wanted to put as much distance between me and the Elenore Fielding House as possible. The sun was hot as it beamed down on me, casting everything in a golden haze. I could feel sweat beading in my hairline. It wouldn't be long until my makeup turned to soup on my face. I slowed down, taking in the old brownstone buildings that used to be so familiar to me. The architecture was always one of my favorite things about Brooklyn. There's something homey about the stone houses being packed so close together you have to share an alleyway. It's as if they were chiseled from one huge mountain like Mount Rushmore.

Although I tried, really tried, I couldn't keep my mind on the houses. I was looking at my feet now, watching my shoes step over the cracks in the sidewalk. It's this Brooklyn kid's superstition along with children from all around the world, that if you step on a crack in a sidewalk, you'll break your mother's back. I never knew my mother, but as a child I was very careful not to step on sidewalk cracks. I didn't want to chance it. I didn't want to break someone else's mother's back or Elenore's. Not that Elenore was my mother, but in many ways she was.

I was so angry with her at the moment, I almost deliberately stepped on a crack. That was silly, I didn't want to hurt her. I wanted to yell at her. It took all of my strength not to call her and have it out over the phone. She was in the middle of a tour and wouldn't answer anyway, but all the same, I was tempted to leave a nasty voicemail. I couldn't believe Elenore's insensitivity. I knew she believed you never die as long as you're remembered, but she didn't consider what it did to Chamberlin to tell the story of how we found our dead parents at the bottom of the elevator. A story he was forced to tell on repeat. Hearing it is different than living it. Perhaps Elenore couldn't understand that. She wasn't there when Chamberlin pried opened the elevator doors. I was.

When he finally forced the doors open, after cutting his hand so badly that he later needed stitches, smoke as dark as night filled the house. But somehow, I could still see. I saw my father and Mrs. Fielding laying amongst strips of torn metal at the bottom of the elevator. They were dead. Anyone could see that. They were dead and they were holding hands just like the story of Emmit and Elenore. Chamberlin didn't mention it on the tour, and I wondered if he had noticed what I had. Over the years, I clung to the small comfort that they had died together, not alone.

I can never forget how Chamberlin climbed over the pieces of metal to his mother. Maybe at the time he thought she was still alive. Maybe he thought she could be resuscitated. He scooped her up in his arms as blood snaked down her face and opened eyes. In life, her eyes had looked just like Chamberlin's—Heaven. In his arms, they were dull like the sea at night—vacant and cold, so very cold. He shook her so hard her hand fell out of my father's, and I cried.

It felt like hours before Mr. Fielding, Elenore, and Maddy made it down the stairs. They all just stood next to me and watched Chamberlin grieve, too shocked to comfort him or do anything. They just stood with me and cried. Poor Chamberlin. He seems to be the unlucky one to find everyone dead—first his mother, then Maddy.

Keeping my head down and watching out for cracks in the sidewalk, I strolled along aimlessly. For how long, I don't know. I just kept walking. It was the sound of crying, a deep, loud sob, that broke me out of my daze. I jerked my head in the direction of the noise to find myself at the cemetery. I could see the Fielding Mausoleum butted into the base of the hill. I also saw the tall guy with coke bottle glasses from the funeral home.

I peered through the bars of the fence just as he had done yesterday, watching him for a long while before I decided to go talk to him. I thought maybe I could cheer him up, but more than that, I was curious about him. No one had introduced or mentioned him, yet his connection to Maddy had to be significant—well, at least to him. And there was that strange exchange at the funeral home. I wanted to know why he gave Chamberlin or X or the both of them the finger.

The graveyard was refreshing. I found that sentiment odd. Cemeteries, burial grounds, graveyards, whatever you want to call them, always freaked me out more than anything, more than ghost stories or haunted houses. There was something about walking through a patch of earth designated for dead bodies that unsettled me. It didn't matter how green the grass was or how neatly the grounds were kept. There was always a stillness there. The stillness you can only get when everyone is dead. It's different than being by yourself or in isolation. In a cemetery, you're not truly flying solo, everyone is just dead and not able to talk to you. It's a different kind of being alone.

Today, today was different. I liked it there today. For the first time, I thought a cemetery was peaceful. It was as if everyone there was meant to be there and, in a strange way, so was I.

The shade was more than welcomed. It was a good ten degrees cooler under the canopy of the trees. The grass at Brooklyn Keeps was always luscious, but today it looked like a green blanket. I half expected to find baby bunnies and fawns nestled in the grass with sleeping faeries and other mystical things.

I smiled at the sound of the wind as it rustled the leaves on the ornamental cherry trees. It sounded like bells. I couldn't help but think of that line from *It's a Wonderful Life* even with the spring sun in the sky: *Every time a bell rings, an angel gets his wings.*

The young man with the glasses recognized me. "Hi, Sister," he said, extending his hand to mine as I came up the lane.

His hand was cold and clammy, I felt like I was shaking hands with a dead fish. "Hi. I didn't get your name yesterday."

"Damian Hurst."

I wanted to wipe my hands on my shorts, but didn't want to come off rude, so I playfully twisted my arms behind my back and wiped them on my butt. "Nice to officially meet you, Damian."

He came right out with it. "I apologize for my behavior at your sister's viewing. It's why I didn't attend the funeral."

I assumed he was talking about resorting to the New York hello. But I didn't know he had been invited to attend the funeral. I thought it was family only. Even X and Tilly weren't invited and now that I knew them, I found that surprising. They were family to Chamberlin. That could explain Tilly's contortions outside the cemetery gate. I'm sure she was upset she was excluded from the funeral.

"So, what *was* that about at the viewing?" I asked.

"I thought I could handle seeing him, and I couldn't."

Well, that settled it. I knew Damian had to have meant the middle finger and all it applies to X. "Yeah X, can be a little aggressive," I said. "I see how he can rub you the wrong way." I was sure X dressing up in what looked like a Halloween costume for the viewing didn't help matters.

With the finesse of a sledgehammer, Damian moved aside a chunk of curls that was obstructing his view. "I mean no disrespect, but I'm talking about your brother. X is just his puppet."

I glanced at the Fielding Mausoleum. My eyes had avoided it for some reason until that moment. Maybe it was because of the wingless angels that kept watch. The iron door was closed, and a wreath of spring flowers hung from it. It looked oddly inviting.

"I don't understand. What did you do?" I asked, my line of vision falling on his fogged glasses. "Chamberlin is a sweetheart. Like the nicest guy in the world."

Damian laughed, throwing his head back like a lunatic. I took a step back. There was something unnerving about the pitch of his laugh. It oscillated in high and low tones like how I'd imagine a demon to sound while watching an Adam Sandler movie.

"It's me?!" Damian said, pointing to himself, which made me read his T-shirt. It was a mockup of one of the shirts from the gift shop. It read: I Hate Chamberlin Fielding. This guy had issues.

"It can't be him, can it?! Damian said, his voice elevating to a near shout. "Guys with looks like that can get away with murder, and he did!"

"What are you talking about?" I asked, my face twisting, despite my attempt to remain deadpan.

He was all energy now, his long arms and legs jerking in ways that made me want to run for it. "Why do you think Maddy's in the ground? It's his fault!"

I didn't correct him. It wasn't worth it. Maddy wasn't in the ground, but in a vault above it. I knew what he was getting at, and I didn't like it. "Hey—listen, it's not Chamberlin's fault Maddy took her own life," I told him in a firm tone of voice, the firmest I could muster. "She didn't have to end things. She could have stayed to fight another day. You, or anyone else, can't put that on him. Shame on you for trying!"

Damian hunched over, making himself my height. We were now face to face, eye to eye. His glasses were a sheet of fog thanks to his dragon-like exhales through his nose. I tried hard not to flinch. "Here's some advice for you, Sister," Damian said nastily. "Look past his pretty face and see the real Chamberlin Fielding."

The sympathy I had felt for Damian yesterday was gone. Hate bubbled up from my stomach.

"I know Chamberlin found out about our engagement," Damian said, inching a little closer to me so that I could feel his hot breath on my face. "I'm sure that praying mantis told him. Your brother would rather see Maddy dead than with me. Well, I guess he's happy. He got his way. Long live the Vampire Chamberlin," he mocked. Damian kissed his fingertips sand pressed them to the mausoleum. Without another word, he walked off, the chimes in the trees ringing.

CHAPTER THIRTEEN
A Different Point of View

My head was spinning. It was like my brain was being tossed around in a food processor. Soon it would be a zombie smoothie. I understood nothing. Maddy was engaged. No one mentioned that. Maddy hadn't had on an engagement ring, or did she? I thought back to the last time I saw my sister—dead in her casket. I could only remember her face, her drawn cheeks, her placid forehead. I couldn't recall how her hands looked, besides them being clasped over her waist. I think I would have noticed an engagement ring. That's the sort of thing one takes notice of. I didn't doubt Damian Hurst was telling the truth about the engagement. A clandestine engagement made perfect sense. Damian being Maddy's fiancée would explain why he was invited to the funeral. He would've been family, if 'until death do you part' hadn't come before they exchanged vows.

But at the same time, Damian being the only distinguished guest at a family-only funeral would imply that someone knew about the not-so-secret engagement. That someone having to be Chamberlin or Elenore. I doubted very much it was Chamberlin. If they embodied the kind of animosity Damian led me to believe was mutual, Chamberlin wouldn't want him there. Then again, Chamberlin did have a noble sense of duty. He would have been a knight, with a gallant steed and a heart of gold, if he had lived in a fairy tale. So maybe he would have invited Damian if he did, in fact, know about the engagement.

Elenore was never much for diplomacy, but I could see her inviting Damian in a moment of kindness. It didn't matter if it was Chamberlin or Elenore who knew about the engagement, or if they even did, Damian could have just said that. I didn't trust him as far as I could throw him. However, it did explain why Maddy wanted to go out on her own and start a new life. It seemed a shame to die when so many people loved her, but my father had died, and I loved him, and Dorothy Fielding had died, and Chamberlin loved her.

I didn't have to wait long for Damian to walk himself out of my sight. I was sure with legs that long he was already across town. Saying my farewell to Maddy, I decided to head home. Despite my run in with Damian, my mood was much improved since leaving the Elenore Fielding House.

I enjoyed the rest of my walk through the shaded path of the cemetery. There were no cracks in the sidewalk. Little brown birds, the size of mice, flittered across my path, pecking at the sidewalk and in the grass. Their songs also reminded me of mice, with little pips and squeaks—nothing like the squawks of Polly the raven.

I closed the gate to the cemetery, casting my eyes on the Fielding Mausoleum one last time.

"Hey, Sister," I heard a voice say from behind me. I hadn't seen anyone as I exited the cemetery and the sound, let alone my name being spoken aloud, made me jump. My heart pounded in my chest as I turned around, my red hair whipping me in the face as I did. It was the man in the leather jacket from Maddy's viewing—Vinney, Elenore's ex-fiancé and the detective assigned to Mr. Fielding's disappearance.

Annoyed and hoping I looked it, I pushed away the strands of hair stuck to my sweaty face.

"Sorry, I didn't mean to scare you," he said.

"Then why are you lurking in a cemetery?"

He gave me a smile that highlighted the dimples in his cheeks. "I'm technically *outside* of the cemetery."

I scoffed, narrowing my eyes. I hated being corrected. He knew what I meant. "You're still lurking."

His smile moved into a sideways grin. "Maybe a little," he admitted. I could see why Elenore liked him. Besides being handsome in a traditional, yet sleazy way, he was the kind of man that wouldn't be scared to challenge her—someone she didn't have to play mother to.

"Sorry about Maddy," he said.

"Yeah, it's a shame. She was so young."

"Yeah, *it* was," he said, like he was fishing for something. I didn't like that. Maybe I was being paranoid or maybe it was just knowing he was a detective that put me on a razor's edge. "I was glad you were able to make it. Elenore didn't give you much time to get here. When *did* your flight come in?"

Not sure if he would follow, and not caring, I headed down the sidewalk in the direction of home. He did follow and I felt oddly obligated to answer. "I took the first flight. You know Elenore, she can't keep the house closed for long."

"I *do* know Elenore," he said, keeping stride with me. He was definitely fishing for something. I wished I had grabbed my purse before I went for my walk. I wondered if my can of mace would've helped Vinney take a hint.

"Is there something you want from me?" I asked as my nose wrinkled. I'd forgotten how much cologne he wore. I was sure he left an oily residue at all of his crime scenes. Forensics would label it 'V' for unidentified oil oozing from Vinney.

"No, there's nothing I want from you," he said nonchalantly, "just catching up with an old friend. We didn't get a chance to talk yesterday."

I could also see how all the cryptic questions and statements would drive Elenore crazy. I'm not a cryptologist, and neither is she. "We're not friends," I stated for the record.

"Aren't we? I thought we were friends?" he asked hurt.

I was beginning to see why Chamberlin thought Elenore should file a restraining order against Vinney; he wouldn't give up.

"No, we are not friends," I said, keeping my eyes straight ahead. "You were one of the detectives assigned to my adoptive father's case. And sorry if it hurts your ego, but I think it can take it—the shitiest one."

He grabbed his chest like I'd shot him. Taking a step back, he asked, "Is that fair?"

I kept walking. "What *is* fair? So, tell me Mr. Big Shot Detective, where's Franklin Fielding? Did you bring his killer to justice?"

Vinney caught up with me. It only took a few large strides. He walked alongside me for some time, rubbing the stubble on his chin. "Who said he was dead?" he asked intuitively, as if I just gave him the big clue to crack his cold case."

I scoffed; it was more of a double scoff. "Of course he's dead. Everyone always thought he was dead. Besides Chamberlin, and even he thinks so now, too. If he wasn't dead, he wouldn't be missing. It wasn't like Mr. Fielding to just disappear and not tell anyone where he was going."

Vinney was back to rubbing his chin. I hoped his five o'clock shadow was chaffing his fingers. "The Fieldings like their secrets," he said. "I learned that the hard way."

I stopped dead in my tracks. "What is that supposed to mean?"

"Why do you think Elenore broke off our engagement?"

I grinned, payback time. "Because you lurk *outside* of cemeteries?"

He mirrored my face. "Because I was getting too close to the truth."

"And what truth would that be?" I asked, lifting an eyebrow.

"I know someone in that house murdered Franklin Fielding. I know that. Between old friends Sister, because that's what we are, if I knew Elenore did it, I would drop it," Vinney said with a seriousness that made me stop and look at him. "Call it a detective's intuition or a hunch, but I know there's more to the story and I was getting too close. Elenore did what she always does and protected her family."

"Sorry for your loss," I said, walking on.

He grabbed my arm. I instinctively pulled away to no avail. He dug his fingers in.

"I like how you would turn the other way for Elenore's sake but are more than willing to crucify her siblings," I hissed. "Maybe that's why she broke off her engagement to you. A man that was willing to put a murder rap on one of her siblings that she considers her children doesn't seem like marriage material to me."

He let my arm go. He seemed dumbstruck, like he hadn't considered what I just said. As if all he had seen before him was the case and solving it, but I didn't care. He already put a bad taste in my mouth.

"Is that why she broke off our engagement?" he asked in a whisper, seemingly mulling it over. "I never would've reported anything, if something turned up on one of you kids. I just wanted to be in on the secret, part of the family. I wanted her to trust me."

"She'll never trust you now," I said spitefully. "You threatened her family. That's the one thing she will never forgive. Family first, it's one of the Fieldings' golden rules."

Vinney stood there doe-eyed, like I really had shot him this time, his hazel eyes wide and glassy. I preferred his police bravado to mopey victim of my own choices. I couldn't look at him, so I kept walking, but I did give him some good advice that I hoped could give him, well—hope, though I knew how stubborn Elenore could be. I called back to him, "Vinney here's an idea, why don't you try protecting us for a change!"

CHAPTER FOURTEEN
A Different Sight

The front door to the Elenore Fielding House was open. I took the steps in a hurry and went to pull the stained-glass doors open. I arrived home in between tours and that meant the portico's stained-glass doors were locked. Elenore always kept the front door open during normal business hours and the portico doors locked until tour time. I didn't grab my key before I left and there was no getting into the house short of breaking the stained-glass doors, and Elenore would kill me if I did that. Without the guiding torches, how would lost spirits find their way home to the Elenore Fielding House?

I wasn't going to line up like a tourist in the entryway. I decided to spend the next thirty minutes in Mikey's next door.

Mikey's was just how I remembered it. My eyes, as always, darted around my head like the room was spinning. Everywhere, on every surface, there were posters, bumper stickers, and car magnets. There were New York snow globes, mugs, and pins. In the very back of the store were T-shirts, hoodies, and hats and what we always called the black light area, designated by fuzzy posters that glowed in the dark along with everything else. The smell of vinyl and starch was thick in the air and everything in the store seemed so trivial it made you feel like you needed it all. I loved Mikey's.

It was good to see old Mikey himself at the register. Mikey was the owner of this fine tourist trap. He had been old since I was a kid and had a son, Mikey Junior, who everyone just called Junior. Junior was about Chamberlin's and my age and was a friend.

"Hey, Mikey," I said, strolling up to the counter that housed hookahs in every color imaginable. The caterpillar from *Alice in Wonderland* could have lived happily behind the glass counter at Mikey's. I imagined the whole cast could.

Mikey pushed the glasses that were sitting on the top of his head into their proper place. "I'll be," he said, patting his stomach like I was a delicious dish he was about to eat. "It's Sister Fielding!"

I put up a hand in a Miss America sort of wave.

"That's not good enough," he said as he came through the swinging door of the counter. He wrapped me in a bear hug. It surprised me to see how much I've grown. That couldn't be right, Mikey must have shrunk. We were almost the same height.

"My stars, you haven't changed a bit. You're just as beautiful as when you left. Now tell me Sister, how are you?" There was no chance to reply. "Elenore fills me in when she can. But that girl is always working. I told her just the other day she was going to work herself into an early grave." He paused at this, realizing what he said. "Sorry, I didn't mean to be insensitive. I'm very sorry about Madelin. Sorry I couldn't make the funeral, I had to man the front," he said, putting his hand to his forehead as if to salute the store. "I hope you understand?" I nodded, having no time to do or say anything else before he continued. "Maddy was a good girl, but I didn't like her boyfriend much. He was a four-eyed giant of a young man. He had the smell of trouble about him. Maddy didn't come in here as much as you and Chamberlin used to. Now Chamberlin," he said, his eyes lighting up like fireworks, his countenance less tired now like Time's hand had turned back, "he grew up to be a strapping lad. His sister tells me he's on his way to becoming famous and putting the Elenore Fielding House on the map again. Won't that be nice?" he said, getting back to his stool behind the counter.

I was about to respond when Mikey beat me to the punch. "No one deserves a little success more than Elenore and Chamberlin. He still comes by once a week, you know?" Mikey told me with a proud smile. I shook my head, I didn't know. "Sits and has dinner with this old man every Thursday. I think he pitties me now that Junior's in California. I let him; I like the company, even if he never has much to say. I never have a problem talking for the both of us," he said with a raspy laugh that made the sound of helium leaving a balloon. "There never was a boy like Chamberlin Fielding, mind Junior. I said it all the time to his mother, God bless her heart. I'd say 'Dottie'—that's what I called her, if you remember?" I nodded. "'I'd say Dottie, there never was a boy like Chamberlin Fielding.'" He tapped the side of his nose. "I knew he'd go places. I'm just happy to say I know him."

Mikey paused to catch his breath, and I took the opportunity to get a word in, not that I minded him rambling on. "California? What's Junior doing in California?"

"School. He wanted to go to school there."

"Wow, that's far."

"Yes siree Bob. If you ask me, he wanted to get as far away from here as he could. I guess he was feeling weighed down by his old dad. But you got to let kids go their own way at some point or they become as rabid as a caged dog. Elenore had to do that with you, you know?"

My cheeks warmed. That, I did know.

"You still living in England?" Mikey asked.

"I was staying with my great aunt and her cat in London, but I'm moving back here." That reminded me, I had to call Great Aunt Girty and call Kris. Great Aunt Girty would be glad I made the decision to move back to Brooklyn, she knew I was homesick. The Grand Duke Wiskerton would be his indifferent self, and Kris, well I wasn't sure how he would take it.

Mikey clapped his hands like one of those toy monkeys that smash symbols together. "That's the best news I've had in a while," he beamed. "That will make Elenore very happy. I don't think there's a day I see her that she doesn't say, 'I hope Sister comes back.'"

A group of teenagers walked in, sounding the little bell above the entry.

"Tell you what Sister, you come by with Chamberlin for dinner tomorrow and we'll catch up some more," he said, keeping his eyes on the teenagers. "I don't want to talk your ear off, and I have to watch these kids. Just last month I was robbed. While I was in the bathroom, someone made off with my gun that I keep behind the counter and some merchandise. It's hard to tell what. The place was trashed, things all knocked about." He shook his earlobes. "My hearing is not so good. I didn't hear a thing. Your brother and Elenore helped me clean the mess up. I say that like I was much help. They did it all really. Junior was going to fly home, but he'd just returned to California after two weeks and tickets to and from there are a small fortune."

"Sorry to hear that Mikey."

He nodded. "Kids today are not like they were even ten years ago. But look around and let me know if you find anything you like. It's on the house of course. I owe your family for cleaning this place up."

I gave him a hug over the counter and went to look around. I still had twenty minutes to burn. I made a beeline for the shirts.

I was looking for a size small 'Brooklyn is for Ballers' gray T-shirt when I noticed the door leading into the upstairs apartment was open. I thought I saw Mrs. Mikey (the loving nickname the neighborhood kids gave Junior's mom).

With my hand on the doorknob, I looked up the stairs. "Mrs. Mikey?" I called. I heard footfalls. I wasn't sure what the state of Mrs. Mikey's hearing was, so I let myself in and headed up the stairs. I knew the way; Chamberlin and I had come into the house through the store entrance with Junior loads of times.

I moved a little slower than I normally would have. There were boxes on both sides of every stair tread. They were overstock from the store. I flipped back the flap of one box to see air fresheners.

"Mrs. Mikey?" I called again, this time from the top of the stairs. There was no sign of her. The upstairs of the house was dark. Boxes were stacked from floor to ceiling like mini carboard skyscrapers, blocking out most of the natural light. Getting to a light switch was out of the question. One wrong turn and the city of boxes would come crashing down. I recalled Junior's house always being cluttered, but I didn't remember it looking like an episode of *Hoarders*.

I was past the point of feeling awkward and felt more than a little crazy for just letting myself into their home. Just as I was about to head back downstairs, I heard a noise. I wasn't sure what it was. It could've been a footstep, or maybe it was a cat. Mikey always liked cats. "Mrs. Mikey?"

The noise came from the first room off the hall. The door was closed. I hesitated for a moment before deciding to open it. It pushed open with a low-grade squeal. The room was empty except for the towers of boxes lining the perimeter of the room like a fence. There were no windows, and the only light was missing. There was a big dark hole in the plaster ceiling where a fixture should have hung. The plaster looked black like there had been an electrical fire or some other sort of damage there.

One thing was clear, Mrs. Mikey wasn't there, and it was time to go. I shrugged off what I thought I heard; old houses make odd noises after all. And Mikey's house was old. It had been, at one time, the Bethany Wing of the Elenore Fielding House.

I turned to leave and stopped dead in my tracks. In front of me, grazing my nose, was a young woman.

Startled, I tried to take a step back and tripped over my feet, falling on my butt. There was something familiar about the woman I almost collided with. I had met her before. I was certain of that. Maybe she was one of Junior's cousins or something.

She had on a royal blue dress with little pink rosebuds on it. The style of the dress was of an antique fashion, complete with a bustle. She must have been hot in all that fabric. Today wasn't a good day to go larping.

I scrambled to my feet. "Sorry, I was looking for Mrs. Mikey.

I thought I heard her."

Being about the same height as the young woman, my line of vision naturally fell on her face. I noticed her dark eyes were clouded over in a white film like she had cataracts, but she was too young for that. There was no way she was over twenty. No, they were dead eyes—soulless eyes. It was at that moment, I recalled how I knew her. I had seen her face in portraits for half my life. It was Bethany Fielding.

Bethany slowly tilted her head toward me, and that's when I noticed her neck. There was a bulge protruding from one side of it like it was broken. It *was* broken. She had hung herself.

I covered my mouth, though no scream escaped.

Her pale, small mouth opened, her message delayed as if it came from far, far away. "Sister . . ."

I screamed. And just like that, she was gone as though she was never there. I wasted no time. In a flash, I was down the stairs, and out the door, not taking a second to wave goodbye to Mikey.

CHAPTER FIFTEEN

A Different Maddy

I was down the block before I stopped running. Placing my hands on my knees, I caught my breath. My chest heaved as little drops of perspiration slid down my face, darkening the sidewalk in a gruesome Rorschach.

That morning, I had made my peace with last night and the rocking bassinet, chalking it up to being overdue for some old-fashioned haunting, having lived in the house for as long as I did without hearing a peep from its ghostly residents. But this was ridiculous.

I was feeling like I was one loose screw short of the looney bin. I had lived in one of America's most haunted houses for years and never saw a thing, and now I saw the ghost of Bethany Fielding. What the hell was going on?!

Maybe the stress of Maddy dying and being home after so long lowered my spirit immunity. I was stressed; therefore, I was more likely to see ghosts. That would explain why I never heard or saw anything before. Regardless of why, the truth remained the same—I saw dead people. I couldn't even think that without the corners of my lips curving into a smile. I saw ghosts, that was a little more accurate. Or, even more to the point, I heard a ghost and saw a ghost. I heard Baby Ivette cry, and I saw Bethany Fielding. And I saw something or someone hovering over X's Ouija mat. I guess, make that two ghosts.

I felt better acknowledging that. It was like I was being honest with myself and that felt good. But it also made me sad. Chamberlin's said the Fielding's can't see their dead, yet I saw Bethany. It was confirmation, delivered with a knife to the heart, that I wasn't a real Fielding. I wasn't Fielding enough for the Fieldings and I was too much Fielding to be with Chamberlin. I felt like a hamster trotting along on a hamster wheel.

As my heartbeat and breathing returned to normal, I realized seeing Bethany wasn't that crazy after all. *That* being the key word. It was still crazy, but Mikey's was originally part of the Elenore Fielding House as none other than the Bethany Wing. Why shouldn't the ghost of Bethany haunt the wing dedicated to her? That, on some level, made sense to me. It's how it all happens—how a spirit gets trapped amongst the living. It becomes an echo, repeating some horrific event from their lives like Bethany's suicide or haunting the place they died. As much as Bethany scared me in the moment, it seemed like Standard Haunting 101. If I avoid the Bethany Wing, logically, I should be able to avoid Bethany. I hoped my new superpower was only temporary and as I settled back into life in Brooklyn, things would return to normal.

I straightened myself out and headed back to the house. I took my time, putting all of my energy into avoiding the cracks in the sidewalk. I was really missing the cobblestone streets of London.

As I walked past Plant Haven, the door opened. It was Tilly. She was in a black skirt and a white polo shirt with her name embroidered on it. She had on white knee-high stockings that had a little black bow below the knees and black Mary Janes that also had bows.

"Hey Trinity."

"Oh hey," I said, still a little out of it. I knew she lived next door but seeing her pop out of Plant Haven seemed strange, like I was trapped in one of Mikey's snow globes—trapped on the same block with the same people and the same ghosts.

"You okay?" she asked. "Chamberlin's looking for you."

"Oh, he is?" I pulled my phone from my jean shorts. I missed several text messages and a call from him.

"He said you were taking a walk around the block and didn't come back."

Wow, he really did tell her everything. I wondered if X got the memo and was scouting the neighborhood for me.

"I lost track of time," I told Tilly as I texted Chamberlin I was with her.

I looked up from my phone to see Tilly smiling at me. I tried not to look at her teeth and focused on her dark eyes. It wasn't working. My eyes drifted lower and lower until they fixated on her lips and the little white pebbles resting on a fleshy, pink shore. "Um. . . I guess you're working?" I said, unsure what else to say.

She inclined her head in the direction of the store. "X, too."

I suppose I was glad he wasn't off looking for me.

"We have to earn our allowance. Working for your parents," she said, with a playful roll of her eyes. "Come and meet my mom."

I had nothing better to do and the air conditioning rushing out of the store felt like heaven on my face. I entered Plant Haven. It really was a haven, well, for air plants. The store was packed with very smartly dressed middle-aged women with well-groomed children. The very opposite of the types of visitors the Elenore Fielding House usually attracted. I don't know how many people were buying, but you'd think air plants were little green aliens from Mars the way people were staring at them.

Tilly's mom in one word: beautiful. She was tall and thin like Tilly, but her teeth were bright white and perfectly straight. It was clear she had a very good relationship with her dentist. Her hair was most likely close to Tilly's shade but was dyed light blonde and fell over her shoulders in spiral waves.

After Mrs. Deedle was done ringing up a customer, Tilly took my hand and dragged me to the counter. "Mom, this is

Chamberlin's sister, Trinity, from London."

She held her hand out to me. "Tiffany Deedle. Pleasure to meet you, Trinity from London." I oddly thought she meant for me to kiss her hand. But that's silly. I think it was just that she was so much taller than me that it made her hand seem directed at my mouth. I was normally not so socially awkward, but there was something about Mrs. Deedle that made me feel like I had two left feet and three hands.

Her hand was very delicate, her nails perfectly manicured and, on each finger, she wore an expensive looking ring. I shook it. It was probably the most awkward handshake in the history of the world, but it didn't last long.

"Hey, Trin," X said from across the store with a wave. I waved back, with half of his enthusiasm. It popped into my head upon seeing him that it was possible that his stupid homemade Ouija mat might have given me a third eye. If we hadn't broken Mr. Fielding's rule of no Ouija boards in the house, maybe I never would have seen Bethany. Hearing a ghost is very different from seeing one, and now that I had seen Bethany, I had a gut feeling she wouldn't be the last ghost I would see. I was really starting to dislike X. I could blame the recent events on stress or on him, but was leaning toward X. He had the kind of face that was easy to hate.

"So glad I got the opportunity to meet you, Trinity," Tilly's mom said. "You were today's breakfast topic."

I smiled, again feeling awkward. "Hopefully a nice breakfast topic."

"Yes, very much so. Tilly and X both like you, so I like you. Boris . . . well," she said, running her hand down Tilly's hair with pride. "He said he has to meet you himself and I hope he does soon. I'm sure he will like you as much as we all do."

I inferred Boris was Tilly's father. "Yes, I hope so, too."

"Mom, Trinity and I are going to hang out in my room for a little bit, she's had a rough day."

"She's already had her break," X said to his mother, coming up behind me and giving me an uncomfortable hug. I really hated him. "I'll go upstairs with Trinity and help her relax."

Mrs. Deedle ignored her son with a grace I wished I possessed. "You two girls have fun." Excusing us, she turned to X. He still had spiky hair and was wearing his dog collar with his Chamberlin locket, but he had on khakis and a work polo. He was wearing less eye liner, which I assumed he did for his mother's benefit. "Xavier Deedle, you keep spritzing the plants," she ordered.

I followed Tilly upstairs, glancing back at X as he spritzed away. The staircase was very similar to the one in the Elenore Fielding House but on a smaller scale. It was identical to the one hidden by boxes at Mikey's. That was the *only* thing Tilly's house had in common with Mikey's. At the top of the stairs, instead of coming to a hall, you were greeted with an open concept living space. Tilly's house looked like one of those houses from TV, were viewers are brought into the living rooms of Hollywood's biggest stars. There was exposed brick, and a gas fireplace, and the kitchen was all white quartz with gold bar stools with adorable white, furry cushions. It looked too nice to sit in.

"Bedrooms are on the third floor," she said. I followed her up the next flight of steps.

She opened the second door on the right. "My room," she said.

I had never seen a room like Tilly's; it was picture perfect, ripped straight from the centerfold of a glamourous home décor magazine. It had fur rugs on the floor, and a crystal chandelier, and what I was sure was a custom day bed. I noticed one corner of her room was set up for a photo shoot, complete with a giant adjustable lamp. I recognized the textured black background. This must be where Chamberlin took his Instagram photos.

Tilly handed me a blue Gatorade from a mini fridge hidden in a wet bar on her back wall. "You look dehydrated."

I greedily drank it, wiping my lips with the back of my hand. "Thanks, I think I am."

"Chain said you were really upset about the tour. He was too when the changes were made." Again, I thought he told her everything. I wondered how he found time to do that between tours, and if X was included in a group text.

"Yeah, I'm sure he was," I said. "It's bizarre how Elenore can just add something so personal and not care how it will affect Chamberlin or me."

Tilly nodded sympathetically. "Elenore says grief sells and it does. It pains me to say she was right, but Chain started getting tips after that. It's pity tips, but it's still money. He never tells her when he gets tipped. He says it's because, like me, he doesn't want to admit she was right but part of me thinks it's because she'd take the money."

I shrugged. I didn't want to admit Elenore was right either and I didn't want to give credibility to their money problems.

"So this is the Elias Wing . . ." I said, wondering if Tilly's bedroom used to look like the room I saw Bethany in. I glanced at the crystal chandelier, at the little glass prisms that hung from it, and wondered if anyone had tried to hang themselves in this room.

My macabre thoughts quickly drifted into happier ones. I had money, that's one thing I always had—my father made sure of that—but never had I had style like this. If I was going to stay at the Elenore Fielding House, which I was, I was going to get the same designer the Deedles used to revamp Mr. Fielding's room. Heck, I would renovate the entire upstairs. Give Elenore her own little retreat to help her relax and whatever Chamberlin wanted, though I knew he would decline a renovation.

"Yep, this was the Elias Wing," Tilly told me.

I was pulled back into the world of doom and gloom and ghosts. "Did you ever see anything in here? Or feel anything?" I asked as Bethany's dead eyes and her bent neck flashed in my head.

"Nope," Tilly said, plopping onto a metallic silver colored beanbag chair. "I've only ever heard Baby Ivette crying. And it was only the two times while I was on the staircase next door."

I folded my hands around the Gatorade bottle to stop them from shaking.

"Did you see something?" Tilly asked intuitively, her brown eyes growing to the size of walnuts. I hate walnuts.

"No, I was just wondering since you said you had a sensitivity," I said, playing it off to the best of my ability.

Tilly sank back in her beanbag chair. "I wish I saw something, but no. My dad says I don't have a sensitivity, that I have intelligence and there's a difference in that. He always talks in terms of intellect or non-intellect." Presumably seeing my knitted eyebrows, she explained. "He's a neurosurgeon, so he talks a little weird."

"Like literally a brain surgeon?" I asked.

She laughed. It sounded like the squeaking of a mouse in the jaws of a cat. "Yes, like literally a brain surgeon. You will never meet anyone as serious as my father. He has what my mother calls a proper mustache to prove it." That made me laugh. I wondered what a proper mustache looked like: thick, thin, or maybe a handlebar. Tilly placed a lock of her hair under her nose. I laughed some more, feeling my tension ease with every outburst. I was positive that was not what a proper mustache looked like.

"I guess the point I'm trying to make," she said, easing back into her metallic pearl, "is that I probably don't have a sensitivity. I'm just intuitive."

"Was it that intuitiveness that helped you find Elias's journal?"

"Nope. That was the intuitiveness of the construction crew." She got up and pulled back the sheer curtain to her window. "This side of the house had no windows because, as you know, it used to be connected to Chamberlin's house. My dad wanted to add windows, not that we have much of a view, but as a fire safety thing. There was a good four feet of dead space on the entire outer wall of the house that we were able to convert into usable square footage. It was like the side of the house was one big servant staircase. There were steps going all over the place like a maze. It's probably the same way at Mikey's house, just a hidden network of stairs to nowhere. It was really cool to see before it got torn down. The journal was tucked behind one of the staircases wrapped up in a cloth."

I was intrigued. My eyes were probably the size of walnuts now. "Did they find anything else?"

"Just the journal and a couple of glass bottles. My dad kept them, but he said they were nothing special. They're in the living room if you want to see them. My dad is a history buff. He's part of some reenactment troupe and everything. He really got into it after he did one of those mail your DNA away kits. It's why he bought this house. He said he would have kept it original but there had been so many bad renovations that there was nothing original left. We still have our condo in New York City that he stays at if he gets stuck at work late, but we all prefer Brooklyn."

"Um, so, your dad bought this house because it used to be part of the Elenore Fielding House?"

Tilly sat back down, crossing her legs. "Not for that explicit reason. My dad's DNA test led him to believe we are distantly, distantly, far off and away related to President George Washington and Emmit Fielding served under him when he was a general. I think it's his dream to buy all three properties one day, although we both know Elenore and Chamberlin will never sell. He has several other properties on watch in case they go up for sale. My dad's realtor called him before the listing went public for this house and he bought it with cash."

"Oh, wow," I said, genuinely surprised. "I had no idea the Elenore Fielding House had ties to George Washington."

"Yep, my father was disappointed there was nothing historical in the tour. I guess there's nothing scary about George Washington besides his teeth," she said with a laugh, pointing to her mouth.

I suppressed my laugh. I didn't like how she felt the need to always poke fun at herself.

"I'm surprised with your dad being into history he'd let you give the journal to Chamberlin."

"After he read it, he thought it should go next door. He's not only very big into history, but big into learning from it. He thought the Fielding family should have it. He had to work the next day, so I offered to drop it off and that's how I met your brother."

"Does Chamberlin know your dad read it? I thought only you and X did." I was sure that was what Chamberlin told me last night.

"Yeah, I told him my father read it, too. I don't think he puts him into the equation. Chain didn't want to show it to Elenore, probably because he thought she would add it to the tour. He doesn't have to worry about my dad mentioning it to her, they've only talked a few times since we moved here."

I took another sip of my Gatorade. "Elenore mentioned your parents aren't a fan of Chamberlin."

"That wasn't always true. My dad really liked him at first. He liked that even though he dropped out of high school, he still got his GED and was taking college classes all while working around the clock. He said it showed he had grit."

"I didn't know Chamberlin dropped out of high school. Elenore never said."

"Yeah, his senior year to help her."

"Wow," I muttered. I was feeling really guilty now. I wished Elenore would have just come to me when they were having money problems. All of her emails and texts to me over the years had been fluff.

"Yeah, I don't think he wanted to but, you know . . ." she said.

I knew. *Family first*, and that meant the family business.

Tilly braided her hair cathartically as she spoke. "My parents think X's change in wardrobe are Chamberlin's influence, which is ridiculous. I told my dad that it was X's idea for Chamberlin to take on the vampire gimmick and is the one who got him all the sponsors, but it didn't matter. X started spiking his hair and wearing eyeliner and the more makeup he wore the less my dad liked Chamberlin."

"Were you close with Maddy?" I asked.

Tilly pulled out her braid. "Um, yes and no. There was a time I was. When I gave Chamberlin the journal it was summer, and he was real close with her then. It was natural for the four of us to hang out. But then when schools started . . . Maddy, well Maddy . . . just hung out with a different crowd that's all."

"She dissed you, didn't she?"

Tilly nodded, her teeth poking out from of her lips.

"Did Chamberlin know?"

"I don't know," Tilly said, working on a new braid. "I never said anything about it to him. I didn't want to make a big deal out of it. If he knew, he never said. Either way, it put a strain on my relationship with Maddy. X and I were still coming over every day and the awkwardness from school carried over. She distanced herself from us and from Chamberlin." Tilly bit her bottom lip in thought. "Chain has always been so nice to me. His kindness doesn't make sense unless it's sincere. But sometimes I wonder, if he didn't drop out of high school, if he would have dissed me like Maddy did or if he would've remained my friend."

"Your friend. Chamberlin and Maddy are very different people. Maddy was selfish."

"I'd like to think he wouldn't leave me out," Tilly told me with a sad smile. "X said Maddy didn't want to be associated with me because everyone was making fun of my teeth. That was true enough, and she did, too." Her eyes moved from her hair to my face. "You know I really want to get my teeth fixed. My mom said the teeth come from her side of the family and I'd look just like her if I got them fixed."

I fully agreed with Mrs. Deedle. "Then why don't you?" I asked. As Elenore had observed, money wasn't the issue. I couldn't believe Tilly was so concerned with looking like a genuine tarot reader that she would let her self-esteem suffer.

"I just feel like if I do, I'll be proving every single person whoever made fun of me right, that there was something wrong with me that had to be fixed."

"Tilly, if you want to do it, do it. Do it for yourself, not them."

"I like that," she said, cheering up. "I'll think about it. Thanks, Trinity."

"And for the record, I used to be teased too. About my red hair and about my freckles, so I get it."

She looked at her freckled arms. "I guess the one good thing about having what X calls shark teeth is that everyone usually looks past my freckles."

We shared a lighthearted giggle. I was feeling almost back to normal now. I was glad I ran into Tilly. I wondered if this was what she did for Chamberlin, made him feel better about everything. There was just one more thing I needed to feel better about. "Do you know Damian Hurst?" I asked.

"Oh yeah, I know Damian. Don't fall for that tumbling over at the viewing thing."

I quirked an eyebrow. "You were at Maddy's viewing? I didn't see you."

"Yeah, I was in the corner. I don't do good with death and crowds."

"I don't think anyone does."

She grinned, leaning further into her chair. It looked like it was swallowing her, soon she would be lost. "Yeah, that has to be true enough."

"I ran into Damian today," I said, trying to stay on track. I wanted to know everything Tilly knew about him.

She abruptly sat up, the beanbag chair crackling as she shifted her weight. "Really?! He came to the house?"

"No, I ran into him at the cemetery."

"Oh," she said thoughtfully.

I guess I was going to have to lead the conversation. "Did you know Maddy was engaged to him?" I asked. I recalled Damian's comment about the praying mantis having told Chamberlin about their engagement and ventured he was talking about Tilly with her long insect-like limbs.

She nibbled on her bottom lip again, making a moaning sound that resonated from her throat. "Okay, so I promised I wouldn't tell anyone," she said, her moaning transforming into words. "And I've kept my promise. But now I feel so guilty. Maddy's dead, so I shouldn't keep it any longer, but I'm so worried he'll be mad."

I squeezed my Gatorade bottle, letting my fingertips crush the plastic. "Who will be? Who's going to be mad?"

"Chamberlin, for keeping it from him."

"The engagement?" I asked, making sure we were talking about the same thing.

Tilly's cheeks were flushed, but other than that she was keeping herself together. "Yeah. A few weeks before Maddy died, things were really bad next door. Like, yelling and screaming all the time. My dad wanted to call the cops. X and I pleaded with him not to."

"What was all the yelling about?"

"About Maddy wanting to leave and money. Chain told me that when their father died, they all got money. There was a life insurance policy. That's the reason Elenore entombed the empty casket. It was the only way to claim Franklin Fielding was officially dead without a body. Elenore got the money and spent it. She spent Chamberlin's and Maddy's money too. Chamberlin tried to reason with Maddy and told her Elenore used the little bit of money they got from the life insurance policy to keep them afloat, but she didn't want to hear it. Maddy kept saying she was going to call you."

The Gatorade bottle imploded in my hands. "Call me?"

She nodded. "And tell you everything. I guess to get you involved. Did she ever call?"

"No," I said, my hands locking around the Gatorade bottle like a vise.

Tilly was back to braiding her hair, her arms and legs moving closer to her core as she overlapped strand after strand of her hair. She really did look like a praying mantis. "Anyways, in the interim, Maddy came over to talk to me, which was really strange, as she hadn't stopped by to hang out since that first summer . . ."

Tilly was spurred into movement, getting to her feet in a leap. She looked like one of those wrestlers on television, getting off the mat without the aid of their hands. Her sudden motion caused me to jump, sending the Gatorade bottle flying from my hands. "Come here," she said. "I want to show you something."

My interest piqued, I rose. I picked up the empty Gatorade bottle and followed her to her dresser. Tilly pulled open the top drawer, pushing everything to the side in her search. As she rummaged, I noticed a pill bottle that sat on the top of her dresser. It was filled with sleeping pills. It was about half full and the same kind I took. If it weren't for her name on the pill bottle, I would've thought it was mine.

Tilly found what she was looking for—a white velvet box. She opened it, showing it to me. "Maddy gave me her engagement ring to hold on to because she thought Elenore would find it during her routine snooping."

My eyebrows furrowed again. I was sure the crease between them had to look profound now. As I had thought, Damian told the truth about his engagement to Maddy, but no one knew, besides Tilly. I was the first Fielding to learn the truth. He wasn't invited to the funeral. He waited outside the cemetery because he wasn't family. He was an outsider. His beef with Chamberlin was happenstance. "She didn't want anyone to know . . . why?" I asked, hoping Tilly could shed some light on the situation. Maddy wasn't the kind of girl who cared if her brother liked her boyfriend.

"I think she was planning on running away with him. I think that's why she was asking for her money from her dad's life insurance policy."

"A fresh start," I mumbled.

Tilly rolled her shoulders. "I have no idea what Maddy saw in Damian, but I told her she had her right to live her life. Which I still believe. I feel the same way about *Chain and you.*"

"Chain and me?" I could feel my face flush. The heat of the springtime sun was back tenfold in my hot cheeks. She really was intuitive.

"Yeah Trinity. It's obvious to anyone with eyes he loves you."

My pulse hiccupped. "He tell you that?"

She shut the velvet box and put it back in her dresser drawer. "Not directly, but I was reading X's and Chain's palm the other week—poor X, his love line is so short. He's definitely dying a virgin." She made eye contact with me, her warm brown eyes not blinking. "But Chamberlin's palm predicts great love. His scar, the one he got when he forced open the elevator doors, runs through his love line. It means his love will be a tremulous one. And what's more tremulous than loving your adopted sister?"

I didn't know what to say. Was there something harder to

overcome than that?

She took my empty Gatorade bottle and tossed it into the trash bin. "He said he only ever loved one girl. I knew he was talking about you. Every time he mentions your name, which is quite a bit, I see it in his eyes. He loves you, Trinity."

"But he's my brother," I said breathlessly. I felt like I was having the same conversation I had with myself for years. I really was a hamster running around and around on a wheel.

Tilly smiled, showing all of her teeth. "He can call you baby, but that doesn't make him your father."

We both laughed. That was one way to look at it.

She took her seat on her bean bag chair while I stood. "You know, when he mentions you, he always calls you Trinity, never Sister. It's because psychologically he doesn't view you as his sister. And let's be honest, you're *not* his sister. Not biologically and not spiritually."

She was dead on about that. I saw Bethany Fielding, and Fieldings don't see their own dead. And, it was true that Chamberlin hadn't called me Sister since I've been home, but he called me that the entire time I lived with him as his sister, which left me on the hamster wheel.

Tilly sighed in what I assumed was relief. "You have no idea how happy I am that you're cool. I would die if Chamberlin was in love with some snobby jerk."

I took a seat at the end of her bed, redirecting the conversation. I couldn't keep running on the proverbial hamster wheel. I wasn't a hamster; I was a sister. "Don't you like him? I thought maybe you did?" I asked. I left out the part about Elenore thinking she was in love with him and was worried about babies with bad dentition.

"Seriously, Trin," she said, laughing into her hand in hiccups. "Who wouldn't like your brother?" Her laughing continued, making me join in. "I should stop calling him that, huh? Of course I like Chain, but I have enough good sense to know we are meant to be friends and am perfectly content with my lot in life. I want him to be happy and I want him to be with someone who's right for him. I'm glad it's you and I'm glad you're here."

"Thanks," I said. "You're great Tilly, really great." I looked down at my hands. I was on that wheel again, spin, spin, spin. "I don't know if Elenore will understand. I mean, that is if Chamberlin still likes me."

I was beginning to think Elenore having everyone call me Sister was her way of discouraging Chamberlin and me as an item, just as treating Tilly coldly was meant to discourage him from having any feelings for her.

"He does still like you," Tilly reassured me. "X is Deedle Dum not me, remember?"

I laughed. I remembered.

"I guess that's what Maddy was dealing with when it came to Damian," Tilly mused. "How to make Elenore understand." She sat up to the best of her ability, the bean bag chair remodeling under her every move. "Hey, do you think you can help me break the news to Chain, so he's not mad at me for keeping Maddy's engagement to Damian a secret. I'm worried the longer it's a secret the worse it will make it. I don't want any secrets between Chain and me. I know he has his and that's okay, but I can't have any from him."

"Yeah, of course."

"Okay, perfect," she said, with what looked to be a grateful smile. "I'm gonna text him and Elenore right now and tell them I have something important to discuss with everyone before we hang out with Allison."

CHAPTER SIXTEEN
A Different Ending

"**P**erfect timing," I said to myself, walking out of Plant Haven. Finally, something was going my way today. A tour just let out next door, that meant the portico doors were open.

The heat seemed oppressive after leaving the air conditioning. It made me feel dizzy, the going in and out of the heat. This must be how a marshmallow over a campfire feels.

I quickly squeezed past the people walking out, past the stained-glass doors and their guiding torches, into the house.

"Sister!" Elenore called from the gift shop.

I turned on my heels, like she just caught me doing something I shouldn't have been doing, my hands instinctively twisting behind my back. "Yes, Elenore?"

I really wanted to tell her I was retiring my nickname. For two reasons, Sister' had to go—Chamberlin being the utmost reason. If the intuitive Tilly was right and he still loved me, Elenore forcing him to call me Sister, as she would, could get really awkward. And then there was Bethany saying my nickname like it was a curse. I can't forget about the creepy shadow from last night either. Scratch that, there are three big reasons 'Sister' was getting buried.

Being that Tilly was going to drop a potential bomb tonight, I decided to wait till tomorrow to drop my own bomb on Elenore. I had no idea how Elenore or Chamberlin, for that matter, would take the news of Madelin's engagement to Damian. I thought Elenore would take the logical approach or maybe the macabre approach and say death saved her from the biggest mistake of her life. But I worried Chamberlin would think knowing this tidbit could have tipped the scales and somehow possibly saved Maddy's life. Chamberlin was a masochist. Punishing himself was right up his alley, but if he went that route, it would also punish Tilly.

I still didn't know what the big deal was about Damian. Tilly warned me he wasn't what he seemed. Just like Damian warned me Chamberlin wasn't what *he* seemed. The difference being I already knew Chamberlin was more than what he *seemed*, not that he was a real-life vampire or anything like that.

"How'd your tour go?" Elenore asked, from behind the gift shop counter.

"Uh, good."

She stopped wiping the counter with a Lysol wipe to look at me, her one eyebrow pitched abnormally high. "You were okay with everything?"

"You're asking me if I'm okay with the part where you exploit my father's death and our brother's guilt?"

She wrinkled her nose like she was about to sneeze. "Yeah, that part. Linnie said you were pissed. Well, I don't think he said that exactly, but he let me know it bothered you."

"It's fine, Elenore. It's part of the tour now, so just leave it be."

She reached over the counter and hugged me. "Oh thank goodness, because according to the surveys we give at the end of the tour," she said, releasing me from her hug and pulling out a stack of papers from under the counter, "eighty percent say the elevator story is their favorite part."

The problem was it was more than a story, it was real life,

my life. I glanced down at the papers. Seemingly satisfied I looked at them, Elenore slid the stack of surveys back under the counter. She attended to her flyaways like she had just won a battle, a smile of victory blooming across her face. I noticed she never got around to doing her hair or makeup.

"Now that you're staying, I *would have* cut it if you found it offensive," Elenore told me.

"Yeah, about that. I'm staying but I don't know about giving tou—"

"There you are," Chamberlin said, coming down the stairs.

He approached quickly, stepping in so close I thought he was going to embrace me, but he didn't. He must have realized he overreacted because he took a step back, his eyes hooded by dark plumes of lashes. "Enjoy your walk?"

"Yeah, I did. Then I stopped at Mikey's. I can't believe Junior went to college in California."

"I was sorry to see him go," Chamberlin said with a nod. "Poor Mikey, he's been very lonely after Mrs. Mikey died. And with Junior in California, he's pretty down in the dumps."

"Oh, Mikey didn't say anything about Mrs. Mikey," I said. So, that was why Mikey couldn't make it to Maddy's viewing. There was no Mrs. Mikey there to cover the shift. I glanced at Elenore. I was surprised she didn't fill me in on that. She shrugged as if to say she thought she had. Then again, she had never mentioned that Chamberlin dropped out of high school or that she was engaged to Vinney. If those things didn't make the 'Tell Sister List', I wasn't surprised I heard nothing about Junior moving to California or Mrs. Mikey dying. It was like in her own way Elenore had punished me for leaving. She told me nothing, she kept me at an arm's length. 'Only the good fluff for Sister. If she cared, she would have stayed.' Talk about passive aggressive. I was feeling lucky I got the call about Maddy.

"Yeah, Mrs. Mikey died last year," Chamberlin said. "Junior was going to come home after that but his father insisted he finish school."

I no longer wanted to talk about Mikey or Junior. I couldn't talk about them without thinking of Bethany. "I went to Plant Haven and met Tilly's and X's mom," I volunteered, changing the subject.

"Haven't met her yet," Elenore said.

I scoffed. "She's been your neighbor for almost four years, and you haven't met her?"

"She could have come over here," Elenore said, going back to wiping the counter. I was sure it was disinfected by now, but Elenore pulled out another wipe and started from the beginning.

"She's just upset Tilly's and X's dad doesn't like me," Chamberlin said.

"He probably just comes off dry. He *is* a neurosurgeon."

Elenore jerked her face in my direction. "What's that supposed to mean?" she asked. "Chamberlin's smart."

I grinned. "Maybe he doesn't want baby vampires in his family."

Elenore laughed, a booming laugh that filled the gift shop.

"Baby vampires?" Chamberlin asked.

I placed my hand on his arm. "Nothing Chamberlin. You guys get a text from Tilly?" I asked.

He nodded.

"Yeah, what's that about?" Elenore asked.

"It's important so make sure you're both available. I'm going to go upstairs and take a nap."

"You're not going to help with the rest of the tours?" Elenore asked.

"Nope. I'm taking a nap. And I'm taking a shirt," I said, fishing for my size on the rack. "I didn't bring a lot of clothes."

I ran past the wingless angel and up the first flight of stairs. I darted past Baby Ivette's room, taking the second flight slower. By the time I got to Mr. Fielding's room, I was exhausted. Too exhausted to shower. I reasoned my skin would absorb the scent of the citrus potpourri, leaving me smelling like an orange. I took off my clothes and slid on my pajamas from last night. The rumpled sheets were irresistible. With my phone in my hand, I dove into them, my eyes already shut. The combination of the heat and the stress of the morning worked better than my sleeping pills.

HOUSES *HAVE* SECRETS

* * *

I looked down at my hands. They were cold—so cold, but the red liquid covering them was warm. The smell of blood clung to my nostrils, metallic and earthy. Mr. Fielding lay on his bed, dead. Maddy and Chamberlin were against the wall again, visible between the drawn bed curtains. Chamberlin was crying, while Maddy just watched me with those dark eyes of hers—dark eyes like her father's. I never liked dark eyes. They were hard to read, not at all like Chamberlin's light blue ones that were as clear and translucent as tropical waters. Dark eyes, like Maddy's, always looked like pits, worse when they dilated. The blackness would fill her almond-shaped eyes as if she was a demon—all black, all evil. I never noticed how much she looked like her father. She inherited the sandy blonde hair from her mother, a trait she shared with her siblings, but her face was more like her father's than I remembered. Her face was like Elenore's.

I didn't approach Chamberlin this time, I let him cry. He didn't have the cut on his face, and I didn't want to see it appear. A sound like glass shattering filled the room. I glanced to the chandelier. It was still high above me and Franklin Fielding's corpse. The brass arms stretched over us like the tentacles of an octopus. We were in its grasp, but the sound didn't come from it.

My eyes went to the painting of the Elenore Fielding House on the wall. I noticed the front door to the house was open, and I could see the stained-glass doors of the portico, see the guiding torches. I thought the house was painted with the front door closed. I crawled closer to the painting, making sure not to touch Mr. Fielding's dead body. A bloodied knife rested near his arm on the bed. It was one from the kitchen. It had the same yellow handle as the rest of the knife set. I wondered if that was how I did it, how I killed Frank Fielding in my dream. It was Sister, with the banana knife, in the master bedroom. What a way to go. He was lucky it was just a dream.

I crawled to the head of the bed. I was directly in front of the painting now. The glass to the frame *was* missing, yet there weren't any signs of broken glass on the bed. I was left unsure. I had

142

no idea where the sound of glass shattering came from.

The painting of the Elenore Fielding House had always amazed me with its detail, but now it seemed to come to life. It was as if the paper held a miniature dollhouse. The front door was opened, and I could see into the house. The torches in the stained-glass panels blazed like they held real fire. I went to touch them, forgetting I had blood on my hands. I pulled my hand away, but it was too late. A red smear soiled the painting. The stained-glass doors were repainted in blood, blotting out the flames meant to guide lost spirits.

"Sister."

It was Chamberlin's voice, but it was distorted by the gargling blood that dripped from his cut lips. The fresh smell of blood seized the room. The same deep cut from last night marred his beautiful face, sawing it in half. "Stay with me," he pleaded, his words slurring.

"No!" I shouted, seeing myself reflected in his eyes. My auburn eyes painted his blue globes red. The top of his face was too heavy under the burden of the cut. It started to slide. "Chamberlin, no!"

* * *

I woke up panting, my heart racing. My eyes were on my hands. There was no blood. Like always, the blood was only in my dream. Sitting up on my elbows, I searched my room with a scrutinizing eye. I was alone.

Resting back on my pillow, my eyes settled on the painting of the Elenore Fielding House above the headboard. I crawled over to it, just as I had done in my dream, but this time I didn't have to watch out for Frank Fielding's corpse. The glass to the frame was intact. The front door was closed and there was no blood.

My phone dinged. It sounded so loud in the quiet room that I instinctually grabbed my chest. Realizing the sound was just my phone, I searched the sea of blankets for it. It was from Chamberlin. Everyone was waiting on me. I had slept for over four hours, not that it felt like it.

As quickly as possible, I got out of bed, fixed my makeup as best I could, tied my hair back in a ponytail, and put on my Vampire

Chamberlin shirt from the gift shop. My jean shorts that I'd worn earlier in the day were still on the floor, so I slipped them back on with a pair of flip-flops to complete the look. The medium t-shirt was unisex and huge on me, making me look like I was ten years old, but I didn't have a lot of options, so I tied a knot in the back of it to make it more form fitting.

When I got to the second story landing, I did what had become habit and ran past Baby Ivette's bedroom and the wingless angel at the foot of the stairs. Clearing the wingless angel, my eyes were drawn to the stained-glass doors. The setting sun beat down on them. They never looked so pretty. I touched the flame of one of the torches. I couldn't help myself. I felt like Sleeping Beauty when she came face to face with a spinning wheel. The panel wobbled in its frame. It made the fire look real, like it did in my dream.

"Hey Trin, we got everyone Starbs," Tilly said from the dining room, having seen me.

"Hi," I said to everyone, taking an empty seat at the head of the table. Tilly and Chamberlin sat to each side of me. To Chamberlin's right sat Elenore and to Tilly's left sat X.

I was feeling underdressed. Tilly had on the same skirt and knee-high stockings, as earlier, but she swapped her flats for stiletto heels and her work polo for a red crop top. She completed her slutty schoolgirl look with black suspenders. X rocked his usual spiky hair and dog collar locket combo. His shirt had so many buckles on it that it looked like a black straight jacket. Chamberlin had also changed his outfit from this morning. He still had on the black boots with red laces but changed into a gifted T-shirt from one of his sponsors that featured a vampire crying blood as they licked a cross. It was pretty much awful, but he pulled it off, as always. His black pants were plentiful with buckles. It looked like he escaped with X from the same insane asylum.

Tilly removed a cup from the cardboard cup holder and handed it to me. "Got you an iced shaken espresso, four shots, no two percent milk, substitute with a splash of vanilla sweet cream, and keep the classic. If your order isn't perfect, blame Chain, he gave it to me."

"Thanks." I took a sip. "It's perfect."

Elenore didn't look happy. It was like she was going out of her way to turn down the corners of her mouth like a dejected clown. "Tilly, thanks for the Starbucks, but you know I'm really busy with Maddy just dying."

Make that an angry clown.

A blush consumed Tilly's freckles, until her face was as red as the crop top she wore. "I'll be quick," she promised. She fished through her bookbag purse and took out the small, white velvet box she had shown me earlier that day. She placed it in the center of the table. "A week before Maddy's death, she gave me this to hold onto."

Chamberlin opened the box. "It's a ring."

"Let me see," Elenore said, snatching it from him. She looked to Tilly. "What is this?"

Tilly in turn glanced at me. I nodded encouragingly.

"It's Maddy's engagement ring from Damian Hurst."

"Engagement ring?" Chamberlin said, his eyes darting back to it. "Wait, you're telling me they were engaged?" He took the box back from Elenore. My guess was to see if it was a real diamond. "Officially engaged?" he asked.

"As official as you can be, I guess," Tilly said, her arms folding into her chest like a bullet proof vest. She never looked more like a praying mantis.

"Why do you have the ring?" he asked.

"She wanted to keep it a secret."

Chamberlin sat back in his seat with his lips pursed, the velvet box still in his hand, though he closed it.

Tilly hurried to explain. "I didn't think it was a big deal. I thought she just didn't say anything to you and Elenore because she was mad and eventually she would."

Chamberlin's eyes cut to Tilly, his dark lashes locking on to her like a tractor beam. "You would have let my sister run off with Damian without telling me?"

She was crimson now. "I . . . I don't know," Tilly stammered. "She asked me to hold on to it and keep it a secret based on the merit she was your sister, and I said I would. I really thought she would tell you soon. It's not like she could keep it a secret forever. But then . . . "

We all knew what happened next. *But then* she died.

Tilly looked to me pleadingly.

"It doesn't matter Tilly didn't tell anyone. It doesn't change anything," I said.

"Doesn't it?" Chamberlin asked, his tone laced with what had to be anger.

Tilly pulled her arms into her body so tightly, I heard her suck air. I thought she was going to faint. Her arms were contorted into her body, there was no way she wasn't cutting off air supply by puncturing a lung. I couldn't help but focus on her. No one seemed to notice. It was as if she was just sitting around the table like everyone else.

"Her suicide makes even less sense now," Chamberlin mused. "Why kill herself when she could have just married Damian and rode off into the sunset?"

Elenore slowly sipped her coffee before placing it on the table, her hands wrapping around it like she was cold. Elenore always drank hot, black coffee. It didn't matter if we were in the middle of a heat wave or how long the coffee was sitting in the pot, she'd microwave it for a few minutes and drink it like it was from the Fountain of Youth.

"I don't know what to think," Elenore finally said, "but it's like Sister said, it doesn't matter. Maddy is dead. Maybe if we had known beforehand, we could have said something to her, but she probably wouldn't have liked what we'd have to say." She looked to me. "We're not fans of Damian."

"Hey, Chantilly," Chamberlin said, reaching his hand across the table to Tilly. I had never heard him call her by her full name. I assumed Tilly *was* it. I wasn't sure if he meant for her to take his hand, but she didn't. She sat across from him like a human insect. Her legs had joined the contortion and were tucked into her chest. "I'm not mad at you," he told her.

Chamberlin confirming he wasn't angry didn't seem to help

Tilly relax. I was really getting worried about her. Even her eyes were bloodshot now. Her blood pressure must've been through the roof.

Chamberlin spoke to her in a kind voice, softer than his usual tone, although he always had a kindness to his speech. "You did keep a secret Tilly, but by doing that, you were being a friend to Maddy. Her suicide proves she needed a friend. Thank you for being there for her and for me. I wish I could have been a better friend to Maddy. If I was, maybe she would still be here."

This exchange of guilt, for that was what it was, instantly made things better. Tilly lowered her arms from her chest to her knees. Chamberlin absolved Tilly of her guilt. It was now for him to carry. His inability to be that better friend to Maddy was his burden to bear.

The sweet moment was ruined by X. He had been so quiet, I forgot he was in the room. "Tilly, for being Deedle Dee, you sure act like Deedle Dum! You should've told Chamberlin and Elenore and you should have told Maddy to stay away from Damian Hurst."

"What's done is done," Elenore said. I think she was also worried Tilly was going to have a stroke in the dining room. "Trust me X, we told her all the time to stay away from Damian. She wouldn't have listened to Tilly. And if we would have told her not to marry him, she would have eloped the next day."

"So, what should we do with the ring?" I asked, trying to end this conversation once and for all for Tilly's sake.

"I could pawn it," Elenore said.

"Elenore!" I chastised. There was just something wrong with pawning our dead sister's engagement ring.

A smile accompanied by a rosy glow highlighted her face. "Kidding," Elenore chuckled.

I was positive if the ring was left with her, that's exactly what she'd do with it.

"We give it back to Damian tonight—if he's home." Chamberlin said.

Elenore adjusted the bun on the top of her head. "Is that a good idea after the last time?"

My eyebrows knitted together. I wondered what they were

talking about.

"I can control myself Elenore. I don't want that creep knocking on Tilly's door asking for it."

That seemed to make Tilly very happy. Her legs were off the seat and her hands loosely hung about her.

Chamberlin took out his phone and texted Damian.

His phone dinged.

"That was fast," I muttered.

"The guy's a loser," X said. "His phone is glued to him."

"He's free now," Chamberlin told us.

"Don't forget you have Allison coming over tonight," Elenore warned.

"I know," Chamberlin said, "but she's not coming till later. We'll be back by then."

Elenore got up and kissed the top of his head. "Okay, just don't do anything stupid. There's still plenty of leftovers in the fridge. I'm going to do some paperwork and go to bed early. Make sure you have your key because I'm not walking down three flights of steps to let you guys back in."

* * *

Damian Hurst lived on the other side of town. It was about a twenty-minute walk. It was still hot out but compared to what it had been that afternoon, it felt nice. I don't think I was ever so happy for the sun to set. It was like I was a vampire awaiting the night, so I could go outside and frolic and not sweat.

It was enjoyable walking with Chamberlin, X, and Tilly. Tilly had the same phobia as me and screamed every time X tried to push her onto a crack in the sidewalk. I also enjoyed the view—more like I relished it. Chamberlin looked otherworldly under the lingering gold hues in the sky. The colors of twilight seemed to wrap him in a new level of mystique and splendor like he controlled the night. Maybe he *was* a vampire.

We got to Damian's place in less time than we anticipated. He lived in an apartment complex. One of those old factories that were upcycled into hipster apartments where the prices were sky-high and there was never any parking. Chamberlin pushed the button labeled: D. Hurst. We waited for Damian to buzz us into the complex. There was no response. Frustrated, Chamberlin pulled out his phone and called Damian.

"Put it on speaker," Tilly said.

He did. We heard the other line pick up.

"Hey, where are you?" Chamberlin asked.

"I'm at your house, dickwad. Where *are* you?"

Damian was completely unmasked. He was the dickwad, whatever that was.

Chamberlin scoffed. "Well idiot, little good that will do. We're supposed to meet at *your* place."

I thought it was cute he couldn't think of a better comeback than 'idiot' and so did Tilly. We both let out a fawning sigh at the same time.

"That's not what the Vampire Chamberlin texted," Damian said in a condescending tone. "Better check your phone brainiac or have one of your groupies do it for you. Try the one that wears the dog collar, I bet he's good with his hands."

My eyes darted to X. He shook his head nonchalantly. "He's not worth it," he said to me. I was glad X had a cool head. Damian was obviously trying to get everyone riled up. I wondered, like Tilly, like everyone, what Maddy saw in him. Sure, he lived in a nice place, but so had she, even if it was haunted.

Chamberlin went back to his messages. We all looked at his phone. In his anger he had made some pretty big typos. His phone read: Meet el ure house. I could see how Damian misread it as 'Meet Elenore house' and how Chamberlin thought it read 'Meet at your house'. It was an honest mistake.

X apparently couldn't help himself. "I'm not going to point out phones have a thing called spell check, or text prediction, or—" Tilly elbowed her brother hard to shut him up. Chamberlin blushed deeply. I felt more than a little bad for him.

"That's the problem with texting. It happens to us all," Tilly said. "He's the stupid one for not asking what you meant. Seriously, he's such a dumbass."

Chamberlin admitted nothing to Damian. "We're on our

way back," he told him.

"Take your time, I've finally met a member of your family I like," Damian said haughtily.

Another scoff from Chamberlin. "Oh really, who's that?"

"Your uncle."

"I don't have an uncle," Chamberlin said. He looked to me to collaborate his claim. I shook my head. We had no uncle I knew of, Fielding or Dunn.

"Urgh, your uncle Elias. Seriously Chamberlin Fielding, you're as dumb as a brick. You better hope nothing puts a hole in that pretty face of yours. Without it, you're screwed."

We heard the scream of a raven. Once you've heard one, you will always be able to pinpoint it as a raven. It squawked, "Poll-ee!"

Chamberlin almost dropped his phone.

"Damian, listen to me," he said, his voice hitching. "I don't have an uncle. Get out of the house!"

The phone clicked. Damian was gone.

"What's going on?" Tilly asked. "What was that noise?"

"It sounded like Polly," I said.

Tilly wiggled her nose. "Polly?"

"Chamberlin's pet raven," I told her.

"The stuffed one on the mantel?" X asked, with a quirked eyebrow.

I nodded. I couldn't explain it. But it sounded just like Polly.

Staring into the blank screen of his phone, Chamberlin nibbled on his bottom lip. I was worried he was going to bite through it. With trembling hands, he dialed Elenore.

"Hey Linnie, what's up?"

"Where are you?!" he asked.

"In my room."

"Lock the door and call Vinney."

"Why, what happened?!" Elenore asked, her tone taking on an intense quality.

Chamberlin's tone was laced with what had to be anxiety. It came out hurriedly. "I think there's a murderer in the house."

"What?! What are you talking about? Who?!" Elenore's voice cracked and it had nothing to do with bad cell reception. I could tell she was scared.

"Lock your bedroom door and call Vinney on his cell. Tell him to come over right away. Don't come out until I'm home." With that, Chamberlin slid his phone into his pants pocket and sprinted down the street. We followed. Tilly took off her heels and ran barefoot. I took my flip-flops off, but I still had a hard time keeping up. It was like I was running with giants.

The last of the sun slipped behind the house-lined street, leaving the sky a grim bruise. The sidewalk and its many cracks were highlighted by the haunting ambiance of streetlights. We ran so quickly, it felt like we flew back to our street. We were passing the light at the corner, now Plant Haven. My throat was dry, and I could hear my heartbeat like it was playing over the radio, my dripping sweat keeping time with the rhythmic tempo of my heart.

Someone from across the street yelled for Chamberlin. We all turned our heads to see Allison. She was everything X and Tilly made her out to be. She was beautiful, just like her pictures. We were too out of breath to say anything, even X. He just waved.

We were on the granite steps to the Elenore Fielding House now. Chamberlin had his key out, but he didn't need it. The front door was open. "Let me go first," he said, breathlessly.

"We're going with you," I said. Tilly and X nodded in agreement. We were a quatrefoil, after all.

"Polly," I whispered to him. He understood. We went in the direction of the living room, passing through the guiding torches and under the scrupulous eyes of the wingless angel.

"Damian!" Chamberlin called.

There was no answer. But I heard something. It sounded like a leaky faucet. And then there was that smell. That earthy, rusty smell, that I knew all too well. But it was different than the smell from my dreams. A smokey scent accompanied it.

"Damian!" he shouted again.

We entered the living room to only have Chamberlin push us back. I gasped, covering my mouth with my hands. It was too late, we all saw the hole blown in the back of Damian Hurst's head, where it hung off the back of the sofa. We all saw the brain matter splattered over the floor. He still wore his glasses, his dead, gray eyes wide-open in what looked like surprise. A gun rested next to him on the sofa, his hand loosely grasping it. The sound I heard when we entered the house was the sound of blood dripping down Damian's curly hair onto the hardwood floor where a large puddle of blood had pooled.

"Hello, Sister."

My eyes darted up at the sound of my name. On the antique sofa across from Damian sat a dapper gentleman in dress slacks and shirt. He wore a vest that had fine pinstriping running through the fabric. He was gripping a cane with a large silver ball handle with the letters "E.F.' engraved on it. I knew I was looking at the ghost of Elias Fielding. His lips curved into a rictus grin. I didn't like that look. It was as though he knew something I didn't know, and I liked that even less.

My heart felt like it stopped and without it, I lost the power to speak. I grabbed Chamberlin's arm, making a strange noise that was strangled by my tongue.

Chamberlin squeezed my hand and just like that Elias Fielding was gone. But the blood, Damian's blood, was everywhere.

CHAPTER SEVENTEEN
A New Investigation

Elenore seemed happily at home in Vinney's arms. The serenade of dripping blood seemed oddly fitting for a Fielding love story. I didn't think she was milking it for Vinney's benefit. Elenore seemed genuinely upset. It wasn't in her to play damsel in distress. It wasn't like her to cry. And to be honest, I'd never seen her so shaken. I wasn't sure if it was the unhappy reality that someone had just killed themselves in our home that forced tears from her normally tearless eyes, or the reality that Damian Hurst's blood ruined a family heirloom, and she was going to have to cancel tomorrow's tours.

Vinney reluctantly let Elenore go when forensics arrived at the house. At that point, she found comfort in Chamberlin's arms. I wondered what it felt like to cry into his chest, for his hand to wrap around my back. I almost faked a tear. I didn't know Damian well and everything I knew about him was bad. After the initial shock wore off, I was okay. I was used to blood. I saw it every night in my dreams—saw it, smelled it, and touched it. X and Tilly, and well, Allison because she followed us into the house, were not as well off.

Allison was doing a lot of crying. She kept making these horrible gasping noises, followed by loud sobs that she attempted to smother with Chamberlin's shirt sleeve. The Deedles, like me, weren't criers. But Tilly was contorted into a human insect again, her arms and legs drawn into her core. X, for the most part, looked like he always did, but he hadn't blinked in over ten minutes. I think he needed medical attention, but I didn't want to get in Vinney's way. He was barking orders in every direction. He clearly knew what he was doing, which impressed me. I'm sure Elenore felt the same way.

Vinney had us sit on the stairs while two medics moved Damian's body. Vinney didn't want us walking around the house; he wanted us where he could see us. I sat on the bottom step, as far away from the wingless angel as I could get, which left my feet on Maddy's duct tape body. Until then, I had been very careful not to tread on it.

I wasn't sure how I felt about the wingless angel after seeing Elias Fielding sitting on the couch like it was just a normal day. If the wingless angel was the embodiment of Angeles Hillings and she was after a new set of wings that fit just right, I didn't want to give her any ideas. I knew I wasn't a real Fielding. Seeing Bethany proved that. Seeing Elias was like beating a dead horse. The Fieldings don't see their dead. Thus, I wasn't a *real* sister, but to a murdering ghost under the guise of an angel I'm sure that was splitting hairs.

When forensics was done and Damian's corpse was removed, Vinney called us into the living room. I'm not sure what Vinney hoped to gain by doing this. It seemed more than a little unethical to put us back in the living room without cleaning up the blood. I suppose it was a scare tactic. I got it, he's a detective, he has a case to solve, although it didn't take a genius to realize Damian committed suicide. The gun was in his hand. Case closed.

It was a challenge to skirt around the flecks of brain matter to get to the other side of the living room. The room smelled heavily of blood and smoke. I assumed the smokey scent must've been the aftermath of firing a gun.

I took a seat where Elias had sat. I hoped he was watching. I wanted him to know I wasn't scared of him. I was there to stay, so he and the rest of the ghosts had better get used to it, Angeles included.

Chamberlin sat next to me with Elenore on his other side. X and Allison sat on the two matching tufted wingback chairs between the two sofas. They pulled the heavily carved chairs, constructed of mahogany with plum-colored cushions, as close to us and as far away from the blood as they could. Tilly sat on the footrest by her brother. Being surrounded by purple made X appear regal, like he was some gothic king, and left Tilly looking like a strange sort of pet. Her brown hair fell over her shoulders. Thanks to her balled up limbs, it looked like her body was made of hair like Cousin Itt from *The Addams Family.*

We all had a lovely view of what was left of Damian Hurst. There was no way Elenore was getting him out of the cream brocade fabric. It was destroyed. What a shame. That antique sofa belonged to Emmit Fielding.

I was thinking we should clean up the puddle of blood before it sank into the hardwood floor but figured Elenore would clean it up as soon as Vinney said he was done. Or maybe she wanted the stain there. It would be one heck of a memorial to Maddy's fiancée—the Fielding way, as part of the tour.

Vinney sat on the armrest of the sofa next to Elenore. She had stopped crying and was wiping her tears on her *Nightmare Before Christmas* sleepshirt.

"So, let me see if I got this straight," Vinney said, taking out a small green pad from his leather jacket's pocket. "You're all here because that stuffed bird," he said, pointing to Polly on the mantel, "said its name?"

"Yes," we all said together. Allison joined in, although her response was delayed. She had no idea what was going on. I think it would be a while before she called Chamberlin to hang out again.

I scrutinized the taxidermied raven from my seat. Her curio case was open, and her glass eyes glistened like onyx in the chandelier light. She almost looked alive. I wondered if Chamberlin thought so too. Normally, Polly's curio cabinet was kept closed, for shock value. When it gets opened during a tour and everyone sees a taxidermied raven, it's a big surprise. But when we got to the house, it was open.

"You see, if the bird says its name, someone dies," Allison told Vinney. Obviously, she took the tour. She glanced at Chamberlin, tears standing in her eyes, her eyeliner and mascara a smear on her face. "Tell him, Chamberlin," she pleaded.

Vinney raised his hand to silence Chamberlin before he could respond. "I know the story. What I don't know is how a stuffed raven says its name. So, let's back up." He looked past Elenore, focusing his hazel eyes on Chamberlin. They looked amber in the light of the room, like they were made of honey. "You called your sister and told her a murderer was in the house, what made you do that?"

"Damian said he was with my Uncle Elias. I don't have an Uncle Elias. Then we heard Polly. The last time I heard her say her name, well you know what happened."

"I've been doing this a long time and a dead bird tipping someone off to a suicide is a first. Ask Polly if she knows the lottery numbers for tomorrow night."

"Vin," Elenore said sharply.

He grinned. "Alright let's back it up a little more. Why was Damian Hurst here?"

"I asked him—well, I thought we were meeting at his house, but he came here, so we came back," Chamberlin said confusedly.

"I thought you two hated each other," Vinney said, glancing at Elenore. "Why would you meet up with him after he tried to press charges on you, Linnie? You almost faced jail time because of that kid."

My eyebrows arched at hearing Vinney call Chamberlin by his nickname. I wasn't sure why that caught me off guard. At one time, Vinney was engaged to Elenore and from his own mouth, Chamberlin had said he used to really like Vinney. They must have been closer than even Chamberlin led on. Elenore and her secrets. I hated playing catch up.

Chamberlin reddened, his head drooping like a wilted flower. "I, um, I wasn't looking for a fight. Tilly had Maddy's engagement ring from Damian and I didn't want him showing up at her house asking for it back."

"I see, protection in numbers," Vinney said.

"Something like that," Chamberlin mumbled.

"You should have called me."

Chamberlin's line of vision was on the floor. "I had Elenore call you."

"That was the right call, but I was talking about when you decided to return the ring."

Chamberlin's blue eyes lifted to Vinney, although they were still hidden behind a thick cloak of lashes and only the faintest hint of blue shone through. "We can't call you for everything."

"Of course you can," Vinney said, his eyes darting to Elenore. "You will always be my family even if you don't think of me as a Fielding."

It was Elenore who blushed now. She played it off by wiping her eyes.

At that moment, a man broke through the police barricade at the door. He was very tall with a perfect mustache. It wasn't too long or too thin. It was full and dark and, in the words of Tilly's mother, 'proper'. I knew at once I was looking at Doctor Deedle. Dr. Deedle was strikingly handsome with jet black wavy hair, the same shade as his mustache. He was wearing a dress shirt with a tie and dress pants. It was hard to imagine him in Civil War reenactment garb.

Tilly, seeing her father, jumped to her feet. She ran to him and wrapped her arms around his waist.

"Chantilly, Xavier, we're going."

Vinney was on his feet. "I don't think so. I'm in the middle of a possible murder investigation."

Dr. Deedle pulled his medical credentials from his wallet like it was a badge. "I'm Dr. Boris Deedle, head neurosurgeon at Mount Sinai Hospital, and this is my daughter and my son, and we are leaving."

"You didn't say he was a *real* neurosurgeon," Elenore whispered to me.

I nodded. "Yeah, he's the real deal."

"I thought doctors wore scrubs."

"Um yeah, when they're in surgery," I said.

She whispered to Chamberlin, "You should have told me X's and Tilly's dad was a brain surgeon."

"What does it matter?" he asked.

She elbowed him. "Seriously Chamberlin, it matters."

"You said you didn't want to hear anything about their parents. I was just doing what you asked."

She sighed in what I guessed was frustration. "Forget it, Linnie."

Vinney took Dr. Deedle's credentials, scanning them over before handing them back to him. "I'm detective Vincent Mallory of the Brooklyn Police Department." He took out his badge and showed it to Dr. Deedle.

It was quite the uncanny coincidence that the original investigator of Emmit and Elenore's murders had been a Mallory. History has repeated itself. Another questionable death in the Elenore Fielding House, and another Mallory to investigate it. Maybe it was why Elenore fell for him—some weird connection to some weird past.

In acknowledgement, Dr. Deedle nodded, and Vinney put his badge away. "Your daughter and son were firsthand witnesses to a murder-suicide. And Chantilly is eighteen. I had enough common sense to ask her."

"Then you're aware Xavier is seventeen and a minor?" Dr. Deedle asked flatly.

Judging by Vinney's face, he wasn't aware. I wasn't either or I would have said something to him. X told me last night he was legal. What a little liar. I guess being a minor would hurt his already doomed chances with Allison. But I couldn't help wondering if in a couple of years, if X grew a mustache and lost the spiky hair and the eyeliner, if he'd look like his dad and suddenly become attractive. I think he would. Maybe there was hope for X yet. Maybe he did have a chance with Allison if he took his sister's advice and was more of himself and less of who he thought people wanted him to be.

Vinney was seasoned, he wasn't going to let this oversight get the best of him. "You're free to stay tonight while I question Chantilly and we can schedule a time for you to bring Xavier to the precinct for a statement."

"I have the time now," Dr. Deedle said, with a shake of his mustache. "You will take both of their statements tonight. But you will not be conducting these interviews in the middle of a crime scene. This is not a safe place for my children or hers," he said, glancing to Elenore.

I really liked Dr. Deedle. He, like Vinney, would not be bested.

We made our way into the dining room. Elenore put a pot of coffee on and brought extra chairs from the kitchen and placed them around the table while Vinney dismissed the other officers.

Vinney took his seat at the head of the table closest to the kitchen, no doubt to be as close to Elenore as possible. Dr. Deedle sat to his right with Tilly on his left. He held her hand, and she folded the other into herself. X sat at the other head of the table. Allison sat between Chamberlin and him. I was next to Vinney, that was until Elenore took the empty seat between us.

"Dr. Deedle, prior to your arrival, I was going over what led your daughter and son and their friends to find Mr. Hurst as he was," Vinney said.

Dr. Deedle shook his mustache again. Presumably by magic, but it must have been the result of moving his upper lip.

"To catch you up to speed, they were meeting with Mr. Hurst to give him back an engagement ring Madelin Fielding gave to your daughter."

Dr. Deedle breathed in heavily. Tilly pulled her free arm closer to herself as if his audible breath was an indication he wasn't happy with her. Maybe he wasn't, but it was endearing how he held her hand on the tabletop for everyone to see. I could tell he was proud of her, and very protective, too. He was like another Elenore. No wonder they didn't get along.

I noticed Vinney adopted a more professional air in front of Dr. Deedle, calling Tilly by her full name. "Chantilly, how did you come to have Madelin Fielding's engagement ring?"

"She asked me to hold onto it."

"Why was that?"

"She wanted to keep it a secret from her brother and sister."

"Why was that?" Vinney repeated.

"She didn't say."

Vinney brought out his little green pad again. "What do you believe is the reason?"

Tilly faltered. "Uh . . . uh . . . um . . ." I was sure she took the presence of the green pad as a sign she did something wrong. Her anxiety was getting the best of her.

"Answer the question," Dr. Deedle said sternly to his daughter.

"I, uh, think because her brother and sister didn't like Damian."

"And you're aware Madelin Fielding died a few days ago?"

Dr. Deedle's eyes moved to a half-lidded position, over the coffee cup Elenore placed in front of him.

"Yes, of course I know," Tilly said. "I thought you knew Chamberlin is X's and my best friend."

Poor Tilly, Vinney was being sarcastic.

"And you didn't think it was important to tell the authorities about this secret?"

Her voice hitched. "Um, I didn't think . . . I didn't know it could help, otherwise I would have. I promise."

"It would have been helpful to know, but it's still helpful now," Vinney said in an even tone.

Elenore placed a carton of creamer and the sugar bowl on the table and headed back into the kitchen.

"How so?" Dr. Deedle asked with the same stern voice he just used with his daughter.

"Madelin Fielding did not commit suicide. She was murdered."

Dr. Deedle's eyes were wide open now. His children inherited their warm brown globes from him. His eyes looked as much like walnuts as Tilly's had earlier that day.

Elenore rushed in from the kitchen with the last of the coffee mugs in her hands. She placed them on the table. "What are you talking about?!"

"I was keeping it hushed to flush out the murderer," Vinney told her, "but my number one suspect, just blew his brains out all over Emmit Fielding's couch."

Dr. Deedle mirrored my reaction. "A damn shame," he said. I knew he was talking about the antique sofa and not Damian Hurst dying. Emmit Fielding served under his far and distant ancestor President George Washington. The sofa was a part of history.

"I don't understand," Elenore said, her eyebrows furrowing into a deep groove. "Why do you think she was murdered?"

"Maddy was found by Chamberlin in her car. The car was running but she didn't die of carbon monoxide poisoning. The tail pipe wasn't blocked. We ran a tox screen and discovered she overdosed on diphenhydramine."

"That's not possible, Maddy didn't do drugs," Chamberlin said. "I would've known."

"Linnie's right. She didn't do drugs," Elenore agreed. "Not my Maddy."

Vinney placed his hand on top of Elenore's, not caring who saw it, and evidently not afraid she would pull it away from him. "It's not the sort of drugs kids get high on. It's a major ingredient found in prescription sleeping pills. It's not an opioid, so it's not street hot."

Elenore nodded, wiping new tears.

"I had a theory that things went south between Maddy and Damian." He glanced at me. "I wasn't following you today, Sister. I was following Damian."

I nodded, but he didn't seem to notice. Vinney's attention was on Tilly. She was crimson again, like she had been earlier when she told Chamberlin about holding on to Maddy's engagement ring. All of her freckles blended into one dark shade of red.

"Are you alright?" Vinney asked her.

"I, I uh, have an anxiety disorder," she spluttered.

He scribbled in his pad. "Do you take medication for that?"

"Sometimes, when it's needed, but it makes my head dull. Anxiety is a disorder of the mind, there are other ways to treat it. I'm pursuing those avenues."

"That sounds like something a doctor would say," Vinney said thoughtfully.

"Well, my father is my doctor, and he is the very best neurological doctor—maybe in the world."

"And these anxiety pills, when you need them, he prescribes them?"

Dr. Deedle answered for her. "I do. As a doctor of neurological disorders, it is perfectly legal and ethical to treat my own daughter. Just as I assume it's not illegal to be the acting detective on a case you have a vested interest in."

Vinney smiled. I could tell he liked Dr. Deedle. "Chantilly take any other pills, sleeping pills, perhaps?"

Dr. Deedle didn't flinch. He gave away no tells that Tilly did, in fact, take sleeping pills. "My daughter's medical history is not a topic for public discussion. It's not only unethical, but as her doctor it's illegal for me to discuss her medical history in front of her peers."

"Understood," Vinney said. "If I have any other questions about Chantilly's medications, I will talk to you both privately." Vinney got up and extended his hand to Dr. Deedle. "Thank you for your time. If I need anything else, I will contact you." Dr. Deedle stood and shook Vinney's hand. He pulled a business card from his wallet and handed it to Vinney.

Based on their introduction in the living room, I knew they didn't know each other, but they at least must have known of each other. Tilly clearly knew Vinney, and Dr. Deedle was her father, and they did live next door. Over the years of dating Elenore, it was likely they crossed paths. He knew Vinney had a history with the Fieldings, but perhaps he ascertained that when Vinney placed his hand on Elenore's. I was sure nothing got past Dr. Deedle.

X and Tilly got up. I could tell Chamberlin wanted to say something to Tilly but didn't. Tilly was barely functioning. I was sure she was going to go home and take a pill for her anxiety, regardless of whether it made her head dull. X helped clear away the coffee mugs. He had been quiet, very quiet for him, but at least he was blinking again.

Dr. Deedle walked around the table to Elenore and gave his condolences for Maddy. He glanced over Chamberlin and looked to me. "You must be Trinity from London." He extended his hand and said, "Nice to meet you. Chantilly and Xavier have told me good things about you."

My hand was very small in his, but the handshake wasn't awkward as it had been with Mrs. Deedle. "You as well, Dr. Deedle."

His eyes again drifted to Chamberlin. I don't think he could have made it any more obvious he didn't like him without coming straight out and saying it. Maybe his dislike was somewhere closer to hate, now that he got his children mixed up in a criminal case.

After letting the Deedles and Allison out and locking the front door, Vinney came back to the dining room, taking up his seat next to Elenore. I was surprised he didn't have anything else official to ask them, but thought it was for the best since they didn't know anything anyway.

"Vinney," Elenore asked, "why would Damian kill Maddy? He loved her. He was a creep, but I think he did really love her."

Vinney ran his hand over his closely cropped hair. "The only motive I could come up with for Damian murdering Maddy is retaliation. My theory is Maddy broke up with him and he killed her. It's possible. I mean, you and Chamberlin were pushing for it for months, maybe something finally got through that thick skull of hers and she told him to hit the road."

"You think it could've been an accidental overdose?" Chamberlin asked.

"No. I don't think so," Vinney said. "Maddy wouldn't take sleeping pills then go for a drive. It just doesn't add up. In my line of work, if things seem off, it's because they're off. You can't force a solution."

"No, I guess not," he said, bowing his head.

"What has me worried is the gun," Vinney told us. "The gun

Damian used to kill himself was stolen from Mikey's."

My eyes grew wide.

"The serial number on the gun found in Damian's hand matched the one Mikey reported stolen. And it was stolen before Maddy gave the ring to Tilly. Thus, I can conclude Damian didn't initially steal the gun to kill himself. Which leads me to ask why *did* he steal it?"

Elenore gasped, covering her mouth with both hands like I had done earlier when I first saw Damian dead on the sofa.

"It was for me," Chamberlin muttered, repeating what Damian had said on the phone. "'You better hope nothing puts a hole in that pretty face of yours.'"

"Maybe," Vinney said. "Mikey's was burglarized shortly after you two had your little brawl. I'm sure he had plenty of opportunities to use it after that and never did. Maybe Maddy's death brought back an old vendetta. Damian did bring the gun to the house knowing he was meeting you. But he didn't use it on you, he turned it on himself instead of his intended target. My question is why?" He exhaled loudly, apparently mulling something over. "I'm not gonna look a gift horse in the mouth, but I think Chamberlin dodged a literal bullet tonight. All of them did. That gun had five rounds in it."

Elenore broke into a sob. The panting cries were hard for me to hear.

"Hey, come on," Vinney said, hugging Elenore to his chest. "That's just one of many possibilities. It's just a theory. A theory is nothing until it's proven. Maybe it wasn't Damian who stole the gun, it could have been another killer. Who's this Uncle Elias?" Before Chamberlin or I could answer, Vinney cut us off. "No, I don't think the ghost of Elias Fielding killed him. I know you guys believe in all of that, but I don't. I've never seen proof of ghosts and trust me I've looked. Either you guys left the front door open or someone flesh and bone opened the front door for Damian."

"The door was locked when we left. I locked it myself," Chamberlin said. "It had to be Elias Fielding. Elenore was in her room."

"What about Maddy's key? Could Damian have it?" I asked. Damian already proved to be a liar. He was never invited to the funeral. Dating Maddy, I was sure he knew the family stories and could have just said Elias's name to get under Chamberlin's skin. If Damian had seen the ghost of Elias Fielding like I had, I doubted he would be chilling with him in the living room. It was way more likely Damian had Maddy's Key.

The key to the front door and the stained-glass portico doors was an antique skeleton key as old as the house. We all had one. I thought it was a possibility Maddy could have given her key to Damian, for the same reason he stole the gun from Mikey's. With Chamberlin and Elenore out of the way, she would be free, and she would be rich, once the Elenore Fielding House was sold.

Vinney rubbed his chin, like he had done outside the cemetery that morning as if the friction of his fingers on his stubble could spark a thought. "That's good, Sister. I'm gonna check his body for that key tonight. If he does have the key, that would really help to tie everything up. The only thing left to solve would be why Damian had a change of heart. Why kill himself?" He scoffed. "Like you said Elenore, the guy was a creep, and I don't really give a shit why he did it. But I hate not knowing and I can't ethically close the case until I feel satisfied that I've exhausted all possibilities."

He glanced at me, his yellow tinted eyes locking with mine for only a moment before going to Elenore. "That is, unless something points back here, including the ghost of Elias Fielding. I'm going to protect you and every Fielding at all costs, ghosts and ghouls included. It makes me sick that kid was able to get a gun in this house. Honestly Elenore, I think I should move back in," he said with a reckless smile.

'Back in'. That was news to me, but he had been engaged to Elenore. I wondered how long he lived here. Vinney calling Chamberlin Linnie was making more and more sense. Vinney was almost family, almost a Fielding. I couldn't help but feel like Vinney, and I'm sure like Damian, that no matter how close I got, I would never be a real Fielding. Elenore had kept so much from me. Deliberately kept it from me. Being called Sister was like dangling a carrot in front of a hungry rabbit. However, there was a silver lining. If I wasn't family, I could be with Chamberlin, but she had to decide. Or maybe I had to.

Elenore laughed into her hand, her tears dried up.

Vinney laughed too. "I'm being serious. I want to move back in."

"I know," she said. I hadn't seen Elenore that happy in a long time, not since Mr. Fielding went missing. "I know it was you who got Damian to drop the charges on Linnie," Elenore said, flushing. "Mikey told me. Thank you."

"It's the least I could do, I'm the one who taught the kid that right hook."

Chamberlin smiled and said, "It *was* your hook."

Vinney looked like a proud father. I suppose in a way he stepped into that role after Mr. Fielding disappeared. Chamberlin was sixteen when he lost his father. He already had a cavernous hole in his heart from his mother's death, a hole made larger by his father's disappearance. I was glad someone was there for him.

"How did you get him to drop it?" Elenore asked.

"I know there's no point in holding out. You'll just bug me till you get your answer," Vinney said.

That was true enough, we all smiled at that. Elenore always got what she wanted; she knew best after all.

Vinney cleared his throat, leaning back in his chair. He seemed excited to tell the story that would paint him as a hero in Elenore's eyes. His amber globes shone like the torches in the stained-glass doors, as if this story was going to lead him home to Elenore for good. I had a feeling he leaked to Mikey he had something to do with the charges being dropped on Chamberlin in hopes it would get back to Elenore and had been waiting ever since to tell her.

"Kid had a hell of a case against our Linnie. Chamberlin did fracture his jaw, and like I said, I felt slightly responsible." Vinney balled his right hand into a fist and glanced at me. "I grew up boxing, taught Chamberlin all the best moves. Every kid needs to know how to defend themself." I nodded, that seemed reasonable. "But, back to the point," Vinney said, "I just flexed a little muscle." He flexed; however, not much of a show was visible through his leather jacket. "I told Damian Hurst if he pressed charges on Chamberlin, I'd say he hit me, and assaulting an officer meant mandatory jail time. It scared him enough to drop the charges."

Elenore pushed her flyaways off her forehead, clearing her line of vision to Vinney. "You do care about us."

Vinney's eyes widened. "Well yeah, Elenore, please tell me you never doubted that? I love you. I love you, still. I'd marry you tomorrow if you let me."

She smiled; it was her real smile. The one only her family saw. "How about we start with breakfast?" she said. "I have the day off tomorrow."

"Okay," he said, "I'd like that. I'll bring the coffee. Your coffee was always shit. Tonight was confirmation."

She playfully slapped his arm. He took her hand.

I became aware of Chamberlin holding my hand under the table. I wasn't sure how it happened. Did he take my hand, or did I take his? Either way, it felt right. It felt natural. Nothing brings people together like a murder.

"Well," Vinney said, getting up and stretching after reluctantly letting go of Elenore's hand, "I'd better get to the office. I have tons of paperwork to do, and I want to check evidence for the house key."

Elenore walked him to the door. Chamberlin and I lingered in the dining room to give them a little privacy, but we could still hear them.

"I have a favor to ask you," Elenore said.

She glanced back at Chamberlin, we acted like we didn't notice, taking a sip of our coffee that was no longer hot. Not that being hot would've helped it. Vinney was right, the coffee was shit. I think it was the worst cup of coffee I had ever had.

"Promise me if anything happens to me, you'll take care of Linnie."

"Nothing is going to happen to him or you," Vinney said with the authority of a police officer.

"Promise," she pleaded in a desperate tone.

"I promise Elenore. You don't have to worry about Damian. He's not coming back, not by *Walking Dead* standards and not even Dr. Deedle could do anything with what was left of his brain."

Her voice dropped. We strained to hear. "I know who killed Damian."

"Who?!" he said, pulling out his phone.

"It's Maddy. She killed him and she's going to kill me next."

Chamberlin was out of his chair. I was behind him.

"Don't do that to yourself Elenore," Vinney said. "You did everything for that kid. Even if ghosts could kill, which in my professional opinion they can't, she'd have no reason to kill you."

"She didn't see it like that. She didn't see what I sacrificed to care for her, and Chamberlin, and Sister. She only saw what I couldn't give her."

I glanced down, I didn't understand it then, but I did now. I was just as selfish as Maddy, and I hated myself for that. Elenore never asked to become our mother.

"Maddy told me that night before she died that I ruined her life, and she was going to ruin mine. I know you don't believe Vinney, it's why I always liked you. I have both feet in the other world, and you were always standing in reality. But I know better than you," she said, playing with the zipper on his jacket.

"I'll stay the night. The paperwork can wait."

"No," she said with a firm shake of her head, "you should look for the key. I'll be fine. I'm just overtired, and besides, Chamberlin and Sister are here."

Vinney dropped his voice, but it was still perfectly audible. He had a tendency to be on the loud side. I recalled him saying once it was a side effect of coming from a family with seven kids. "I don't like leaving you like this. Give me permission to stay and I'll stay."

"That'll ruin breakfast."

"I don't know," he said with a sly smile. "I think it will make it all the sweeter."

"We're taking it slow, remember?" Elenore said like she was reprimanding a child.

Vinney scratched his forehead. I was sure it was for mere effect. "I could stay in a professional capacity," he offered Elenore. "I'll stay on the couch. Shit, I'll stay on the bloody couch."

She pressed her lips to his cheek. "Thank you, Vinney."

He turned as red as Tilly. It was sweet to see. "I'm going to have the boys drive by the house, keep an eye on it," he told her. "If you get spooked, call me." He ran his finger down her hand. "Seriously Elenore, I'm only a call away. I will do everything in my power to protect you and your family. Like I said, we *are* family in my eyes. I would never betray that, not even if I found out Chamberlin killed your father."

Chamberlin thought Vinney was talking hypothetically, I was sure of that. But I knew, from our earlier conversation, that that was the elephant in the room, the thing that had separated Vinney and Elenore. Vinney thought Chamberlin had something to do with Mr. Fielding's disappearance and Elenore thought he was getting too close to the truth, whatever the truth behind Mr. Fielding's disappearance was. I wondered if Inspector Mallory of old had protected the Fieldings when Emmit and Elenore were found dead. He never did make an arrest.

Elenore threw her arms around Vinney. "I love you, you stupid detective. It's about time you've learned family *always* comes first."

"Oh I've learned it, and I'm looking very forward to breakfast, lunch, dinner, and the rest of my life with you."

She pressed a quick kiss to his lips before pulling herself away to wipe new tears.

Vinney looked to Chamberlin. "Take care of her."

"I will Vinney. Thank you," he said, approaching to shake his hand. "Thank you for all your help and getting the charges against me dropped. And sorry for giving you a hard time."

"Water under the bridge kid." Vinney waved to me. "Night, Sister. Thanks."

He glanced one last time at Elenore, a blush still visible on his cheeks.

Elenore shut and locked the front door, pulling on it to

make sure it was locked. Then she locked the stained-glass doors, a precaution she normally didn't take at night. Those doors were only ever locked during the day to keep guests in the entryway until the next tour began. You would need a battering ram to get through the front door and that was usually good enough for Elenore.

Chamberlin wrapped Elenore in a warm embrace. "Maddy doesn't want you dead. She loved you, Elenore. You were her mother and her sister."

His words brought about another torrent of sobs. I never heard Elenore cry like that. It was like she was gasping to live. There was so much raw emotion in it, so much pain. It made me shed tears.

"I love you Chamberlin," she said, her words sounding like they came from under water. "I hope you know that. I'm sorry I couldn't have done more to give you a better life."

"Stop Elenore. I love you. I love my life. I think of myself as lucky, to have you as my Frankenstein mother sister."

"I love you, too," Elenore said to me, over Chamberlin's shoulder. "Even if I didn't always show it and you didn't always think it. I did. I do. You're a part of this family Sister. You belong here."

"I love you, too, Elenore," I said, stifling my tears.

She released Chamberlin to hug me. "Now you two get to bed. I'm gonna go scrub the couch really quick, hopefully we won't have to reupholster it. But I'm gonna leave the blood on the floor until tomorrow," she said with a smile. "I think a genuine blood stain would be cool to add to the tour."

I laughed. "I thought you'd do that."

"Business first," she said. "Well, family first, business second."

CHAPTER EIGHTEEN

A New Life

I got out of the shower feeling clean in body and soul, like the water washed away all the bad and ugly of the day, only to put on my dirty pajamas. I really needed to do laundry, go shopping, or make the hard call to Kris and have my things from the flat sent. I'll do laundry.

I grabbed my dirty clothes and went to the rec room where the washer and dryer were located. I was in luck, the washer was empty. I put my clothes in, sprinkled powder detergent, and pushed start. The washer came to life with a series of squeaks and groans that would make any haunted house owner happy. They didn't have a high-efficiency washer and dryer like I had in London but a small stackable meant for an apartment. It was a good thing I only had a small load. I didn't think the old stackable could handle more than that.

I couldn't see the clothes spinning around getting full of soapsuds, but I imagined it. I had a healthy imagination. But I knew I couldn't dream up my own version of Elias Fielding. I wasn't *that* creative.

HOUSES *HAVE* SECRETS

There were no paintings or photographs of an old Elias Fielding. Something, I didn't realize until I saw him on the couch. I wondered if Chamberlin and Elenore realized how odd this was. The paintings of Elias Fielding as a boy were all over the house. He was the Fieldings' first and only son and heir to the Fielding fortune. The Fielding's were obviously proud of their son, but the sheer number of paintings of Elias approached obsession. You couldn't go into a room without seeing his dark hair combed to the side, his dark eyes blank, as if the artists left them unfinished.

Oddly enough, all of the paintings were rendered around the same time period. Judging by the soft, round face and hands, I'd say under ten. If I didn't know better, I'd think he died as a child because the paintings just stopped. I wondered if that had something to do with his sister Ivette's death. According to Chamberlin, Elias Fielding was eight years old when his little sister died. Maybe his parents didn't want to hang a bunch of paintings of a murderer up. Perhaps, the earlier childhood ones were precious, he was innocent then, so they stayed, and no new paintings were ever commissioned.

No, Elias Fielding wasn't a figment of my imagination or stress. I knew what he was as soon as I saw him. I didn't like how he said my name and how he smiled at me. Not one bit.

"You just need to go to sleep and start over tomorrow," I said to myself in something like a pep talk. I internally groaned. Going to sleep meant living through some version of Frank Fielding dying. Meant I would be covered in blood. And if my dreams followed their recent pattern, Chamberlin's face would go splat on the floor.

My vision glided down the hall to Chamberlin's bedroom door. I knew he was still awake. His door was open a sliver. Light bled into the hallway in a yellow line.

I knocked on his bedroom door. When he didn't answer, I let myself in. I heard him in his bathroom. As if hearing me enter, the bathroom door opened. Chamberlin was wearing only a towel wrapped around his waist. I tried not to stare, but that was impossible. This was better than any of his videos. Each little muscle, that I was sure had some fancy name, seemed highlighted and perfected under the chandelier above. It was like I was seeing living art. I don't know what was more beautiful, his face, his eyes, or his body. I found myself quite speechless.

"I'm gonna get dressed," he said.

"Uh yeah, of course, should I step out?"

"Not necessary."

He took a pair of basketball shorts out of his dresser and pulled them up under the towel. No longer needing it as a cover up, he towel-dried his hair. Balling his towel up like a basketball, he took aim at his hamper and missed. It landed at my feet.

"You always sucked at sports," I said, picking up his towel for him and helping it the rest of the two feet to the hamper. I noticed it was oddly dry.

He chuckled, which I took as his way of letting me know I was right without admitting it out loud. He quickly slipped into a T-shirt and combed his damp hair back before taking a seat next to me on his bed. "Today was crazy," Chamberlin sighed. "I swear it's not always like this."

"It must be me. I must bring the crazy out."

He shook his head, a wet bang falling in front of his eye. "No, you being home is a good thing."

He looked like he meant it, his eyes beaming in an honest blue. The scratch on his cheek was almost faded to nothing now.

"I thought you said I should go."

A rosy hue colored his complexion. He looked more handsome now. I could see the blood heating under his skin, as I knew mine was from just sitting close to him.

He brushed the loose bang away from his face just for another one to take its place. "I did say that," he acknowledged. "I was mad at you for leaving. That's why I never talked to you once you moved to London."

"Oh, you don't say," I said, with a playful nudge. It was just an excuse to touch him. But it worked, he nudged me back.

"I do say," he said, his playfulness lost. "I guess I'm still mad."

"Will you ever forgive me?" I asked, mockingly batting my

eyelashes, doing my best Puss in Boots impression.

He laughed, a quick titter. "Well, if we learned anything from Elenore and Vinney tonight, it's to forgive. So, in the spirit of that, yes. I forgive you for running off to London without me."

I narrowed my eyes, studying him. "Would you've come with me?"

He shook his head. "No. I could never have left Elenore or Maddy, but it would have been nice to be asked."

"A bruised ego," I teased.

"Very bruised," he admitted. "Crushed even."

I knew I was wrong when I left, I didn't want to talk about how selfish I was and how I left them high and dry. He was right, I never asked him to go with me, but I should have. Even if I knew he would never abandon Elenore and Maddy, it would have let him know how I felt about him.

I had made a mistake. I had made many mistakes. I just didn't have the energy to face the past. The past was too real. It hurt too much, him and me. I took the opportunity to redirect the conversation to something that I was dying to know that wouldn't fill me with leaded guilt.

"So, what's the story with Vinney teaching you a right hook and you *crushing* Damian's jaw with it."

"Damian Hurst," he said, leaning back on his bed with an exaggerated sigh that reminded me of the noise a tea kettle makes right before it whistles. "I was completely fooled by that guy. I should have listened to X. He said from the second he saw him he was no good."

"I guess he's as intuitive as his sister."

Chamberlin's eyes lit up with my recognition of this. "Yeah, they both are. I think it's because they're both geniuses."

Genius was a strong word. I could tell X and Tilly were very smart, but I wasn't putting them on the same level as Albert Einstein just yet. "I'm surprised with a father like that Tilly's allowed to go to psychic school," I said. "Seems a waste of her genius."

"Well, that's only because Dr. Deedle or the Big B as Tilly calls him—"

"Big Boris," I interrupted with a giggle.

"It's Big Bear actually, it's her pet name for him. He's Big Bear and she's Little Bear."

"Oh," I said with a smile, thinking of my opposition to my nickname regarding the Berenstain Bears. "And I'm Sister Bear."

"Not that again," Chamberlin said with a laugh I hadn't heard him use since we were kids. "I'm not Brother Bear."

"I'm very glad about that," I said, taking on a serious air.

He gave me a curious smile as if he was trying to ascertain if there was a hidden meaning in what I just said. To my disappointment he shrugged it off. "But uh, yeah, no one calls Dr. Deedle that but Tilly, but we all use it when we talk about him. He's cool with the psychic school because he thinks of it as a second major, really like a third. Tilly is a premedical major with a minor in Latin. Oh yeah, and she's already received her early acceptance letter from NYU's school of Medicine. She killed the MCAT exam. Um, that's the entrance exam for medical school, if you didn't know."

Okay, maybe Tilly *was* a genius. I was starting to feel a little threatened by her. I wished her nickname was Sister Bear. "Oh wow, that's great," I said, not a hundred percent meaning it.

He enthusiastically nodded. "X is just as smart. He has a 4.0 grade point average and has never studied a day in his life." It looked like Chamberlin was in just as much awe of his friends as they were of him. "X helped revamp the family business, making it profitable. We were bleeding cash before he stepped in. Both of them, really. We owe them a lot."

"Does Elenore know? She seems to appreciate X, but when it comes to Tilly . . ."

"Yeah, once Elenore saw the money coming in, she thought X was a genius too. But as you hinted, she hates Tilly. I don't understand why. The more I mentioned her, the more Elenore didn't like her. So, I stopped mentioning her all together. I guess it's like Tilly said, she's safeguarding my virginity or something. Not that Tilly's slutty or anything like that."

"You know Elenore," I said, "but what I don't get is how this guy Damian got past her."

He raked his fingers through his hair. It was almost dry now. "Elenore was fooled, like the rest of us. Well, besides X. Damian met Maddy on a tour. After the tour was over, he stayed behind to talk to her. He's a movie prop guy. Well—was. He worked on big films out of NYC and offered to help us in any way he could. The guy was a master at makeup and prosthetics. You should have seen some of the transformations he worked on me. I was a mummy one weekend, a vampire the next." His blue eyes sparkled. "Oh, the best was the zombie. I looked so real, I scared myself." I smiled. Only Chamberlin Fielding could be scared by his own costumed reflection. "The werewolf was really good too. X and Tilly made the scariest dead clowns you ever saw. Pennywise has nothing on them. I think the pictures are on my Instagram. I'm not sure though, that's X's thing."

"He sounds like he was very talented."

"He was. Elenore and I were impressed, and obviously so was Maddy. Elenore took him up on his offer to help and before her Night-ins, we were doing catered scaring for high-end clients on the weekends. With the help of Damian in the props department, we created what the person was most afraid of and well, scared them. It was very successful while it lasted. Damian set up cameras in the house, in the hallways, and in certain rooms where we would have planned interactions with guests. The cameras were designed to let us know where guests were so we could find them to scare them. Tilly, X, and Maddy all helped, even Elenore did sometimes. It was a lot of fun."

He took a deep breath. "But then one night everything changed. It was just the four of us that night. X, Tilly, Damian, and me. Maddy had a school thing. Damian went to the bathroom, and he'd been gone awhile. We were getting bored, so I checked his phone to see where the guests were and that's when I saw the videos. He had set up cameras in our bedrooms in the attic. He had videos saved of Maddy undressing, some really embarrassing ones of me, and the thing that put me over the top was a video of Elenore getting dressed in the morning. When he came back to the group, I swung.

He hit the ground, and I pounced on him. I was completely out of control. It was like I was removed from my body and someone else was controlling me. I was just watching, not able to stop myself. If it weren't for X, I would have killed him. I know that." He bowed his head, his eyes hidden behind his thick lashes and shadows. "X hit me to snap me out of it. And I'm so glad he did. It worked. It woke me up from this crazed frenzy. X hitting me saved me. That and Tilly telling the cops Damian hit me first. Seriously, she's so smart. Without that, I couldn't have claimed self-defense. Tilly and X both lied for me, Damian never got a hit off. Then you heard how Vinney stepped in afterwards."

"That's nuts." I muttered. I really didn't see what Maddy saw in him now. They say love is blind, maybe it's dumb, too.

Chamberlin pushed his hair out of his eyes. "Yeah, it was. I had a little bruise on my cheek from X and some cuts on my knuckles. Damian looked like raw meat. Maddy was furious. Of course, he deleted the videos so only X and Tilly saw them, and it was easy for Maddy to call them my puppets, my cult followers, and a whole bunch of other names. I guess they did lie for me . . . Damian *was* telling the truth about never touching me."

"Either way he was a creep," I said. "It sounds like he was asking for a good punch in the face."

Chamberlin shook his head, a gesture I assumed was meant for Maddy. "Before that night, I had never hit anyone. You'd think Maddy would take it as a sign I was telling the truth, but she wouldn't break up with him. Elenore believed me without seeing the videos, but Maddy wouldn't believe me even after I pulled down the cameras Damian hid in her room. After that, things were different between Maddy and me. And with Elenore, too." He dropped his voice, his eyes still cast in shadows. "I thought Damian was so cool, and this whole time he was fake. I felt stupid for not seeing what was right in front of me."

I thought of Tilly. He didn't see it, see that she loved him. I was okay with that. I wanted him to only see me. And Tilly was okay with that as long as they were best friends, so there was no point in bringing it to his attention.

Chamberlin spoke in a whisper. "Do you think Damian really came here tonight to kill me?"

"I hope not."

He exhaled slowly. "I could've gotten everyone killed."

I took his hand. It was soft in mine. It felt just as natural as it did downstairs in the dining room when we held hands. "You didn't."

"I wonder if Elenore was right and Maddy did kill him. Do you think when we die, we suddenly know all truths?"

"I can't say, Chamberlin. Maybe it was suicide or maybe it was Elias. He does have a thing for murdering. But it doesn't matter who or what killed him. If Vinney was right about Damian's intentions, his death saved you." This realization made me feel a lot better. It didn't matter that creepy Elias Fielding was, well, creepy. Even if he did have a thing for murder, he seemed to be on our side. Or at least on Chamberlin's side. Chamberlin was a Fielding, but then again so was Baby Ivette. If I believed the rumors, she was only Elias's half-sister. I wasn't even that to Chamberlin. I was adopted. That didn't make me feel the safest. But I wasn't in the house to kill Chamberlin like Damian was believed to be, I was there to love him.

Chamberlin smiled softly. "I guess it's like Vinney said, let's not look a gift horse in the mouth."

I felt my eyebrows stitch together. "What does that even mean?"

"It means were not going to be ungrateful for a gift even if we don't like how it came about."

"Yeah, true. I'm grateful. The alternative is too awful to think about. I didn't know Damian well, but I feel a lot safer with him gone."

"It's funny, I'm not really that upset," Chamberlin said. "I feel a little guilty about that. I mean, a man did just die downstairs. I should be upset, but I guess you and I have seen our fair share of death. Seeing a loved one dead is on a different scale than what we saw tonight."

My fingers ran along the scar on his palm, the one he got the day our parents died. It was raised and rough, so very different from the rest of his soft hand. "Tilly says your scar runs through your love line."

He opened his hand to look at it. "I always think of it as some cruel cosmic joke. A physical commiseration of the day we were separated from our parents and each other."

"Tilly said you don't have to let it end there. You could overcome the scar and grow."

"It's probably for the best it ends. What if the Fielding curse that claimed Emmit and Elenore comes true? *True love breathes death.* I know you always thought it was romantic they were found holding hands, but they still died. And then there were our parents . . . they were holding hands when we found them."

He *had* noticed.

I took his hand in mine again, feeling his elevated scar against my palm. "If I'm going to die, I want to be holding your hand Chamberlin."

His blue eyes locked onto mine, his dark lashes holding me in his intense gaze. His free hand went to the side of my face, where his thumb traced my lips. His finger was soft and gentle. "I want the same thing," he said in a murmur, "but there's so much in our way."

My pulse surged with every brush of his finger on my lips. "My last name, my nickname," I whispered as if my name was the curse. It felt that way.

"The universe doesn't want us together. My scar is proof."

My heart beat like ten hearts in my chest. I spoke with bated breath, like each word could be my last. "I don't care what the universe wants. I care what I want."

"If we cross this line, there's no going back," he warned.

"Who says I want to go back? I want to move forward. I'm here to stay. You're my home, Chamberlin Fielding."

I pressed my lips to his. His tender lips were softer than I remembered them in our youth. Magic sparked between us, as it could be nothing else. It was an electrifying energy that pulled our bodies together. He closed his eyes and deepened the kiss, our bodies twisting into one. His long lashes fluttered against my cheeks, more magic. It was a race to undress. His hands traveled under my pajama top and up my spine, setting every nerve in my body on fire. I didn't want to be saved, I wanted to burn in Hell with Chamberlin Fielding.

* * *

The familiar scent of metal filled the air. I rubbed my blood drenched fingers together, the blood like warm oil, silky and smooth. I was back in Mr. Fielding's room. I was hovering over his corpse. The blood stain on his white dress shirt spread like a virus, its virulency coloring his chest red. There was a noise, a soft cry. It was Chamberlin. He was against the wall with Maddy by his side. Chamberlin was again a teenager, his face soft and young with no flaws, no scratch. The door to the Elenore Fielding House in the painting was open, the blood smear was where I left it, as if my last dream had changed this one somehow. I heard a loud bang followed by thumps. The sound continued to grow, echoing around the room, until it hit an intolerable pitch. I glanced at Chamberlin and Maddy. It was like they couldn't hear it. The scratch was upon Chamberlin's face again. Little trickles of blood began their descent, dripping down his cheek. I couldn't take the noise any longer. Forgetting about the blood on my hands, I covered my ears. Its warmth heated the sides of my face. I yanked my hands away. On my red hands were strands of blonde hair.

* * *

I woke up as I usually did after my nightmare, out of breath, my heart pounding in my chest like a little engine. Chamberlin's bedroom was dark except for the thin trail of moonlight filtering in through the dormer window. It focused like a perfect beam on Chamberlin's face, like he was in the middle of a photo shoot in his bed. I bet his Instagram followers would've loved this picture. He looked flawless. He looked every bit as supernatural as some of his fans thought he was—ageless, timeless perfection. Again, I thought maybe he *was* a vampire.

He was fast asleep on his back; a sheet just covered his nether region. His toned body looked like it was chiseled from marble. His golden hair cradled his face as his dark lashes curled against his smooth cheeks. His lips were separated, only slightly, just enough for me to feel his breath. I tucked my head under his shoulder, wrapping my hand around his bare waist. That's when I heard it. It was muffled and hard to make out, but I'm positive I heard it.

"I'm going to kill you."

I shot up, pushing Chamberlin's limp arm off of me. "What'd you say?!" My heart was pounding again. I kept my eyes locked on his angelic face. He didn't stir, he was sound asleep. I looked around the room. Was someone else there? No—it was Chamberlin's voice I heard.

I shook him.

He let out a groan.

"Chamberlin!"

His dark lashes fluttered like the wings of a hummingbird before he opened his eyes. Seeing me sitting up, he sat up. "Is everything okay?"

I tried to act natural. I was grateful for the cover of darkness. "Uh yeah, you were talking in your sleep."

"Oh, sorry," he said, rubbing sleep from his eyes. "I didn't mean to wake you." He put his arm around me and brought me down on his chest. I could hear his heart beating. It was slow and rhythmic. He kissed my forehead. "What did I say?"

I couldn't repeat it. "I don't know," I lied.

"Sorry, I wasn't aware I talk in my sleep. No one has ever said. But I guess it would be hard to hear anything over X's snoring."

I let out a quick laugh. Maybe I was just hearing things. I did just wake up from my nightmare. I wasn't one hundred percent sure what I heard.

"The last two nights, since you've been home, or maybe it's you sleeping by my side, I've slept better than I have in years," Chamberlin said, lifting my face to his. There was a sparkle in his eyes, like the moon's reflection in the glistening ocean. He pressed a kiss to my lips. The kiss was soft and sweet like him, a spark igniting between us again. I yearned to have him closer. "I love you, Trinity Dunn. I have only ever loved you."

I kissed him back, all of my worries disappearing as his hand held mine.

* * *

Chamberlin's phone rang. I let out a groan of disapproval. He reached over me to grab it off his nightstand. "Hey, is everything okay, Vinney?"

Vinney was so loud on the other end of the call it was like he was on speaker. I thought for a second maybe Chamberlin accidently pushed the speaker button by mistake, but he didn't. Vinney was just that loud. "You tell me," Vinney blared. "Your sister invites me for breakfast and now she's not answering her phone or the door. She must be listening to music or something. Come let me in. It's hot as balls out here already. I can't wait for this heat wave to kick it. And bad news, no key; four eyes didn't have it."

"Coming."

Chamberlin turned to me, our noses touching, a soft brush of skin on skin. "It's Vinney, he's at the front door," he said to me, as if I didn't just hear their conversation. "Hopefully he has coffee for us, too." He pressed a quick kiss to my lips. "Let's get something to drink and eat, then I want to spend the rest of the day in bed counting your freckles."

"That sounds boring," I said.

He beamed. "Not at all. I'm gonna kiss every one I count."

"Oh," I smiled, as he took my two hands and pulled me out of bed.

He wrapped his arms around me so I couldn't move. "I'm so happy, Trinity." He pressed another kiss to my lips, letting them linger there for a moment before he pulled himself away. I felt this separation keenly, a remorse penetrating my heart. The desire—no, more like a need—to touch him overtook me. Lip to lip, holding his hand, it didn't matter. I wanted him, any part of him, touching me.

We got dressed quickly, throwing on anything we found, and raced down the stairs hand in hand like it was Christmas morning. As we rounded the corner of the second story, Chamberlin stopped.

"What's wrong?" I asked, tugging on his hand. I didn't like being this close to Baby Ivette's bedroom. Friend or foe, I wasn't a fan of ghosts. Then I saw it. I saw what was wrong. I had no control,

I screamed, and I screamed. I screamed so loud my ears popped. At the foot of the stairs, over Maddy's duct tape body, was Elenore. Her head was turned around like she was an owl.

Chamberlin darted down the stairs to her. Vinney pounded on the front door. The sound was distorted like each pound had its own echo, but pound after pound eventually brought me back to reality. I ran down the stairs and rushed to the door. I unlocked the stained-glass doors and pulled them open in a frenzy. I felt like if I could just get Vinney in the house, he could fix everything.

I did the same with the front door, throwing it open so hard the doorknob struck the wall. Vinney rushed in. He wasn't alone. Dr. Deedle must have heard me scream and was right behind him.

Elenore was in Chamberlin's arms. He looked so much like he did that day he held his dead mother in the elevator. He turned Elenore for Vinney to see. "She's dead Vinney, she's dead! Elenore is dead!" He buried his face in her chest. Vinney fell to his knees at Elenore's side along with the coffees, and the hopes of their new life together.

Dr. Deedle must have known Elenore was dead, just as I had known from the second story balustrade. Nevertheless, he played the part of a doctor and felt for a pulse in vain. "I'm sorry, there's nothing I can do."

CHAPTER NINETEEN
A New Warning

Everyone left—the ambulance, the police, Vinney, the Deedles. The Deedles went as far as to leave the neighborhood and headed to New York City for a couple of days. Vinney would be back, but he had to check in at the police station. Chamberlin and I were alone in the house. It had always been a monstrosity of a home, with huge rooms, tall ceilings, and wide staircases, but I never felt alone in it. For some reason, I did now, even with Chamberlin.

Chamberlin sat at the foot of the stairs with his knees tucked into his chest, staring up at the wingless angel on the newel post. He had been like that since he was made to let go of Elenore's body. Not even Tilly could stir him. Vinney said to let him be, so we did.

Chamberlin had been sitting there for hours when I brought him a glass of water. He took it, but he wouldn't take anything else. He said thank you with a kind smile, not expressing anything in spoken words. I feared there was going to be a period of silence like there had been after his father's disappearance.

It was dusk now. The sun moved to set. The house was

always dim thanks to the thick curtains hanging over the windows. It was part of the moodiness the Fieldings sought to create, but at dusk a natural melancholy settled in over the antique furnishings, blanketing everything from the floorboards to the house's occupants in gloom.

I sat next to Chamberlin at the foot of the stairs, but I wouldn't look at the carving that sat on the newel post. I would only look at him.

"It's just like my father said," Chamberlin mumbled, breaking his silence.

I sighed in relief that he spoke, interlocking my arm with his. I rested my head on his shoulder. "It's not your fault Chamberlin. Elenore fell down the stairs."

"He warned me. He told me to always look out for them or death would find them."

"Chamberlin, what happened to Elenore was an accident."

"No. It only looks like an accident. Just like Maddy's death looked like a suicide. You heard Vinney, he thinks Maddy was murdered. Either way, I'm at the heart of it. I'm sure of that. It's no different than Baby Ivette's death being called an accident, or how my father's sisters deaths looked like an accident. . . ." He leaned his face closer to mine, his voice sounding very deep. "Remember when we were kids, and you used to talk about those gut feelings of yours?"

"Yes . . ." I said reluctantly. Chamberlin knew about my so-called gut feelings. I had told him about them when we first met, but I had been very careful not to mention them after our parents died.

"I have one. One of your gut feelings. I know Maddy and Elenore were both murdered. My life's like a damn prophecy."

My tone took on a sterner intonation. "Chamberlin, it wasn't your fault," I told him again. "Elenore's death, and Maddy's too, is not part of some Fielding curse for brothers to murder their sisters. Think of Bethany; she hung herself. Elias was too young to have forced her to do it."

"It looked like it was her doing," he said, "but her brother Elias was behind her death. Not physically, you're right, he was too young for that, but Bethany took her own life because of him. He was the catalyst. It was guilt over what he'd done that drove her to it. He's still to blame. Just like I'm to blame for what transpired between Maddy and Damian. I let it get out of hand, and she died because of it. By her own choice or by someone else's, she's dead. And Elenore . . . it only looks like she fell down the stairs. It was my fault. Somehow it was my fault," he said, his eyes coming to rest on the wingless angel as if he thought she played a part in Elenore's fall.

I squeezed his arm. There was no point arguing with him. In this state of mind, he couldn't be reasoned with. Maybe Elias had killed his little sister and was to blame for his older sister's suicide, and maybe Mr. Fielding did deliberately make it so his sisters' blanket sleigh ride ended with them tumbling down the stairs to their deaths, but I knew Chamberlin, and I knew for a fact he didn't kill Maddy. And the same went for Elenore. He was with me all night.

If Angeles Hillings did curse the Fielding men, dooming them to repeat history by killing their sisters as she hung from the other end of a rope, she missed out. She may have a new pair of wings to try on for size, but it wasn't because of Chamberlin. He didn't do it. But there was this small part of me that was uneasy Elenore died on the stairs. If Elias Fielding could somehow force Damian to turn the gun on himself, then it was possible the wingless angel, the embodiment of Angeles Hillings, could have killed Elenore. I was in full blown Fielding mode, believing ghosts could kill. However, it was much more likely Elenore had slipped and fell to her death. I, myself, had stumbled up and down the stairs many times over the years.

"My mother believed it too," he told me in a whisper.

I wrinkled my nose, not quite following what he was getting at. "Believed you would kill your sisters?"

"Yes," he said, his eyes never leaving the wingless angel. He watched her like his life—like my life—depended on it. It was as if his watchful eye was the only thing stopping her from climbing down from the head of the staircase and slaughtering people.

"At night, every night, my mother would come into my room

once she thought I was asleep and say a prayer over me."

"W—what?" I stammered.

He turned his face to gaze into my eyes. His eyelids were puffy and swollen. His blue globes were webbed over in little red veins that forked off until there was no trace of white. His dark lashes were slick with tears, but the scratch that haunted my dreams was gone. His skin was flawless. All of his wounds were internal now.

"I'd pretend to be asleep as she folded her hands over my chest and said, like she said every night, 'Dear Lord, please keep my boy the angel I know he is in his heart. Do not let the sins of his family turn him into a murderer.'"

I brought myself closer to Chamberlin, if that was even possible. I buried my chin in the crook of his armpit. "Oh my goodness."

I knew Mrs. Fielding was vigilant when it came to Chamberlin. I just figured he was her favorite. I reasoned it was because he was so much like her. Where the girls inherited their father's aggression and stubbornness, Chamberlin inherited his mother's patience and grace. I never would have guessed the real reason Dottie Fielding watched her son was to make sure he didn't murder his sisters. Wow, the Fieldings were more messed up than they let on.

"You never told your mother you heard her?"

He shook his head, his bangs falling in line with the high cut of his cheekbones. "No, and she came to my room every night since I can remember. I got so used to it, I couldn't sleep until she came and said her prayer over me. After she died, I went on saying it for her. It killed me that I worried her so much. That I, being alive, caused her so much pain. She would cry after her little prayer. She was so in earnest when she faithfully said it night after night. Her words never lost conviction and hope. She knew what I would grow to become." Chamberlin wiped a tear. "I stopped saying my mother's prayer when Maddy died. I knew then that there's no stopping what I am. There's no hope for me."

"Chamberlin, you're not a murderer."

"There's so much you don't know, Trinity." My hand

trembled against our interlocked arms. There was something in the way he said that that scared me. "I have tried to honor my mother's prayer for me. I tried so hard to be that angel she thought I could be. I tried so hard," he repeated, clenching his fist. "There's just too much of my father in me."

He bowed his head, no longer committing his gaze to the wingless angel or me. We sat in silence for a long time, the room growing darker as the amber light filtering in from the torches diminished with the setting sun.

"I'm going to go clean the blood off the floor in the living room," I told Chamberlin reluctantly. I didn't want to leave him, but Damian's blood had to be wiped up before it became a real nightmare.

* * *

I grabbed the mop from the pantry and bleach and a bucket from under the sink in the kitchen. The rubber gloves weren't with the bucket. There was no way I was touching blood with my bare hands, that was a pleasure reserved for my nightmares. I checked the junk drawer. An empty little orange pill bottle was mixed in with the rest of the random crap thrown in. Picking it up, I examined it to find it was for sleeping pills prescribed to Chantilly Deedle by Dr. Boris Deedle, the same kind I saw atop her dresser. I wondered if it was that exact pill bottle.

Placing the empty bottle back in the drawer, I continued to rummage for the rubber gloves. Finally, I spotted yellow rubber gloves rolled up in a Ziploc bag. It was amazing the amount of junk Elenore fit in that drawer. I grabbed them and headed toward the living room.

Chamberlin's dark-lidded eyes followed me. I was hoping he would join me in the living room, but he continued to sit at the base of the stairs. I let him. I didn't want to be pushy. Watching me clean up blood was probably not the best thing for his already shaken psyche.

Elenore did a good job cleaning Emmit Fielding's sofa. There was still a visible stain, that couldn't be helped as the sofa was upholstered in light fabric, but it didn't look like if you sat on it, you would be covered in blood. I slid the antique sofa away from the blood stain on the floor to gain easier access to it. The edges were dried and flaky. Its texture reminded me of the old houses in the neighborhood that desperately needed to be scraped and repainted. The center of the blood puddle was thick and sticky like syrup. Old blood was a lot different than the oil-like blood of my dreams and took a lot longer to clean up than I thought possible. I had to scrape at it with my nails through the gloves. The smell of bleach and blood made the living room smell like a hospital.

A noise, similar to rustling leaves in the wind, made me look up. It was accompanied by the unmistakable sound of footfalls, like the kind a cat would make when it's hunting—scarcely audible, just the impression of a sound. The Grand Duke Wiskerton was famous for doing that right before he would jump out from under the couch with a cat toy pressed between his teeth.

I knew I wasn't at my Great Aunt Girty's, but instinctively I did what I would have done if I was at her flat in London and looked under the couch for The Grand Duke. He wasn't there. Nothing was under the antique sofa Damian Hurst had bled all over. But under the sofa parallel to it, the sofa I had seen Elias Fielding sitting on yesterday, I saw feet. Two sets of small feet, belonging not to a cat, but to children. The feet were dressed in white socks with decorative lace at the ankles. My chest tightened along with my extremities. I felt rigid and slow but my heart beat faster. I felt it thudding in my chest like bass on a stereo.

A small head popped out from the back of the sofa. I gasped, but I wasn't able to do much more. My body felt like it was made of lead or maybe tin. I was as immobilized as Dorothy's Tinman in *The Wizard of Oz* when she first found him seized in the forest. The little girl who peered at me from behind the sofa was about six years old. Her face was pale, her complexion lighter than I was. She had dark hair, as dark as an oil spill, that hung in waves around her heart-shaped face. Her dark eyes filled her orbits like the eyes of a snake. She giggled. It was this high-pitched sound that could have cracked glass. From the other end of the couch another little girl's head darted out. She had the same dark hair and eyes and the same placid skin. They could have been twins, but the second girl was clearly a few years older, judging by her height.

I didn't dare move, even if I could. "Who are you both?" I asked in a whisper.

The older of the two girls answered first in a squeaky voice. "I'm Sister."

The little one answered in a similar tone. "I'm Sister."

"I'm Sister, too," I said, wondering if I was looking at Mr. Fielding's sisters. It took me a moment to recall their names. Lillian and Clementine. Yes—that was it. Lillian and Clementine for whom Chamberlin was named. Could this be them?

They giggled at my response. Their high-pitched laughter becoming deep, deeper now, too deep for little girls. Their small doll-like hands crept out from behind the sofa clinging to the mahogany armrests, their nails long and yellowed like claws of an animal, their hands red up to the wrists in blood.

I felt the forced air in my ear before I heard it. "Sister, you're next." I turned to see Bethany—her bent neck, her cloudy dead eyes.

My body was electrified as if I was just struck by lightning. Every nerve fiber in me burned. I pushed myself away from her, but it didn't matter. Bethany was already gone—vanished—and so were the little girls. But their giggle, this deep, maleficent giggle, I still heard. Polly's curio cabinet opened with a groan, her steely, black eyes locking on to mine like a laser beam.

I scrambled to my feet and ran to the stairs. "Chamberlin!" I shouted. He wasn't there. I frantically turned around in the foyer. He wasn't there. "Chamberlin!" I heard a noise coming from the direction of the kitchen. The crooked fan popped into my head. "Oh God, no!"

I raced into the kitchen. Chamberlin was on the kitchen table, his back turned to me. "Don't kill yourself! You didn't kill Maddy, it was—"

Chamberlin turned around, pulling out his earbuds. "Trin, you say something?" My body shook like a leaf stuck on the windshield of a Mack truck. He jumped off the table and wrapped his arms around me, bringing me close to his chest. I pulled him closer. I could barely hear him over my own heartbeat. "What happened? What's wrong?" he asked.

Tears streamed from my eyes. I had held them in since we found Elenore. I had tried to be a rock for Chamberlin, but I wasn't a rock. I was Play-Doh, and I was crumbling. "Don't kill yourself. Please, I'm sorry."

"Hey, hey calm down," he pleaded, running his hand down my hair. "What are you talking about?"

I sniffled, trying to take back everything I just let out. "Elenore told me after Maddy died you tried to hang yourself from the kitchen fan. Don't deny it. I know the truth."

"What?!"

"That's why the fan looks like that," I said, separating myself from him just enough to glance at the fan. It wasn't there. There was just a large hole with wires hanging from it. I pulled myself further from him, searching. There it was, the fan was sitting on a kitchen chair.

Chamberlin laughed. It was a strained laugh, somewhere between a laugh and a cry. It scared me. I had never heard him laugh like that before.

I put distance between us, taking a few steps back. "Why are you laughing?" The horrible promise I thought I heard him mutter in his sleep last night raced through my mind. *I'm going to kill you.* My heart sped up. Bethany said I was next.

"Sorry," he said, reaching for my hand.

I pulled away.

His face screwed up. "Trin, what's wrong with you?"

"Tell me why you're laughing," I demanded in the sternest voice I could marshal.

He gave me an unsure smile. "I'm laughing because of Elenore."

I raised my eyebrows as I sucked air. My heartbeat was in my ears again, my body ready to move into a fight or flight response. "Because she's dead?"

"What, no!" he said, pushing his hair away from his face and taking on an earnest countenance. "Because of what she said. I never tried to hang myself from the fan. It looked all wacky because she tried to take it down herself. She wanted to replace it because the blades had warped. I said I'd do it, but she lost her patience waiting on me and attempted to do it herself. She didn't take into consideration changing out a fixture isn't that easy when you have plaster ceilings. She stopped mid-project when the plaster began to crumble, and duct taped everything back together."

I had a splitting headache now. "So . . . you didn't hang yourself? She didn't cut you down?"

He shook his head. "No. Nothing like that at all."

"And you weren't in here trying to hang yourself?"

He pointed to a box on the kitchen counter that was open. It was a new fan. "No, I was replacing the fan for Elenore. You were cleaning up Damian's blood in the living room, and I thought I should follow your example and try to make Elenore happy. Sitting by the stairs wasn't helping anyone." He smiled. A trace of sadness haunted the way the corners of his mouth pulled up. "Better late than never, right? I've been meaning to change out the fan, I just never got around to it."

He reached out for my hand again. I let him take it. I nibbled on my bottom lip. I agree he wasn't helping anything or anyone, including himself, by sitting at the foot of the stairs all day, but this was a drastic change in mood, even for a Fielding. "I saw the rope burn on your neck," I said like an accusation.

"Trin, we don't even have rope, and I shave every day, sometimes twice a day. I get a rash from shaving when it's really hot out. It's actually called heat rash."

"Oh," I said, feeling silly. "So, you really didn't try to kill yourself?"

He hugged me to him. "No. I would never. So don't worry about me. I'm fine now. No more moping."

It appeared me needing him broke Chamberlin out of his funk. I suppose he was trying to be my rock. "Why would Elenore say something so awful?" I asked.

"Was it really awful if it got you to stay?" he mused, his dark plumed lashes holding me in his gaze. "That's why I was laughing. I knew when you said that, that that was the reason why you stayed. Elenore told you that lie so you wouldn't go back to London."

I laughed, a laugh of relief. "You're right. She told me that and I told her I was staying."

"To keep me safe," he said, brushing my hair away from my face to gaze into my eyes. I wondered what he saw when he stared into my auburn globes. Not heavens, my eyes were too dark for that. I was hoping he didn't see blood in their ruddy brown hue.

I took in his bloodshot heavens, the cut of his cheeks, his soft mouth. "To keep you safe," I confirmed.

"I'm lucky to have had someone like Elenore and to have someone like you worry about me."

A toothy grin spread across my face. "I agree."

His lips found my neck, where he pressed soft kisses to it. Traveling north, he found my lips.

"Is it true what you said during the tour?" I asked between kisses.

He kept his lips close to mine. "Is what true?"

"About the Fieldings never seeing their own dead?"

He gave us space, his arms loosely gathered around my waist. "I think it is. I've never seen anything or felt anything. On this one tour, I had a group leave early because a cold spot was following us around the house. I never felt it. Everyone around me did, but I couldn't. I guess, the first time you can say something supernatural happened would have been yesterday when I heard Polly over the phone. I know it was her I heard." He let out an exaggerated sigh. "Maybe we only heard it because modern technology trumps the spirit world. Like how those paranormal investigators were able to capture all those little orbs in the house on video."

"Did Elenore or Maddy ever experience anything?" I asked. I didn't like that the ghosts of the Elenore Fielding House were popping in more frequently now and in numbers. More so, I didn't like what they were trying to tell me. I would feel a lot better if I wasn't the only Fielding to have seen things in the house. It would be nice to know that the ghosts were just pranksters and not fortune tellers like Polly.

He thought for a moment before shaking his head. "Not that I know of."

"Your dad?"

"No, if he did, he would have had the newspaper print it."

Normally, I would have laughed at that. Chamberlin was right, Mr. Fielding would have written a book about a real-life interaction with a ghost, but I wasn't in the mood to laugh anymore. I couldn't get the images of Lillian and Clementine out of my head, let alone Bethany's broken neck.

"Your mom?"

He ran his hands down my arms. "My mom . . . I think she *did* see things or felt them. It's why I assumed she said her prayer every night, but she never told me directly." He narrowed his eyes. They looked like blue slits. "Why are you asking? Did *you* see something?"

"No," I lied. "I guess I'm just wondering why you were trying to summon your father with a homemade Ouija board if you didn't see something. It wasn't for Maddy, and according to X, it was a typical way to spend a night for you three."

"I've been trying to talk to my father."

"Yeah, but why?"

"I want to know if he passed on to the life beyond. I want to know if he found peace. It seemed like a hard and fast rule that a Fielding can't see anything in the house. I thought maybe the Ouija board could change that. Why bother? I don't know. I guess I want to feel better about his disappearance. Not hearing from him is a good thing. Every time he doesn't respond I feel relief."

"Why didn't your dad like spirit boards? He brought home a doomsday raven, why not a Hasbro board game?"

"Despite the fact that he couldn't see the ghosts in the house, he believed they were there. He also believed ghosts under normal circumstances couldn't hurt the living. He thought of them as shadows of their former selves. They can make a noise or cause a cold spot here or there, but that was it. They weren't physically there. It may be scary to experience, but they didn't physically harm anyone because ghosts *can't* physically harm you. Yet he believed that a Ouija board could change all that. A Ouija board is like a conductor for ghosts, letting them amplify their power and take on a physical form, or so my dad thought."

"Like the shadow the other night?" I said, a shiver running down my spine. Just thinking about it and hearing it say my name made me want to head back to my aunt's flat.

"I have a confession," Chamberlin said. "I didn't see the shadow. I just went along with it because you guys were all freaking out."

I scoffed. "You're kidding me?!"

"No."

"You really didn't see or hear anything? You didn't hear it say my name?"

He leaned against the kitchen table, pulling me to him. "I heard nothing, and I didn't see a shadow, but I did see the candles flicker. I thought there was a chance Maddy was there, and because I'm a Fielding, I couldn't see her. So, I asked X to tell her I was sorry just in case."

"You're unreal! X and Tilly saw and heard it."

He shrugged. "Maybe they did."

"Maybe! You think I made it up?!"

"I didn't say that."

Anger bubbled over in my stomach; I couldn't believe he faked it. "How long does the Ouija board give a ghost strength?"

"Um . . . if I had to guess, I'd say until the circle is broken." He ran his hands down my arms again as if to warm me up. "Trin, you're not scared of the house now, are you? I'll never use a Ouija board or X's homemade mat again."

I did my best to act indifferent. "I'm not a fan of them." I said impassively. I felt like I got kicked in the gut when I was already lying face down in the dirt. I got the message loud and clear. The house didn't consider me a Fielding. A hate for the Elenore Fielding Housed burned in me. I tried to push the thought away. After what transpired between Chamberlin and me last night, it was a good thing I wasn't his sister, but it still stung. It was like the house didn't think I was good enough. I wasn't good enough and it was trying to scare me away like I was some common tourist. But I wasn't a tourist, I was Trinity Dunm Fielding. The house was stuck with me.

"Never again, no more Ouija," he said. "I'm sorry, I don't want you scared of our home. I never should've broken one of the golden rules."

"Don't worry about it, Chamberlin. It's like your dad always said, 'Old houses make odd noises'. I'm sure whatever I thought I saw and heard was nothing. Besides, ghosts can't hurt you, right?"

"No," he said, pressing a kiss to my lips. "Only people."

CHAPTER TWENTY

A New Face in the Casket

It was different seeing Elenore in the casket. It wasn't until I saw her, saw her hands folded over her waist like she was sleeping, that I realized I was suffering my first big loss since my father. When my father died, I had also lost Chamberlin, but that was a different kind of loss. When I moved to London, the sense of loss grew. It was angst filled, but I knew he was still there, just a phone call or a flight away. There was still hope. With Elenore dead, there was no hope. No nothing. No meaning to it. It must be how Chamberlin felt when he decided to no longer recite his mother's prayer.

Maddy and Elenore looked so much alike they would have been twins if they were the same age. This comparison made me think of Lillian and Clementine peeking out from behind the sofa in the living room. I fought a shudder. I wondered if Elenore and Maddy would be reunited in death like they were. I wondered if one day I would hear them giggling and calling me by my loathed nickname. I wondered and I feared.

I had felt like Sleeping Beauty when I was compelled to

touch the torch in the stained-glass door after my dream, but it was Elenore who looked like her. She reminded me so much of Disney's Sleeping Beauty: how her light blonde hair curled around her face in spirals, how her cheeks and eyes were brushed with a soft pink, how her red rose lips were slightly apart as if she was awaiting Prince Charming's kiss. Vinney had kissed her and kissed her, but there was no magic in the adult world. There was no spell to bring her back. No matter how much he loved her, she was gone. A token of his love would be buried with her. Elenore wore her engagement ring from Vinney. Chamberlin suggested it, repeating to Vinney his own sentiments: He was family. He would always be family even with Elenore gone. It was an act of kindness Vinney took to heart, swearing his allegiance to us like he was a medieval knight, which I believe Prince Charming was. I supposed both Chamberlin and Vinney would have been knights in another life, but in this life, they were mourners.

Vinney wept by Chamberlin's side. It was family only. It was just the three of us. The doors to Christie's Funeral Home were shut to everyone else. So, it was okay to cry, and we did. Elenore may have been a pain in the butt, but she was our pain in the butt, and she was irreplaceable.

Being a Fielding, and thus born with an innate sense of the macabre, Elenore had told Chamberlin repeatedly how she wanted her funeral to go: buried in white, family only, no flowers, in lieu of flowers donations to the upkeep of the Elenore Fielding House would be accepted. We honored her wishes.

The trip to the cemetery was just as somber. The priest, the same one that presided over Maddy's funeral, said a prayer. And that was that. It was over. Elenore was laid to rest in the crypt next to Maddy's—the wingless angels and gargoyle her keepers.

It seemed fitting the sky was overcast, rain clouds hung low, blocking out the sun. The heat wave had ended with a shower and the ground was still moist. The smell of earth was thick in the air as if we had buried Elenore in the ground.

"See you in a few," Vinney said, after giving us each a hug. It felt strange parting with him at the cemetery, if only for a few hours. Chamberlin had asked him to move in, an honor Vinney took with another pledge of knightly loyalty. Vinney had work at the station he had to finish, and then he was going to his apartment to grab some clothes. I think he just needed to be alone, and we respected that, not poking holes in the injustice that he had to work on the day his fiancé was entombed.

Chamberlin and I walked through the cemetery holding hands. The last of the teardrop petals from the cherry tree fell in our hair like springtime snow. It would have been a magical moment if we weren't surrounded by the dead. Like I could ever forget I was in a cemetery. I stepped on the brown petals that had fallen before, their beauty gone. They were wilted and brown, decay wafting from them like the corpses under our feet.

All of the beauty was in Chamberlin. He looked ethereal, his eyes burned brighter than ever in the monotonous gloom, his lashes in distinct contrast to his eyes and fair complexion. With the scratch on his cheek long gone, he looked like he was made of fine china, flawless and immortal.

We walked to the other end of the cemetery, to Damian Hurst's grave. His name hadn't been added to the headstone yet, but it read Hurst in large letters. Old flowers and new ones marked it as a fresh grave. Finding a small stick, Chamberlin dug a little hole near the headstone. The soil was easily tilled, thanks to last night's rain, and within a few seconds the hole was large enough. He pulled the white velvet box Tilly had given him from his jacket pocket. He took out the ring and placed it in the hole he made, covering it with the loose soil.

"In pace requiescat," Chamberlin said.

"What does that mean?" I asked.

He brushed his hands on his pants. "It means rest in peace in Latin."

"I didn't know you knew Latin."

"I don't, Tilly does."

"Oh yeah, a genius with a minor in Latin."

He smiled as soft rain drops fell from the sky like tears. "She taught X and me some cool lines. It felt fitting. In Latin, rest in peace takes on a darker tone."

* * *

Chamberlin and I were in the kitchen when the doorbell rang. It sounded like bells ringing and again I thought of the line from *It's a Wonderful Life*: *Every time a bell rings, an angel gets his wings.* Maddy clearly didn't cut it. I wondered if Elenore's death satisfied the bloodthirsty Angeles.

"That's Tilly and X," Chamberlin said, getting to his feet.

I nodded, feeling uneasy about the doorbell. I had a gut feeling it wasn't just Tilly and X, but the entire Deedle family. I was sure it was Dr. Deedle who pushed the doorbell. It was the proper thing to do, he probably pushed it while he wiggled that proper mustache of his.

As predicted, Chamberlin opened the door to the Deedle family. Dr. Deedle and his wife were at the head of the pack. Mrs. Deedle handed me a large tray of sandwiches. "We are so sorry for your loss. The both of you," she said.

I took the tray from her as Tilly pushed past her parents and wrapped her arms around Chamberlin's waist. "I missed you. My father's been holding me captive, help!"

Chamberlin laughed and so did Mrs. Deedle, and me. X rolled his eyes, but in a playful way. Chamberlin and I hadn't seen Tilly and X since the day Elenore died. They had texted him a dozen times a day, each of them, but it wasn't the same.

"Chantilly, that's enough," Dr. Deedle said, shaking my hand, then Chamberlin's.

We went into the living room where I opened the sandwich tray from the Deedles. X helped himself before I came back from the kitchen with a stack of paper plates and a pitcher of iced tea. Dr. Deedle gave his son a reproachful look that seemed to please X.

X looked extra clownlike today. He was in all black as always but in addition to his thick eyeliner, his eyelids were painted black, and he was still wearing that absurd dog collar locket combo. Tilly, like her mother, had on a simple formfitting black dress. It may have been the same dress, but Tilly spiced hers up with a black velvet choker. Dr. Deedle was also all in black, tie included. I took the all black attire of the Deedles as a sign of respect for Elenore, that would have even pleased her. I sat in the open seat between Chamberlin and Tilly. I was glad we still had on our funeral attire, although Chamberlin had taken off his suit jacket with the sewn in skull pocket square.

The Deedles had been very good to us, sending us a different tray or platter of food every day they were in New York City, and had made a large donation to the Elenore Fielding House in Elenore's name. Chamberlin truly made friends worth keeping. I couldn't say the same for myself back in the UK. There was Kris and he did keep calling and texting. But Kris was no Chamberlin and could never be.

Chamberlin was seated at the head of the table, to his right sat Dr. Deedle. Dr. Deedle got up and shifted his chair, pointing it in Chamberlin's direction and sat back down. He faced him like they were the only two people in the room. This took Chamberlin off guard. He dropped the sandwich he was reaching for on the table, missing his plate. He quickly scooped it up along with all of the stuff that fell out of it. His cheeks burned with what I knew had to be embarrassment.

"I lost my parents young," Dr. Deedle said, in a lecturer's tone. "When it happened, I had a choice to make. I could give up or I could succeed. I have already known you to have exceptional grit and with the house's haunted history and its American history, I know you will do good things here."

"Thanks Mr. Deedle, um, Dr. Deedle," Chamberlin said, trying to maintain eye contact with him, but I could tell Dr. Deedle made him very nervous. Chamberlin drummed his fingers on the side of his thigh. "It's funny you should mention the house's American history. My great-great-great-grandfather served under general George Washington in the Battle of New York. I've been wanting to add a historical segment to the tour, but Elenore thought it was too stuffy. I think I finally found a way to make it all fit."

Dr. Deedle's mustache was doing that weird twitching thing. He put his hand on Chamberlin's shoulder and said, "I knew I liked you."

Chamberlin's jaw dropped. It wasn't overly dramatic, but it was noticeable. Just like the deep red blush spreading over his cheeks and the bridge of his nose.

"General George Washington lost the Battle of New York, but his grit and determination kept his army together," Dr. Deedle said, his large brown eyes as expressive as his mustache. "He wouldn't give up, and because of that, he led us to the greatest victory of all. There is a lesson in that for all of us."

"Dad," X griped, "you're being creepy."

Tilly giggled. His wife tried hard not to; she turned her head and coughed to mask her laugh.

Dr. Deedle withdrew his hand from Chamberlin's shoulder and cleared his throat as if to rid himself of any awkwardness on his part. "I wasn't aware you knew about the house's ties to the greatest President that ever lived. I suppose Chantilly told you."

"I've always known," Chamberlin said, seemingly relaxing. His fingers were still drumming, but they went from a war drum to a bass drum. "There's a funny letter he wrote to Emmit Fielding about the house."

Dr. Deedle's eyes widened. "That President George Washington wrote?"

"Uh, yeah."

Dr. Deedle's mustache twitched like an electric current ran through it. He seemed over stimulated. If his mustache was any indication of what was going on with his pulse, Big B was about to have a big stroke. "You have a letter from President George Washington in the house?!"

"Uh yeah, I can show it to you, if you want? We don't keep it out with the other letters. George Washington visited the house during construction but refused to come after it was finished. He penned his excuse to Emmit Fielding stating, 'The house has eyes and a house that has eyes has secrets.'"

Dr. Deedle had a smile on his face that I hadn't seen him wear. It was somewhere between euphoria and shock. "Well," he said, gaining control of his mustachio, "what a treasure. I'd love to see it."

"Maybe another time Boris, darling," his wife said, putting her hand on his arm. "Chamberlin hasn't eaten yet and I'm sure it would take time for him to dig out the letter."

"Of course," Dr. Deedle said, disappointed, his dark mustache frowning. I held back a chuckle. His mustache reminded me of a cat's tail, giving away their mood. "I can wait." Dr. Deedle stood up and adjusted his chair back to its original position. Before sitting down, he took a chicken bacon wrap from the sandwich tray. "How long have you been interested in history Chamberlin?"

"Dad!" X grumbled.

Chamberlin's eyelashes fluttered. "Uh, I guess always. I'm minoring in American history at school."

Dr. Deedle's eyes darted to his daughter. "Little B said business."

"I said business and history, Big B."

"Maybe you did," he said thoughtfully, taking a bite of his wrap.

Tilly shook her head. "I did. See Mom," she said, glancing to her mother, "I told you he only half listens. He makes up his mind with only half of the story."

* * *

After lunch, Dr. Deedle and his wife left. X and Tilly decided to stay for a while, and we made our way into the living room. "I think you gave my dad a boner," X said to Chamberlin as he took a seat on the blood-stained sofa. "Great, now he even likes you more than me. Did you hear him? 'I knew I liked you,'" X said, imitating his father's voice.

"Dad loves you X. He just doesn't love that you wear more makeup than a circus clown. You know he hates clowns." Tilly turned to me where I sat in the same spot I had sat the night Damian killed himself, Chamberlin next to me. "X almost gave Dad a heart attack when he went home dressed as an evil clown."

"The one Damian designed?" I asked.

"Yeah," Tilly said like she was surprised I knew about that, her eyebrows reaching her hairline.

X scoffed. "I'll say this, it feels good to be sitting on what's left of his blood splatter. I think I'll piss on his grave later."

"You're so morbid," Tilly said, shooting her brother a nasty glare from the armrest of the tufted wingback chair. "Chamberlin probably didn't miss us at all."

"I missed you both very much. We both did," he said, taking my hand. "Life is boring without the Deedles."

Tilly's eyes narrowed to teeny tiny slits. "Are you two . . ." she contemplated, pointing at our hands. "Are you two together?"

Chamberlin nodded.

She let out a high-pitched squeal that sounded like a siren. Springing to her feet, she hugged me first, then Chamberlin. "I'm so, so happy for the both of you!"

"Major props for boning your sister, Chain," X said with a big grin.

Chamberlin laughed. I did too. It was in X's delivery. He was so proud of himself.

"Tilly's not half bad looking if she keeps her mouth closed, but I'd rather die a virgin than bang my sister."

She scoffed, taking her seat on the armrest of the chair. "That's because we're real brother and sister, Deedle Dum. That's too gross to even think about, but even if we weren't related, I'd never get with a guy who wears more makeup than me. So yeah, you're most likely dying a virgin."

"Only confident men wear makeup. And you're just jealous because I wear it better than you. Maddy said she liked my eyeliner."

"Please X, you looked like a gothic clown and Maddy was engaged to Damian Hurst. She didn't have the highest standards." Tilly blushed, turning to Chamberlin. "No offense, Chain."

He dismissed it with a wave of his hand. "You have a point," he said with a light laugh.

I couldn't laugh. I saw the little toes of socked feet wiggle from behind the sofa X sat on. The socks weren't white, like they had been the last time I saw those feet, but red, like they stepped in Damian's blood.

Tilly made the shape of a heart with her hands. "I called it, didn't I Trin?"

"Hmm?" I mused distractedly.

"I said you and Chain were meant to be."

"You did," I said, glancing up for only a moment before fixing my gaze back on the sofa. I kept waiting for the little hands with claws to appear.

"That's right," Tilly said, pointing to herself. "Deedle Dee." She obnoxiously pointed at her brother. "And Deedle Dum."

Reaching, X slapped her hand.

Tilly jumped to her feet. I thought it was to do battle with her brother, but she ran to the fireplace. "Hey, Polly's looking at us!"

"That's strange," Chamberlin said, letting go of my hand to join Tilly by her side. He closed the curio cabinet door. "That's the second time I've noticed it open . . . I guess from opening and closing it with each tour, I must've messed up the locking mechanism." He opened it and closed it again, checking the lock.

"Or," X said matter-of-factly, "Polly's getting ready to say her name."

"Morbid," Tilly said, elbowing her brother in the back of the head.

"Hey, watch the hair, or it will be you Polly caws for."

Tilly scoffed. "Crows caw, ravens croak, idiot."

CHAPTER TWENTY-ONE
A New Revelation

Vinney returned to the Elenore Fielding House in his go-to-leather jacket, like it was another day on the job. He had a restless energy about him. After a sandwich, he took out the trash, cleaned out the garbage disposal, and fixed the drip in the kitchen sink. Before he decided to scrub the floor with a toothbrush, Chamberlin suggested they head back to his apartment and box up more of his stuff. Vinney jumped at the idea.

I couldn't bring myself to go with them. The stress of the morning had left me exhausted. Between Elenore's funeral and seeing the bloodied socks in the living room, all I wanted to do was sleep. After Tilly and X left, that was what I planned on doing, but then Vinney came home. I wasn't going to miss this opportunity to go up to the attic for some shut eye.

I wasted no time running up the stairs. I kept my eyes directly in front of me. I saw only one step after the other. There was no wingless angel, no bassinet rocking, no apparitions of any kind—just stairs. I slammed Mr. Fielding's door behind me and locked it. I had been spending the nights in Chamberlin's room, but that was *his* room. It felt strange to take a nap in there without him.

I slipped off my black dress. Lured to the bed by orange citrus, I nosedived into the covers. It was so soft. It was like all the peace I sought was in those sheets. The pitter-patter of rain hitting the window of the dormer was the perfect lullaby.

* * *

Mr. Fielding's dead body was before me. My hands trembled with the burden of his blood as the smell of death clung to every inch of me. I was in his room. I was sure of that. I saw the dark wallpaper with the green leaves, their jagged edges connecting to each other in stripes, but something was different. The painting of the Elenore Fielding House in all of her glory was no longer in front of me. I quickly realized this was because the bed was pushed away from the wall, off centered. I assumed Young Chamberlin and Maddy moved the bed because they stood where it should have been. I watched them intently as they removed the painting of the Elenore Fielding House from its hanging bracket and leaned it against the wall by the door.

Together they walked around the bed to the footboard. Chamberlin locked eyes with me for a split second before rolling his father on to the floor. Chamberlin's tears were gone, but their stains remained, stealing his innocence. Frank Fielding's body struck the hardwood with a loud thud, making me gasp. I jumped off the bed, my legs trembling beneath me. Chamberlin and Maddy each grabbed one of their father's feet and dragged the corpse around the bed, his body squelching as it left a trail of blood in its wake.

I looked around confused. The wall the bed had been pushed against—the wall the painting of the Elenore Fielding House had been hanging on—was missing. It was like it vanished into thin air. There was nothing there now, just darkness. I met Chamberlin and Maddy at the head of the bed, going around the other way as not to step in blood. Where the wall had been, there was now a deep alcove. I marveled at this hidden space—at this secret. Where did the wall go? Alone, Chamberlin propped his father's corpse against the back of the alcove like his father had fallen asleep. He stood. Our eyes met. His face was reflected in his eyes, not mine. I couldn't see myself; I could only see the cut as it became visible, the blood beginning to drip its crimson tide. He spoke, his words clear despite the welling of blood. "What now Elenore?"

* * *

I woke up screaming. My hands acted to smother the sound while my eyes instinctively went to the painting of the Elenore Fielding House. With my heart still pounding in my chest, I got out of bed to examine the wall. I ran my hand down the glossy wallpaper looking for the false door I thought I bore witness to in my dream. My dream, as always, seemed more real than reality. It left me feeling disoriented and dizzy as my brain struggled to comprehend the difference between the two. It seemed perfectly plausible there was a false door in Mr. Fielding's room. It could have been a fragment of one of the old corridors that had been boarded up during the addition or demolition of the wings of the house.

I couldn't budge the bed on my own and I didn't see a doorknob. All I could do, not that it was helpful, was bite my nails. My mind was reeling. I was beginning to think my perpetual nightmare was more than a dream. Could that really be it? The mystery behind Mr. Fielding's disappearance? Was Franklin Fielding dead and stuffed behind the wall in his bedroom? Was it his own children who did it? His own flesh and blood that murdered him? Chamberlin, did he help cover it up?

But could I truly trust my dream? I was a Dunn. If anything I saw the future, or at least got a feeling about it. I didn't see the past. My father never told me I could see the past.

I needed to talk to someone. Not Chamberlin. No—not him. I didn't want to say anything to Chamberlin until I was sure. Tilly— I would talk to Tilly. I didn't have her number in my phone, which seemed crazy to me. In a very short period of time, she had become a staple in my life. I'd have to go to her.

I threw on the first shirt I found. It happened to be the Vampire Chamberlin shirt I'd swiped from the gift shop. It would do. I put on a pair of shorts and flip-flops and ran down the stairs, keeping my eyes in front of me as I took tread after tread. I kept this laser focus as I ran through the stained-glass doors, through the front door, and all the way to Plant Haven.

Mrs. Deedle was manning the store alone. She had changed out of her black dress and into her embroidered polo shirt and black skirt.

"Hi Mrs. Deedle, I was looking for Tilly."

"Hello Trinity. She's in her room. You can head up."

"Thank you."

I took the stairs leading to the second-story apartment at the same speed as if I was passing the wingless angel. I reached the top of the stairs to see Dr. Deedle on the couch smoking. He was still in his all-black attire, although his tie had been loosened, and the first two buttons of his dress shirt unfastened. "Oh, hi, Dr. Deedle, your wife said it was okay to come up. I'm looking for Tilly."

He put out his cigarette in the ash tray he held out the window. "I quit five years ago," he said, his eyes fixed on me.

I stood awkwardly at the threshold of the living room, feeling like I needed his permission to go to Tilly's room.

"That brother of yours is a good kid."

It was way worse to hear Chamberlin referred to as my brother now that I saw him naked. I nodded. I wished X was here to tell his father he was being awkward.

"Like I said, I had to face similar pitfalls."

I wanted to talk to Tilly ASAP, wanted her to make me feel better, but I got the feeling Dr. Deedle wanted me to ask him about his past and was going to keep me in limbo until I did. "Do you mind me asking what happened to your parents?"

"Not at all," Dr. Deedle said, taking a cigarette from the silver case that sat beside him on the couch. "It's a fascinating story actually. It's the reason I became a doctor. You see, it was because of my father. My father was different than other people's fathers."

He lit the cigarette and took a puff. I moved in closer as not to be rude but wasn't sure if I should sit. Sensing my deliberation, he gestured for me to take a seat. Nodding graciously, I settled down on the couch across from him.

"It wasn't the way my father spoke or how he dressed," Dr. Deedle told me. "On the contrary, my father was a professional. A lot of good men looked up to him. He was a county clerk. A job he did with pride, dressing in a suit every day to go to work. After work, he came home to his loving wife, and my sister, Chantilly, and me."

Dr. Deedle exhaled out the window, staring off into the distance. "It was his eyes. That's what made my father different. It was like you could see the gears turning in them, actually see him thinking. I was thirteen years old when I lost my parents. The same age Chamberlin was when he lost his mother. Thirteen," he said with derision. "There's something to that number. Bad things happen in accordance with the number thirteen. I suppose Hollywood got that right."

I would have to agree. I was thirteen when I lost my father. I wasn't sure if Dr. Deedle knew that, but I didn't want to interrupt him.

"It happened on a day like any other day," he said after taking a long drag. "Nothing particular had happened. Nothing stands out to me. It was just a normal day, just a normal dinner. My mother had just put dessert on the table. She had made peach cobbler. My mother made an amazing cobbler. We were just about to dig in when my father told us he had inadvertently corrupted us, his family—because he, himself, was corrupted, and it was his duty to rectify his mistakes. He pulled a gun out of his suit jacket that he'd left hanging on the back of his chair. I had never seen a gun in real life before," Dr. Deedle told me as if he was a little boy again. "They're so much bigger than they seem on television, or maybe it was because I was so much smaller then. But I digress—he shot my mother first, then Chantilly, then me, and then himself."

The little hairs on the back of my arms stood up. I was speechless.

"My mother died from her gunshot wound to her chest, and my father had put the gun in his mouth and blew out his brains like our friend Mr. Damian Hurst. Chantilly, my beloved sister, was shot in the head. She lived, but I can't really call it that. I should have said she survived. I," he said, pulling his shirt to the side so I could see his scar, "was lucky. The bullet went clean through my shoulder. Barely a flesh wound. But I had a choice to make after that. It would have been easy for me to give up. My family was gone. I was alone. No one would have blamed me. But I couldn't. You see, that day right before my father shot my mother, I saw the truth. It wasn't my father's eyes that made him different as my pubescent self had first believed, it was his brain. His eyes were just windows to the inside. I knew then, my father had always been different inside, but his good looks, nice clothes, and nice family served as a mask. I'd be damned if I'm not the spitting image of my father, and Xavier the spitting image of me." He shook his head. "No, I wouldn't give up. I would help people like my father and people like my sister."

"You act as a psychiatrist and a surgeon to your patients?" I asked curiously.

"Yes. I have two PhDs and a medical license."

"Wow, that's impressive." I saw where Tilly and X got their genius from.

"You can never learn enough. I'm glad Chantilly and Xavier are following after me and not . . ." He paused here, for a long while. I thought he was going to say his wife, but he said, "My father."

"I operated on my sister several times, but bullet wounds . . ." he said, his voice dropping. "I've seen bullets do next to nothing and I've seen them destroy a brain. My sister was unfortunately the latter. She died about five years ago in a home, not knowing her name or me, but I still visited her every day and had Chantilly and Xavier accompany me. It's important to remember where you come from. If you don't, history will always repeat itself. You can't run from your past, and you can't run from your family. I understand why you went to London, Trinity, even if Elenore, Chamberlin, and Madelin did not. But it's important to stop running at some point."

I was right, nothing got past Dr. Deedle, and I knew *he* was right—I couldn't run from my problems or my family.

CHAPTER TWENTY-TWO
A New Me

The end of Dr. Deedle's cigarette had turned to ash. He tapped it on the ashtray, taking one last inhale before putting it out. I had forgotten about the cigarette. The smokey scent brought me back to the night we found Damian Hurst dead. The lingering smell of gunfire and the smell of blood had made an unlawful marriage in the living room. I wondered if that was how it was for Dr. Deedle when he came through to find his parents dead and his sister brain dead. Did he smell blood and smoke? He must have. I couldn't imagine what it was like for Dr. Deedle to walk into the Elenore Fielding House and see the blood and the pieces of brain splattered on the floor. It must have felt all too familiar to him, like he stepped back in time.

"Well, don't let me keep you," Dr. Deedle said. "I took the day off to drive the kids home and I'm already bored and smoking." He laughed, a short chuckle that made his mustache jump. "I guess I'll go help Tiffany with her plants."

"Thank you for sharing your past with me Dr. Deedle, and for the advice too."

With that, I hurried up the stairs to the third floor and lightly knocked on Tilly's bedroom door as Dr. Deedle's story buzzed around in my head. His life was tragic. It seemed worse than my own tragedy. But it was inspiring. I had lost my father, and because of that drifted through life. He had lost both of his parents and his sister by his father's own hand and became a neurosurgeon. Scratch that—the head neurosurgeon at Mount Sinai Hospital. I learned a lot from Dr. Deedle. I had to stop running from my problems. I had to face them.

Tilly opened her bedroom door cautiously before flinging it open. "Hey Trin! Come in, X never knocks, and Chamberlin's knock is different. I didn't know who was at the door, kinda freaked me out a little."

"Oh, sorry. I would have called—"

She stuck her head into the hall. "No Chamberlin?"

I took a seat on her bed. "No, he's helping Vinney pack."

"Perfect," she said, dragging her silver beanbag chair in front of the bed where I sat. She plopped into it. "So dish on the Chamberlin thing."

"Uh . . . " I said, my eyebrows furrowing. There was no way she knew about my dream. She said so herself, she didn't have a sensitivity, she was just intuitive. There was no way she was *that* intuitive."

"You guys have sex yet?"

I blushed; heat radiated from my cheeks in what must have looked like two tomatoes.

"Omg you did! Was he really a virgin? Was it good? Is he big?"

I laughed, more from embarrassment than anything else. "I—I don't know."

She huffed, leaning back in her beanbag chair like it was a throne. "Fine, keep the details to yourself. I shouldn't be fantasizing about him any longer, not now that you two are official. I guess I need to find some other beautiful goth boy to love."

"Someone say beautiful goth boy?" X said, letting himself into his sister's room.

Tilly reached for a pillow from her bed and threw it at her brother. She missed. "Not now X, we're having girl talk. Go play with one of your dolls."

"They're collectibles, not dolls and why play with them when I can play with Trinity?"

"You're really creepy sometimes," I said to X.

He smiled, delighted. "Coming from a Fielding, that's a real compliment. Thanks, Trin."

X took a seat on the bean bag chair with his sister. "So, what are we talking about?" he asked.

"You are way too close," Tilly said, trying to push her brother off her chair. They were cute together. I wondered if that was what Dr. Deedle was like with his sister before she was shot. Xavier was the spitting image of his father. I wondered if Tilly was the spitting image of her aunt. No—that was stupid. Tilly looked like her mother, but I wondered if her carefree spirit was her aunt's. No wonder her father was so protective of her.

I considered what it must be like to be named for someone who met with a tragic end. Tilly for her aunt, Chamberlin for his father's sisters, and Elenore for Elenore Fielding who was found dead in her husband's bed, her hand clasped around his. Something like that has to affect you—it has to. Were they buried under the burden of living for themselves and the person(s) they were named for? Was it like that creepy professor from *Harry Potter* with the stutter that had to carry Voldemort around on the back of his head? I hoped it wasn't that bad.

"So . . . fill me in, what were you guys talking about?" X asked curiously.

"Nothing now that you're here, you gigantic parasite," Tilly said, giving him a shove to his back.

Dr. Deedle had a greater effect on me than even I first believed. I couldn't stop thinking about what he said: 'You can't run from your past, and you can't run from your family.' I was unsure when I left the Elenore Fielding House, but I was certain now. My mind was made up. I was going to do more than confide in Tilly, I was going to ask her for her help and X too.

"I came over to ask Tilly for help moving my bed," I told X. "Chamberlin's at Vinney's and he's taking forever and I'm feeling impatient." Now that I had my mind set on moving the bed, I was anxious. I wanted to move it before Chamberlin got home. I wanted it to be just Tilly and me, but the bed was heavy. I doubted we could move it ourselves. "You should help X," I said. "It's really heavy. Like really heavy. Antique bed, heavy."

"I'm game," X said, taking his sister's hand and yanking her to her feet. "Happy to lend my muscles to any woman in peril."

We had just entered Plant Haven when Dr. Deedle stopped us by the counter. His shirt and tie were back in place. "Where are you three going?"

"Helping Trinity move her bed," Tilly said.

"You need any help?"

"Um, I don't think so Big B, X is going to help."

"I'll help," he volunteered. "Moving a bed has to be more stimulating than spritzing plants. It will be my pleasure."

"Thanks Dr. Deedle," I said, hoping X would step in and tell his dad to stay put, but he didn't. Maybe I scared X by saying the bed was really heavy. Curse my dramatization.

Dr. Deedle kissed his wife goodbye, and together we headed next door to the Elenore Fielding House. It was still drizzling out, so we ran indoors which helped to ease my anxiety. Nothing could get the bed moved quick enough.

We took the servant staircase. Chamberlin, Vinney, and I had been avoiding taking the main stairs out of respect for Elenore. The house felt abnormally cold even for a rainy day. I wondered if Chamberlin turned up the air. Something about the chilled atmosphere felt dreamlike.

I opened the door to my now bedroom. Heat rushed to my cheeks. I quickly picked my clothes up off the floor. I hadn't realized I left the room in such a mess. But then again, tidying up was the furthest thing from my mind when I ran to Tilly's. It was too late to make the bed. I shrugged it off. "Sorry, I should've cleaned up," I mumbled. At least the room smelled fresh. The citrus potpourri still perfumed the air.

"Where's Chamberlin?" Dr. Deedle asked, as if he expected to see him waiting for us in my room. Maybe that's why he volunteered to help. Maybe he was hoping Chamberlin would offer to show him the letter from George Washington again. Without his wife there to tell him it wasn't a good time, he could indulge.

"He's out with Vinney helping him bring some stuff over. I could wait . . ."

"Nonsense," Dr. Deedle said with a disappointed droop of his mustache. "We're here and I'm bored."

X chuckled. "And then you can tell Mom you threw out your back."

"Not a bad idea Xavier. I think even sitting on the couch is more stimulating than spritzing plants."

"It may not be a lie," Tilly said. "That's one huge bed."

Dr. Deedle nodded. "It's a very sturdy bed, indeed. I'll take one side and Xavier will take the other. But I don't want to scratch the floors." He turned to me. "Trinity, do you have any towels that we can lay on the floor?"

My anxiety was mounting. I almost rolled my eyes. I didn't care about the floor. I cared about what was behind the bed, behind the wall. Every second wasted was a second Chamberlin was closer to home.

I grabbed towels from the rec room and was back in a flash. One by one, Dr. Deedle lifted a corner of the bed and X slid a towel under the post. Once there was a towel under the four posters, they slid the bed into the center of the room, away from the wall.

"That's good," I said. "While you're both here do you mind moving the painting for me too?"

"Not at all," Dr. Deedle said. He stood to one side of the Elenore Fielding House painting and X stood to the other. Together, they lifted the painting off the hanging bracket.

"Uh, where to?" X asked.

I pointed to the wall by the door, the place it had been put in my dream by Chamberlin and Maddy. "There against the wall."

"Anything else?" X teased. "Want us to make your bed?"

Tilly laughed. "He doesn't even make his own."

I ran my hand down the wall the headboard of the bed had rested against. There was no doorknob, no way I could see that the wall opened. I didn't want Dr. Deedle's help, that would unnecessarily complicate things if my dream was more than a dream, but I saw no way out of it. I could really use his affinity for not missing things.

"Since you asked X, is there a door in the wall the bed was against?"

Dr. Deedle's mustache twisted to the side. "A door?" I stepped aside to make room for him and X. Apparently intrigued, Tilly moved closer.

Dr. Deedle ran his hand over the wallpaper, like I had just done. "There's something here," he said. "I can feel a seam in the wall, it's not as easy to detect by eye, but I definitely feel something. Yes, someone took great care making sure the wallpaper lined up perfectly to keep it hidden." He turned to me. "Maybe it's a pocket door. Our house had a lot of them before the reno."

It hadn't dawned on me that the wall behind the bed could be a pocket door, and all I had to do was slide it open. The Elenore Fielding House, like the Deedles' home, like most historical homes, was full of pocket doors. Pocket doors were between every entry way downstairs though we usually left them open because of the tours. And of course, there was one leading into the attic space. I felt really stupid, but then again all of the Deedles were geniuses.

Dr. Deedle placed his hands on the wall and attempted to slide the hidden door to the left. When that didn't work, he tried sliding it to the right.

"Let me try," X said. He couldn't get it to budge either. I didn't think he could, if Dr. Deedle couldn't, but that's X for you.

Dr. Deedle smiled at his son, seemingly very glad he tagged along to move my bed. "We are going about this the wrong way, Watson. The door goes up."

"Up?" X said.

"Up," Dr. Deedle repeated, his smile widening. "Look at the room's roof line, it's pitched on this wall, to make room for the door to go up."

"Like a garage door," X mused.

Dr. Deedle's mustache shifted side to side in what had to be excitement. It was like his mustache had a mind of his own and thought we were about to discover buried treasure. "Sort of," Dr. Deedle told his son. "But this door is solid and will go straight up. Observe." Placing his hands on the wallpaper again, he pushed up, and the wall disappeared into the roof line. We heard the door snap in place. "Careful," Dr. Deedle warned, "I don't trust the locking mechanism."

My pulse surged, my heart drumming away in my chest and head. There it was, the dark passageway from my dream.

"Uh, Dad," X said, tugging on his father's arm like he was a little boy.

Dr. Deedle ran his hands down his face. "Oh, that's interesting."

"What's that?" Tilly asked, covering her nose and mouth with her hands and taking a step closer. The stale air from the alcove filled the room consuming the citrus potpourri. On the air was the stench of old decay.

"It's my adoptive father. It's Franklin Fielding."

Distractedly, Dr. Deedle raked his fingers through his wavy hair, disrupting its perfect order. I was sure this was not the sort of buried treasure he was looking to unearth. His professional diagnosis was not a shocker. "He's very dead."

Dr. Deedle was right about that. Mr. Fielding was beyond dead. He was leaning against the wall as I had seen him in my dream, but his skin was dried out like jerky. I could see Maddy and Elenore in his mummified face. For even like that, you could see the traces of his once handsome aspect, and the resemblance his daughters bore to him. I could still make out the blood stain on his shirt, even though the stain was dark now, almost the color of black ink, but there was still a ruddy hue that shone through. Air fresheners, with the slogan 'Brooklyn Does it Better', were all over the floor and hanging from him like he was a serial killer's Christmas tree.

"What's going on?" *Chamberlin* asked, entering the room with Vinney.

I sucked air. Upon seeing Chamberlin, I felt a punch to my gut that almost knocked me to my butt. I clung to the dark wallpaper with its little jagged leaves for support. It was one of my feelings. My stomach tied into tiny knots then did a back flip. I was at its mercy. It was one of those gut feelings that the Dunn women have claimed are the gift of the future. I knew then that I was next. That I was going to be the next 'sister' to die. The house had warned me. Bethany and Mr. Fielding's sisters had warned me. My father had even warned me through X's stupid homemade Ouija mat. Geez, even Chamberlin warned me. I was next. Chamberlin was going to fulfill his dark prophecy and kill his sister courtesy of Angeles Hillings. My father's words rung in my ears, *'My li'l Trinity Dunn, trust your gut. It's more than just a feeling, it's a fact.'*

Vinney put the box he was carrying down by the door next to the painting. "Holy shit, it's Frank!"

"Don't look," Dr. Deedle cautioned, putting his arm around Chamberlin to shield his vision.

"He knows, Dr. Deedle," I said. "Don't you, Chamberlin," I said accusatorily. "You know, because you helped put him in there."

All eyes were on Chamberlin. Dr. Deedle's mustache was twitching uncontrollably.

Chamberlin put the box in his hands down on top of Vinney's. He didn't look at his father. In fact, he positioned his back to him so he couldn't. "It's not how it looks," he said, his face a crimson bloom.

"It looks bad," Vinney said. "Real bad." Vinney went over to the corpse, kneeling to get a better look at it.

"He didn't kill him Vinney," I said. "It was Elenore. She killed him and she had Chamberlin and Maddy help her hide the body in that secret room behind the wall." I knew now that somehow my dream *was* a dream of the past. My dream wasn't a perfect playback of events. I was never there, and Chamberlin's face didn't slump off, but still the truth was all there. Had been there this whole time. I had seen the murder of Frank Fielding through Elenore's eyes. She used one of those yellow-handled knives from the kitchen that always made me think of bananas. It was her hands that were coated in her father's blood, not mine.

Vinney's eyebrows knitted together. He poked the blood stain on Mr. Fielding's discolored shirt with the pencil he kept with his little green pad. "Elenore wanted me to solve her father's disappearance . . . Or maybe, she didn't," he said, standing up and rubbing the stubble on his chin. "Maybe she didn't," he repeated, looking to Chamberlin. "She didn't want me to solve it, did she?"

He shook his head, his bangs falling into his eyes. "She broke off her engagement to you because she thought you were getting close to solving it and she didn't know what you would do if you found out."

"I would have done nothing," he said. "Like we are going to do *nothing* now. We are just going to close this door and forget we ever found Frank. Anyone have a problem with that?"

Everyone, including Dr. Deedle, shook their heads. I was positive he wished he'd stayed at Plant Haven to spritz plants.

"Why would Elenore kill her own father?" Tilly asked. "The way you always talk about him Chain, I thought he was great."

Chamberlin didn't need coaxing. He was ready to speak; tears had already rolled from his eyes. "Because he killed my mother and Mr. Dunn. He tampered with the tension wire in the elevator." His eyes darted to me. "I'm so sorry Trinity."

I felt frozen, like time had stopped.

"Why would he do that?!" Dr. Deedle asked before Vinney could.

Taking a deep breath, Chamberlin brushed back his bangs, his line of vision resting on the floor. "Before my mother's death, my father would take the three of us to see a Mets game once every season. It was a big deal for us, and we all looked forward to it. Maddy forgot her glove, so my dad turned around. I went inside to help her find it. She wasn't sure where she left it, and we were already going to be late. She thought it was likely she left her glove in my parent's room, so we started our search there. The door was open a little and we saw . . ." He bowed his head, his eyes hidden by shadows. I could see his bottom lip trembling. "We saw our mother with Trinity's father. They didn't see us. Before they could, I grabbed Maddy's hand and brought her downstairs. I made her promise me that she would never tell my father what she saw."

He took another deep breath as if to collect his thoughts. "Everyone knew my father as this fun, eccentric guy—he was, but there was another side to him that only Elenore, Maddy, and I knew." He lifted his face, his blue eyes darting to me. They looked extra light against his dark lashes, like Heaven was trapped inside them. "You never saw it Trinity. You don't know. I told Maddy, that no matter what, she couldn't tell Dad what she saw and that we could never talk about it. She promised."

He sighed in what could only be frustration. "Her stupid glove was never in my parent's room. It was on the dining room table. She grabbed her glove, and we never talked about it again. Then the elevator crashed. I was beside myself after it happened. I think he was trying to console me, so that's why he said what he said, but that night my father took my hand and told me not to cry for my mother because she made her choice when she chose Tim Dunn over him. I knew then that he killed them."

Vinney rubbed Chamberlin's shoulder. "Shit, man."

I was beginning to think my father may not have saved the Elenore Fielding House for the most beautiful boy in the world, but for his beautiful starlet mother.

With the back of his hand, Chamberlin wiped his tears. "Besides Trinity, you all didn't know my mother. She was the kindest person in the world. I don't care that she cheated on my father, that doesn't change how I see her. She didn't deserve to die or Mr. Dunn either, who had always been very good to our family."

Chamberlin was right, history did repeat itself. Frank Fielding killed my father to free the house of his wife's lover and consequently his wife, just as it was believed Elias framed the servant Angeles to rid the house of his father's lover.

"Maddy had not only told my father what she had seen, but she had also told Elenore. Like me, Elenore knew the elevator accident was no accident. She did nothing and said nothing for a long time, but then we got worried."

He avoided looking in my direction as he spoke. "Trinity had lived with us for about two years as our sister when my father started to add his name to her bank accounts," he said in a low voice. "It was little accounts at first but then he started making large changes and he was battling with Trinity's lawyer for executive power over her inheritance. Elenore—all of us—thought he was going to kill Trinity for her money. My mother may have been the professional actress, but my father was just as talented. He hated Trinity. Hated how much she was like her father. Trinity had no clue, but we all saw the truth. We all knew it was just a matter of time. Together we made a tough choice. We had to kill him to protect Trinity."

Hot tears blinded me. I knew Chamberlin was telling the truth, just as I knew he was going to kill me. He was right, I had no idea Mr. Fielding hated me, but in the dream I'd had since Mr. Fielding's disappearance, I had always understood that he was going to hurt me. I had always known I had killed him in self-defense. But my dream didn't get it quite right. I didn't kill Franklin Fielding in self-defense, Elenore killed him for me.

Chamberlin shook his head, his eyes darting to Vinney. "I know you're thinking we should have gone to the cops, Vinney. But no one would have believed us. No one had detected that my father tampered with the elevator. He had gotten away with two murders for three years. And he would get away with murdering Trinity. Like I said, it was only the three of us who knew my real father. I loved him, but there was something wrong with him."

That seemed to resonate with Dr. Deedle. He nodded.

"Elenore did it and Maddy and I hid the body. That way we were all implicated in his murder. That way no one would or could rat on each other without getting in trouble themselves. It was our secret, and we bore it."

I understood why Chamberlin wanted to commune with his father through X's homemade Ouija mat now. He knew for a fact his father wasn't missing, he was dead. He wanted to know if he was able to find peace after what they did to him.

"I harbored a lot of guilt over not telling Trinity the truth about her father's death, and for the part I played in my father's murder and cover up," Chamberlin said, still avoiding my gaze. "Because of that, I was silent for a long time. I felt better after we entombed my father's empty coffin. That way Trinity knew he was dead too, even if she didn't know what he had done."

Chamberlin kept his stream of vision on the floor, tears beading on his lower lashes. "We could never tell you the truth, Trinity, and I'm sorry for that. We were afraid you would want justice for your father, and we couldn't let you tell the world your father was murdered. It wasn't because we were worried about ruining my father's good name but because it would fall back on Elenore. Maddy and I were minors at the time of my father's murder, but Elenore wasn't. My mother's death and Mr. Dunn's had to remain an accident and my father's fate had to remain a mystery to protect the family."

Chamberlin's head slowly lifted, and we locked eyes from across the room. "Maddy had been pushing to tell you, threatening to tell you. Elenore and I said no, but I'm glad you know the truth now."

It was strange to be scared of Chamberlin. Part of me wanted to run and wrap my arms around him and kiss his tears away, but the other part of me told me to run, run back to London and never see Chamberlin Fielding again. I was surprised Tilly hadn't gone to him, but that was because her father was holding her hand. X stood next to them, blank, not blinking.

"Family first," Vinney said, echoing Elenore.

Chamberlin nodded, breaking his hold on me.

"But Maddy," Vinney said, back to rubbing his chin, "Elenore didn't, she couldn't. I can't imagine her drugging Maddy even if she did threaten to tell Trinity the truth. Elenore was so fiercely protective of the both of you."

"I don't know," Chamberlin said. "Maddy had been threatening to call Trinity and tell her everything for a while. Maybe Elenore thought she was going to make good on her threat and got scared." He raked his fingers through his hair. "Maybe Elenore did do it. We were always unsure how Trinity would take the news of her father being murdered. But, if she did, she regretted it. Maybe that's why she took the pills that night."

Vinney ran his hand over his lips. "What pills?"

"Elenore had sleeping pills that she kept in the junk drawer. The day she was found, after everyone left, I went into the junk drawer looking for a screwdriver to replace the ceiling fan in the kitchen and noticed that the bottle was empty. Earlier in the week it was full."

"Your sister didn't take sleeping pills," Vinney said. "I'd think I'd know something like that."

"I gave them to her," Tilly admitted. "She'd been having a hard time getting to sleep after you guys broke up, so I gave her some of mine."

Vinney's glare narrowed in on Tilly like she was the lowliest of criminals. His golden eyes resembled a hawk's, right before it lunged for prey. Dr. Deedle, as if by instinct, took a step forward, moving Tilly behind him, his body her shield, their hands still clasped.

Tilly's complexion immediately turned red. Her freckles vanished into her flushed face. "I was only trying to help," Tilly said in a low voice. "She didn't have insurance to get her own. I thought Elenore took them. I didn't know she saved them. I swear." Her eyes darted to Chamberlin. "I swear Chamberlin." With her free hand, she ran her finger up and down the back of her father's arm, tracing something only she could see. "I'm sorry Dad, I know I shouldn't have."

X took his sister's free hand. "It's not your fault," he whispered to her. "You wanted Elenore to like you. There's nothing wrong with that."

"There is something very wrong with that," Dr. Deedle corrected in a stern voice. "And we will be discussing that at length when we get home."

Tilly's already scarlet face somehow deepened in hue. X holding her hand didn't help her calm down.

I shook. My legs were like spaghetti under my frame. That was the one thing that had been missing. The one thing that had me second guessing myself. How did Chamberlin do it? How did he kill Elenore? Now I knew, he used sleeping pills. She had fallen asleep, maybe even overdosed like Maddy, while she was climbing the stairs and fell to her death. It looked like an accident, but it wasn't. I had noticed the pill bottle was empty when I was looking for the rubber gloves to clean up Damian's blood. I didn't know how long it had been empty, but Chamberlin just told me—told all of us.

"That can't be right," Vinney said, more to himself than anyone in particular. "It feels wrong. Elenore wouldn't kill herself. Would she kill Maddy to protect Chamberlin? Yeah, I can see that making sense to her. But kill herself? No, never."

The time had come to protect myself and protect Chamberlin from himself. Tears rolled down my cheeks, sobs stinging the back of my throat at the thought of what I knew had to come next. "Chamberlin killed Elenore," I said firm of voice.

The sound of everyone sucking air at the same time sounded like a hurricane forming over the ocean. Chamberlin honed in on me, his eyes and voice unsure. "Trinity . . . what are you saying?"

"I said exactly what I meant, Chamberlin. You killed Elenore. I can't run from my past or my family any longer. You tried to confess to me the other night and I wouldn't let you."

Dr. Deedle's mustache did a dance, no doubt from hearing his advice used so promptly. X stared at Chamberlin, not blinking. Tilly's mouth was open, her crooked teeth exposed like a frightened animal locked in a cage.

"Oh no, Trinity," Chamberlin said, taking a step toward me.

I took a step back. "Stay where you are," I said, throwing my arms out in front of me to protect myself. "I know you killed Elenore and you're going to kill me next."

He looked to Vinney for help. "I don't know what she's talking about. I don't know where this is coming from." He glanced at Tilly and X. He looked them over as if he was unsure how to read them. His blue globes found their way back to me. "Trinity, what's going on?"

The hurt on his face was too much to bear, I had to look

away. "He did it Vinney. I know he killed Elenore. He's covering his tracks. He knows Elenore's tox screen is going to show she overdosed. That's why he mentioned the pill bottle was empty, because he emptied it."

"How can you think that of me, Trinity? I thought you loved me," Chamberlin said with a pleading quality to his voice.

My eyes lifted to his. His dark lashes were weighed down in tears. "I do love you Chamberlin, that's why I'm saying this. Because I don't want my death on your hands. I know what it would do to you. It's not your fault, it's like you said, it's your destiny. You said you were destined to kill your sisters. It's why you kept Elias Fielding's journal a secret from Elenore. You didn't want to scare her. I didn't want to believe you when you said you had too much of your father in you." I glanced at Frank Fielding's mummified corpse. "But I can see now that you do."

"Trinity," Chamberlin said, trying to sound stern, but his voice failed him, "I didn't kill Elenore. I said that about the pills because I thought maybe that would prove she killed Maddy and herself."

"And throw the guilt off of you," Vinney said.

Chamberlin's head snapped in Vinney's direction. "No!" His hands were gesticulating like he was at Mr. Miyagi's—wax on, wax off.

X grabbed Chamberlin by the collar of his shirt. "Did you kill Maddy?! Tell me the truth!"

Chamberlin didn't fight back or push his friend off of him. "No, X! You know me. You know I don't have it in me."

Dr. Deedle got between them. "Xavier, let Detective Mallory do his job."

Chamberlin covered his face with his hands, little sobs breaking through. Dr. Deedle kept a firm grip on Tilly's shoulder to stop her from comforting Chamberlin. Her arms were contorted into her chest. She was transforming into a human insect again.

Vinney was tugging on the hair he didn't have. "We all need to settle down. I need to think." He looked at me with bloodshot eyes. "You're making a very serious accusation, Trinity. This is huge. It will change your life and Chamberlin's forever. And mine. Do you know what you're saying?"

"I'm telling the truth, Vinney."

Chamberlin's frustration broke out into a loud sob. "Trinity, please stop."

"Ask Chamberlin if on the night Elenore died if he went back downstairs after we went up to our rooms for the night. Ask him, Vinney!" I demanded.

"Linnie?"

Chamberlin didn't answer. He just made gasping noises into his palms. His face was completely obstructed by his hands and bangs.

"I went to his room that night after I took a shower and threw my laundry in the wash. He came out of his bathroom in a towel, like he had just taken a shower. His hair was wet, but his towel was dry. He missed the hamper, and I tossed it in there for him. The towel was dry, because he never showered. And he didn't shower because he went back downstairs to see Elenore. He came on to me that night, so he'd have an alibi in the morning when Elenore was found dead."

Chamberlin pulled his hands from his face, fists balling at his sides. "This is crazy! *You* came to *my* room. *You* kissed *me*. I can't believe you're cheapening everything. I didn't use you! I don't need an alibi. I didn't kill Elenore!"

His words cut me. I felt like my heart was torn wide open and I was losing blood. It wouldn't be long now until I died. "I didn't cheapen anything. You did. You waited till the night you killed Elenore to tell me you love me. You did that Chamberlin, not me!"

"Linnie," Vinney said, "I don't need to hear about the bedroom stuff. I just need to know if you went back downstairs. It's a simple question. Yes or no?"

"Yes."

"No, no, no," Vinney said, pacing. "This isn't happening."

"It's not like that, Vinney. I can explain," Chamberlin said, his face bright red as the color traveled down his neck in blotches. "I did go back downstairs, but I didn't kill Elenore or drug her. I helped her clean the blood off the sofa. I didn't tell Trinity I was heading back downstairs because I didn't want to make her feel bad for not helping."

"And the fake shower?" I said.

"You're being ridiculous Trinity. I never told you I took a shower. I was about to get into the shower when you came into my room. I had just shaved and trimmed my hair, that's why my hair was wet, and my towel was dry."

I shook my head. "Check Elenore's blood work Vinney," I said, my heart pounding in my chest. There were more actors in the family besides Dorothy and Franklin Fielding. This whole time I thought Chamberlin was something he wasn't. What he was is a murderer. "See if the sleeping pills were in her bloodstream when she died."

"Even if it shows up in her blood report," Chamberlin said, "what does that prove?"

"It proves you killed her. You already admitted to going back downstairs. And you already admitted the pill bottle was emptied the night she died."

Vinney made the call. "I need that tox screen on Elenore Fielding. Anything popping? I need it now!"

Vinney hung up, his eyes webbed in red. "Diphenhydramine overdose, the same thing that killed Maddy."

"Vinney," Chamberlin whimpered. "I didn't do it. You have to believe me."

Vinney slammed Chamberlin against the wall, pressing his face to the jagged little leaves on the wallpaper and pulling his arms behind his back. "You're under arrest for the murder of Madelin and Elenore Fielding. You have the right to remain silent."

Tears gushed from Chamberlin's squashed face. "You promised Elenore you'd watch out for me."

"That's before you killed her, you son of a bitch. Elenore gave you everything. She knew that night. She knew you might kill her, and she still asked me to protect you. God bless that woman. She had a heart of gold."

Vinney clasped handcuffs on Chamberlin's wrists. The

scrape of the metal sliding reminded me of the sound the elevator made when it crashed, but only one person was going down today.

"Vinney, you're making a big mistake," Chamberlin pleaded. "What about motive?! What reason would I have for murdering Elenore? I loved her. Think about it. There's no motive."

Vinney hesitated. I could see a gleam of hope in his eyes.

X stepped forward. "He hated Elenore. He complained about her all the time."

"What? No!" Chamberlin said.

"He always went on about how much better the house would be if he was in control so he could add stupid American history to the tour. He was just talking about it earlier today with my dad. Elenore thought his ideas made the tour stuffy but he's going to change all that now. Ask my dad, he'll tell you."

Dr. Deedle pressed his lips, his mustache an apparent flat line of disgust.

"He wanted Elenore out of the way because she was bleeding the business dry with misadventure after misadventure," X said. "My sister and I both know that." He turned to Tilly. "It's like you said, you can't trust someone who is too pretty."

Tilly's face was so red it took on a purple shade. "Do not include me in this, X!"

"Well," X said nonchalantly, "either way, there's your motive. He did it. He killed Elenore. Probably Maddy, too. He deserves to rot in jail as some hairy man's boytoy."

Chamberlin looked to Tilly, his tears a silent stream now. "Please Chantilly, tell me *you* believe me?

"Don't talk to my sister, you murderer," X said, taking up Tilly's hand again.

She pulled away from her brother. "I know you better than you know yourself, Chamberlin Fielding. And I know that you didn't kill anyone. Or could ever. I cannot believe everyone here thinks you can. Has everyone gone mad?!"

"Chantilly," Dr. Deedle said, "get control of yourself."

She turned to her father. "No, Dad! I know he didn't do it.

He can't even crush a spider let alone kill someone he loves. This is a huge mistake." She focused her attention back on Chamberlin. "I don't know what's happening, but I will fix this. I will get you the best lawyer. I will not give up on you. I see the real you, I always have."

Chamberlin kept his eyes on Tilly as Vinney pushed him through the door. "Thank you for believing in me," he said, closing his eyelids, his face all dark lashes and gloom.

Tilly followed Chamberlin and Vinney, and Mr. Deedle and X followed suit. I was left alone with Mr. Fielding, my father's murderer, eye to eye. The Fielding curse was over. Chamberlin would not be able to kill me. I saved myself and, more importantly, I saved him.

CHAPTER TWENTY-THREE
A New Dawn

I played with my overnight bag where it sat on the dining room chair next to me. My anxious fingers twisted the black cord hanging from the zipper into all sorts of knots that would've impressed the most seaworthy of sailors. It wouldn't be long now. Soon, I would be back at my London flat, back with Great Aunt Girty and The Grand Duke Wiskerton and back to Kris with a 'K'. I looked at my phone and sighed. Only a minute had passed since I contacted my Uber driver. Waiting to leave was worse than leaving.

There was a knock on the door. I checked my phone again, one minute and thirty seconds since I contacted Uber. Uber doesn't knock, and there wasn't a missed text from Vinney. Maybe the 'House Closed' sign fell off.

"Trinity, are you home?!" rumbled through the front door. It was Tilly. I was grateful she didn't ring the doorbell. I quickly went to the door before she could, keeping my eyes on the torches of the stained-glass doors, not the one the wingless angel held out in her outstretched arms.

I unlocked the portico doors. The one door's stained-glass

panel shook in its frame. The front door gave me a little grief. It had swelled shut from the change in temperature and was stuck, but with a hard yank, it soon opened. Tilly wasn't alone, she was with X. That wasn't a surprise, they seemed to travel as a pair. They really were like Lewis Carroll's strange Wonderland twins.

I couldn't help myself from instantly blushing when I saw them. My face was so hot it felt like I had a sunburn. I hadn't seen them since Chamberlin was arrested. It didn't help Tilly had on an 'I Love Chamberlin Fielding' T-shirt. It was like she brought Chamberlin, with those heavenly eyes of his, back into the house.

"Brought your Starbucks order as a final farewell," X said, handing me a coffee.

"Thanks," I said, taking the cup from him and letting them in. I didn't offer them to sit in the living room or dining room. This was going to be a quick visit. I was leaving, no sense in them getting cozy.

"Vinney told my dad you're leaving today," Tilly said. "I just wanted to say bye before you're off to London." Unexpectedly, she bent her frame, wrapping her arms around my waist in a hug. I almost spilt my coffee on her; it took a balancing act not to. "I'm glad I met you."

I wondered if she meant that now that her best friend was in jail. "You too, Tilly." I glanced to X and added, "you too, X."

He smiled a smile of all lips.

Tilly released me and pulled down her red pleather skirt. "I'm going to see Chamberlin after I leave here. You could come with me if you want, and I'll drop you off at the airport. I know he'd love to see you before you head out."

"Chantilly Deedle, forever the optimist," X said, leaning on the newel post. He was too close to the wingless angel for my comfort. "I think that makes you Tweedle Dum, sis."

She elbowed him, an act I was grateful for. It moved him closer to the living room and further from the stairs.

I shook my head. I couldn't face Chamberlin. "I don't think that's the best idea Tilly, and I already called the Uber. I'm gonna wait at the airport."

"I understand," she said, folding her hands in front of her. "You know . . . he's not mad at you. He blames himself for scaring you."

"Tilly, give it a rest already," X snapped.

She ignored her brother. "I know sometimes he gets really dark when he talks, but there's nothing to it. It's just words. It's how he deals with what happened. It's like therapy for his depression. That stuff he said about his father and the curse, it's not real. Sometimes he just talks like it is. He'd like to explain." She smiled, her teeth poking out over her bottom lip. "So, uh, maybe you could take one of his calls once you're settled in back home."

Home. I felt like I had no real home, but that Tilly Deedle, she really was a ray of sunshine on a rainy day, in a rainy year, on a God forsaken rainy planet. Chamberlin *had* called me. The house line rang, and it was him. He sounded different. Drained, sad. He had limited calls he could make. I think it was once a day so I told him to call Tilly, that I couldn't talk to him yet and I didn't know when I could. I couldn't—I didn't know what to say or think. I was still sorting everything out in my head and my head was as cluttered as Elenore's infamous junk drawer.

"Can I ask a favor?" Tilly said, her hands still folded, her arms constricted into her chest like a creature of the night. "It's okay if you say no."

"Um, sure, shoot," I said, taking a sip of my coffee, doing what I could to avoid making eye contact with her or Chamberlin on her T-shirt.

"Chain would never ask, so I'm going to . . . You see, I, um, I want to get him the very best lawyer, but I don't have money and my father's refusing to help." In presumed frustration, she tossed her hands into the air, unfolding herself to do so. "He's embarrassed he made a public decree of always liking Chamberlin to only have him arrested that same day for a double homicide. He's being really stubborn on the point of not helping. Chamberlin said to sell the house, but I can't. He loves this house, its family. It's his legacy. And even if I did, he'd get next to nothing with all the bad press, and it would be months before he saw a penny and by then it may be too late." She was rambling now, her fingers and hands twisted in front of her like her limbs were made of rubber. This was very different than her usual stiff, insect-like anxiety. More than nervousness fueled her limbs. She was scared for Chamberlin and was asking for my help. "I can't get a loan; I tried," she told me. "But I promise to pay you back once I finish medical school. With interest. I'm good for it Trinity. I swear."

"Whatever you need Tilly."

Her eyes watered.

"Don't waste your money, Trin," X said. "Chamberlin's a lost cause."

Tilly shot daggers at her brother with her eyes. "She's not wasting her money," she said. "Chamberlin is innocent, and a really good lawyer will prove that."

"Thank you for your concern, X," I said, "but it's my money and I want Chamberlin to have a good lawyer."

I went to my overnight bag in the dining room and pulled out my wallet. Plucking my accountant's business card from it, I handed it to Tilly. "Call him when you find the lawyer you want. I'll give him the heads up to expect a call from you and to authorize whatever you need."

Chamberlin *was* going to need the *very* best lawyer. Vinney was throwing everything, including the kitchen sink, at him. His 'we're going to do nothing and walk away' approach that he'd initially adopted upon seeing Frank Fielding's corpse went in the complete opposite direction when he believed Chamberlin murdered Elenore. Vinney sent in a forensics team, who found Chamberlin's fingerprints all over his father's corpse. It was tallied up against Chamberlin, not as another murder charge, Vinney didn't stoop that low, but to show a defect in character—a character capable of murder. The case was stacked against Chamberlin, using him dropping out of high school and assaulting Damian Hurst as evidence. The prosecutor was even going as far to use Chamberlin's Vampire gimmick against him, claiming he's the leader of a Satanic cult. You name it, they were calling Chamberlin Fielding it. Vinney was out for blood, and it looked like he'd have it.

Chamberlin was denied bail while he awaited his trial. He was also denied leave to go to his father's real funeral, a thing no one attended. Franklin Fielding's real interment was the last thing keeping me in Brooklyn. With him resting in peace and the bill paid, I could leave.

Tilly hugged me again. "Text me when you get to the airport. Oh, wait," she said, "I don't have your number. Chain didn't have it memorized," she said. "And they don't allow cell phones in jail."

"Duh," X said, poking the side of his sister's head. She swatted his hand away and took my phone from me. She put her number in and texted herself. "Got it. Now promise to text me when you get to the airport and right before you take off, that way I can let Chain know."

Maddy was right, about Tilly anyway: she was Chamberlin's little follower. She'd follow him to the ends of the Earth. She was just like Emmit's Elenore. In the name of love, she would follow him to the grave. I admired that in her. I wish I had her conviction and devotion. Even if Dr. Deedle didn't approve, I'm sure he was proud of his daughter.

"I promise," I said, meaning it. Tilly was doing something for me I couldn't do. She was going to take care of Chamberlin now that Vinney and I had abandoned him. Elenore would have been pissed. Vinney was right, even if he murdered her, she'd want her Linnie protected. Unquestionably, the Rolling Stones had it right, *You Can't Always Get What You Want.* The universe was really good at handing out cosmic shit storms in the name of what you need. Mick Jagger must have originally been a redhead.

After another hug goodbye from Tilly and one from X, I let them out and locked the front door. I didn't want any tour seekers popping in unexpectedly. I pulled a dining room chair to the window and waited for my Uber driver. I was really tired. I texted my accountant to expect a call from Tilly before I forgot. Leaning my elbow on the windowsill, I sipped my coffee. It was extra sweet, but that was okay. I needed a pick me up. I hadn't slept well since the arrest.

I was happy to be leaving. I was ready to leave the Elenore

Fielding House in the past for good and, as much as it pained me, Chamberlin Fielding, too. I wasn't running away from my past and my family; I was looking forward to my future. Besides, I was never really a Fielding. It was funny how blood separated us, but it was also blood, the blood of my father and their mother, that had made us a family.

Finally, the Uber driver arrived. I glanced at my phone; he was five minutes late. I went to stand and stumbled to my knees. My phone skittered across the floor. My legs wouldn't work, it was as if my bones had turned to jelly. I reached for my cellphone to dial 911 but the darkness crept in so quickly I lost sight of my phone. I reached in the darkness, my hand no longer under my control, my brain powering down despite the thumping of my heart willing me to stay awake. I was powerless against the oncoming darkness. I succumbed to it like it was Death calling for me, flopping on the floor like a wet noodle.

* * *

I opened my eyes to darkness, feeling woozy and disoriented. I panicked, struggling against the duct tape around my wrists and ankles. A piece was also placed over my mouth. My pulse spiked. An instant migraine pounded in my head as I fought to breathe. This was not the future I was looking forward to.

My hands were bound behind my back, giving me no choice but to wiggle my body like a worm to assess my situation. I was lying on coarse carpet. I stretched my legs out, striking something right away. I was in a compact space. There was no doubt I was locked in the trunk of a car.

I heard a noise—footsteps. Someone was coming. I squirmed as far into the trunk as I could, pretending to still be unconscious. The trunk opened, and so did my eyes, only a sliver. It was X. Relieved, I wiggled toward him to make sure he saw me. Only muffled moans were audible through the duct tape.

Seeing me, X smiled. It was dark out—a starless, moonless night. The streetlight across the way back lit him. His braces transformed his mouth into a gaping hole. Only the corners of his lips hinted at the fact he was smiling. It wasn't the smile of a hero—

no, it wasn't that.

"This won't take long, Trin," he told me in a whisper, grabbing me by my feet as Chamberlin and Maddy had done in my dream to their father. Oh, God, no—history was repeating itself.

I hit the ground like a ton of bricks. An amber haze from the streetlights filled the night. It was foggy now that the cold front had finally made its way up the East Coast, but even so, there was enough light to see where I was. The knowledge of that sent a shudder through my body that made it convulse. We were on the other side of Brooklyn Keeps Cemetery—behind the hill the Fielding Mausoleum backed up to. I struggled in vain, pulling up tufts of damp grass and cool dirt with my fingers as X dragged me up the hill.

We reached the apex. I looked up to see that smile on his face again. From the ground, he looked like a giant, or some evil god with his spikey hair resembling instruments of death. He didn't dawdle. He kicked my back, sending me rolling down the other side of the hill. I landed near the front of the Fielding Mausoleum, breathless.

I knew what X was planning, but he had made a miscalculation. I was waiting for the moment when he realized it and his whole plan went kaboom. He didn't have the key to get into the mausoleum. If he broke in, someone would hear him. He had no choice but to untie me and beg for my forgiveness. Which I would never give him. He could have the cell right next to Chamberlin.

"I'm just as smart as Tilly," he told me as he fished around in his pocket. He pulled out a key. He flashed it at me, my eyes growing wide. He didn't make a miscalculation. I was screwed.

"Damian's key," he said haughtily. "I found it wedged in the sofa. It looks like Maddy did give him the key after all. Lucky for us, Elenore didn't find it." He brought the key close to his face and examined it. "I know skeleton keys typically open all doors in a house, but I made sure, ahead of time, it also worked on the mausoleum door. I'm not an idiot, Trin. This is your last stop."

He opened the iron door to the mausoleum. The wreath from Maddy's funeral was still on it, brown and dried and dead. I screamed, but no sound came out. He took me by my feet again and dragged me into the mausoleum, closing the door behind us.

The stone floor was cold and moist and the smell of earth, though we were above it, was rich. It smelled of clay and rain. I couldn't see a thing; it was pitch dark. I already felt like I was buried alive. I was grateful for the sound of X breathing, it let me know I wasn't alone yet.

He struck a match and used it to light a candle. It looked like the same kind of candle Tilly had pulled out of her purse when we tried to summon the spirit of Frank Fielding on X's homemade Ouija mat. I hadn't noticed he had a candle with him. He either pulled it from his pocket or, the more likely scenario, he had it waiting there for him.

The fog from outside drifted into the center chamber of the mausoleum, washing everything in gray. My heart, along with my head, pounded so quickly that I thought I was having a heart attack. Everything hurt.

"Well, Trin," X said, once he was satisfied the candle's flame wasn't going to go out, "who do you want to be entombed with? Maddy, Elenore, or Frank?" I shook my head, a cramp running down the right side of my body. "How about with Elenore?" he asked, his eyebrows rising in right angles. "Elenore ruined my life. It's all her fault, you know? I loved Maddy. Like Romeo loved Juliet. Like mosquitos love blood. I adored her from the moment I saw her. She was like this angel on Earth, but no one is good enough for Elenore. I had to prove myself. Why do you think I dress like this?"

He kneeled next to me to move the hair out of my face. I had broken out into a sweat, despite the cool evening. Little beads of perspiration trickled down the side of my face like tears, my tousled hair sticking to it like a fly in Vaseline.

"It was to impress Elenore. To let her know I was down with the darkness. It's why I helped Chamberlin with his Vampire gimmick and helped him start his modeling career. I wanted to prove I was good for business. That I, Xavier Deedle, was worthy of Madelin Fielding, dark princess of the Fielding clan."

He flicked my nose. "But as I was working hard to help your stupid family, Damian Hurst comes along and Maddy falls in love with him instead of me! I tell Chamberlin he's no good. Does Chamberlin listen to me? Did he watch out for me? No—he thinks Damian is the best. Damian is so talented. Damian is so clever. Damian is good for business! Then finally, they see what I always knew." He took a seat next to me on the floor. "Tilly knew Damian was scum, but she didn't want to burst Chamberlin's bubble. Heaven forbid if Chamberlin Fielding is made to suffer. We lied for him, getting him out of trouble with the cops, though Damian more than deserved the beating he got. I wish I could've been the one to give it to him."

I rotated my hands trying to stretch out the duct tape.

X sighed. "Everything was set for Maddy to notice me. She was coming around. I was so close. Allison was the icing on the cake." He leaned in, stopping an inch from my face. His eyes looked black. I stopped breathing, stopped wiggling my wrists. There was something in his stare that made everything stop.

"I pretended to like Allison to make Maddy jealous. It was working. She would get pissy every time I mentioned how hot Allison was." He shook his head as if in remembrance. "But Allison is nothing compared to Maddy. All my hard work was about to pay off and what does Elenore do?—She kills her!"

There was so much pain in his voice it frightened me. I knew that pain. I scooted myself back on my butt, hitting the wall.

X leaned back against the wall with me, staring up at the candle. I noticed how very young he was; he was just a kid. His tone was calm as he continued. "For a second, I thought maybe it wasn't Elenore who murdered Maddy. I thought maybe it *was* Chamberlin. You seemed so sure he was a murderer. But I looked into his eyes and all I saw was fear. It wasn't him." He glanced at me out of the corner of his eye. "You're wrong about your brother. He didn't murder Maddy, and he didn't murder Elenore. He doesn't have the balls to kill someone, but I do. And I did. I put those sleeping pills from the junk drawer into the coffee pot when I helped clear the table after Vinney's so-called interrogation, knowing Elenore would stay up to clean the blood off the couch and drink that shitty coffee that no one else would touch."

He drew a deep breath. "I did it. I did it for Maddy. Elenore stole her from me."

He turned his body, his one shoulder resting against the wall of the mausoleum as he studied me. I couldn't look away. I couldn't believe I was wrong. Couldn't believe that it was X who killed Elenore. Couldn't believe that Chamberlin was innocent, and I sent him to jail. What did I do?!

"I should be thanking you, Trinity. You made an airtight case against Chamberlin. You completely covered my tracks. Of course, I did help sell the whole Chamberlin hates Elenore motive, but it was you who pointed your finger at him. You who validated the accusation." He nibbled on his nails as he spoke, chipping away his black nail polish. "I did it, not really in the right frame of mind. I accepted Maddy's suicide because she left this world on her terms. I missed her terribly, but I accepted it. Learning she was murdered filled me with something. I thought of the shadow we saw hovering over my Ouija mat and thought she appeared to us because she couldn't rest in peace. When Vinney said Maddy overdosed on sleeping pills, my mind went straight to Elenore. I knew Tilly was giving Elenore pills, her way of getting Elenore to like her. I don't know, I just snapped. I found the pills in the drawer in the kitchen when I was looking for a clean washcloth and dumped them in the coffee pot. I didn't know if anything would come of it. I didn't know it would actually kill her. I don't know much about pills, but when we heard the screams in the morning, and I saw her dead, I was happy. I felt I avenged Maddy."

He let out an exaggerated sigh. "So now it's just you and me, Trinity . . . This must have been what Frank Fielding felt like killing his wife and your dad and getting away with it. It feels pretty good. It gives you this high, I guess. I feel untouchable. Like I can't get caught because I'm smart." He let out another sigh. "The smart part of my brain is telling me to let you go to London. I know once you're there, you're not coming back, and I will never see you again. But the Deedle Dum part of my brain is telling me this is all your fault and I have to do something about it. Things were going well with Elenore. She trusted me. She knew my worth. She was bragging about me to everyone including Maddy. Maddy had even told me she liked my eyeliner. And then there was the talk of you and the threat to call you. I kept thinking you're at the center of it all. You're the reason Maddy was murdered. If it weren't for you, she would be alive. And I would be happy." He locked eyes with me, his eyes like black pits. "You see, the happiness upon seeing Elenore dead has faded and I'm miserable again. Because of that, I have to kill you, Trinity. I need to be happy again. I need to know I can be happy again. You're the last Fielding, with you gone I'll be happy. I killed Elenore for Maddy but I'm killing you for me and then it will be all blue skies and unicorns."

I shook my head, my tears burning my eyes. "Hey, don't cry," he said, using his shirt sleeve to dry my tears. "I'm sorry you're awake. You weren't supposed to be awake, but like I said I don't know much about pills." He moved my hair away from my face for me again. "But I'm glad we got to talk. I liked you from the first time I met you outside the house. It's like I knew you were a Fielding." He opened the locket on the dog collar he wore. "I loved the Fieldings. Loved Maddy. Loved them just as much as I love Tilly. I loved Elenore even though she treated my sister like shit. I would have taken a bullet for Chamberlin, for any of them, for you."

He closed his locket and rested his head against the wall, exposing his neck to the glow of the candle. "Oh Trinity, I'm changed. Learning Elenore killed Maddy changed me, there's no going back now. Everything's changed. Tilly could never understand . . . Maybe, maybe she could have, if Chamberlin was the one murdered. I think only then she could. It's like a switch got thrown that can never be thrown back. All that love has turned to hate. This blinding hate." He unfastened his dog collar and held it in the palm of his hands, his eyes fixated on it. "I hate them all. I hate Elenore, I hate Chamberlin. Trinity," he said, his dark eyes darting to me, "I hate you." His lips quivered. "I hate you so much. It's bad luck you're some weird Fielding hybrid. I need all of the Fieldings dead. Chamberlin will be in jail forever, that's probably worse than death, and that will mean the Elenore Fielding House will be closed for good. The Fieldings will all be buried in one way or another and then I can move on."

Tears rolled down his youthful face. "I hope you understand. And for the friend I used to consider you, I'm sorry." He wiped his tears away with his inner arm, getting to his feet. "I decided I'm going to stick you with Elenore. It was Elenore who made me a murderer after all." He pulled Elenore's casket from the vault. I shook my head violently, scooting away from him on my butt.

"What the hell are you doing, Xavier Deedle?!" Tilly said from the mausoleum door.

I tried to scream. My cries were muffled, but she saw me.

"What the hell, untie her!"

"Tilly, listen to me."

"I just listened more than enough to you. X, you're out of your mind. You're acting like Grandpa. Remember what Dad said about him. He said it was like a switch went off. Think of Auntie Tills. You need to untie Trinity and come home."

Abased he got caught, he bowed his head. "How did you know I was here?"

"The 360 on your phone, Deedle Dum. It gives me your location. You weren't home when I got back from visiting Chain, so I checked the 360 and saw you were at the cemetery. When I saw that, I worried there was a spiky haired reason Trinity never texted me she was at the airport or landed."

"Shit," he mumbled.

Tilly made her way to me. "Yeah Deedle Dum, you know Dad turned it on after Vinney said Maddy was murdered. I'm glad, for both our sakes, I'm smarter than you."

She crouched on the other side of me from where X stood. "I'm going to untie Trinity. No harm done right, Trin?"

I nodded, enthusiastically.

"Then we're going to go tell Vinney Chamberlin didn't kill Elenore."

"And tell him what? That I did?!"

Tilly reached for the duct tape on my mouth.

"Don't touch her!" he yelled.

"Okay," she said, standing up with her palms out in surrender.

X licked his lips, pointing at his sister. "You have two choices Chantilly. You can help me get rid of Trinity's body or you can join her."

I glanced at Tilly, all my hopes riding on her. But this was X, her little brother.

"X," she said, with tears rolling down her freckled face, "you know I love you. And I will visit you every day, like we did with Auntie Tills. And Dad will help you get better."

X's voice cracked. It was laced with pain. "You choose them over me?"

"X," she said pleadingly, "of course not. You're my brother. I love you above all."

He pointed at her shirt. "Above him?!"

"Yes, even above Chamberlin. We have a special bond, and you know it, but I can't let you hurt Trinity. What's done is done with Elenore, we can't change the past. It's like Dad always says, we must learn from it. We have to understand why you did what you did, so you don't do it again. Me letting you do it again would only hurt you X, and hurt me. Do you want to hurt *me*?"

Tears streamed from his dark eyes. His eyeliner streaked down his cheeks like the clowns his father feared. "No Tilly. I don't want to hurt you."

She nodded. "Then help me do what's right. We can fix this. I will never abandon you X, because I love you."

Her words stung. She would never abandon her little brother because she loves him. It didn't matter that he'd committed murder. I abandoned Chamberlin. What did that mean about us? What did that mean about me?

X picked at his black nail polish with his front teeth. "I don't want to go to jail."

"X, I can't control that. But help me set things right. And then we will go home and ask Vinney to come over. Let Dad see if

Vinney can help with damage control."

"You don't get it, Tilly. I murdered Elenore! There's no fixing that. I'll go to jail." He spoke hurriedly. "But we don't have to tell anyone. I got away with it. Help me put Trinity in Elenore's casket and we can go home together, and no one will ever know. They'll think she went to London. By the time they find out she didn't, we'll be in the clear."

She shook her head. "I'll know."

X straightened up, taking on a stern demeanor that resembled his father. "Tilly, as my sister I'm asking you to help me with this. Help me with this and I will help you with your free Chamberlin campaign."

She shook her head again, this time very slowly. I didn't dare move a muscle. X was on edge. He was capable of anything. I feared for Tilly. He had given her an ultimatum: Help him or join me.

His tears and words became erratic. He folded his hands together in supplication. "Please Tilly. Think about it. Elenore deserved it. She killed Maddy and she always treated you like dirt. And with Trinity out of the picture for good, who knows, maybe Chamberlin will fall for you."

Tilly's arms were contorted, her face ruby red as tears fell.

"X, I'm going to untie Trinity."

She pulled the duct tape off my mouth. He pushed her away from me. Tilly wobbled on her heels. Falling back, she struck her head on Elenore's casket.

The metallic scent of blood filled the mausoleum, washing away the smell of clay and earth. A bright red pool dampened Tilly's hair and the stone floor. "Tilly!" X shrieked, scrambling to her. He knelt by her side. "Tilly, are you okay?! I'm sorry. I didn't mean it. Please Tilly, say something!"

Rallying my bravery, I seized the moment. It was fight or die. While X was distracted, I threw my legs over his head, trapping his neck between my thighs. He tried to throw me off; nevertheless, I was able to lock my hold. I forced him onto his side and squeezed.

He pinched my legs, and tried to bite me, but I wouldn't let go. I could feel his strength fading as I choked the life from him. "I have something to tell you X," I said through gritted teeth. "Elenore didn't murder Maddy. I did. I take the same sleeping pills as Tilly. I drugged Maddy because it's her fault my father's dead. Maddy called me after her huge fight with Elenore and Chamberlin and asked me to fly home. She told me she knew the truth behind my father's death. I came and she told me everything Chamberlin had told us when we found Frank Fielding's body. She wanted me to take her side against Elenore and Chamberlin and give her money. Selfish. Maddy was so selfish," I said with venomous disgust. "I asked Maddy why she told her father about the affair after Chamberlin made her promise not to, and do you know what she told me? For attention. My father was murdered so Maddy could have her father's attention. Well, she got *my* attention, but things didn't work out the way she thought."

X was gasping for air now. I saw the gears turning in his eyes just like Dr. Deedle had described. I also saw my reflection in X's glassy eyes and the gears working in my own. I knew exactly what X was talking about when he said he was changed. *I was changed.* I let Maddy do that to me and lost myself. I lost Elenore and I lost Chamberlin forever. Maddy made me a murderer and I made X a murderer.

"In pace requiescat. Rest in peace, X," I said, squeezing so hard, I thought X's head was going to pop off. When he went limp, I loosened my grip, keeping my legs wrapped around his neck. I twisted my body and grabbed Tilly's purse with my fingertips. I felt for the phone. Finding it, I slid it to my side so I could see it. Inverting my back, I stretched my arms as far as I could to the side and with the tips of my fingers dialed 911.

CHAPTER TWENTY-FOUR
A New Story

I knocked on the front door to the Elenore Fielding House. It was a mild day. The heatwave was long over, and X's blue skies were here. My heart was in my throat. I hadn't seen Chamberlin since the day he was arrested. I had stayed at the hotel with the mildew stain on the ceiling for the last few days. Chamberlin and Vinney said I didn't have to stay there, that the Elenore Fielding House was my home and always would be, but I felt differently.

After what I had done to Chamberlin and to Vinney, I couldn't call that place home. I had abandoned Chamberlin. It was him or me and I chose me. I didn't save him, I saved myself. Just like I had always done in my perpetual nightmare. I chose *me.* My love for Chamberlin was less than my love for myself. I was not a Fielding and didn't have the heart to be one. I didn't live by the Fielding's golden rule of family first.

The gut feeling I had all those years ago as a child was wrong. All of the Dunn family foresight handed down from generation to generation in our red hair was wrong. I didn't belong with Chamberlin or as a part of his family. Chamberlin was never going to kill me. Trusting in my gut feelings had ruined my life. My father should have told me *not* to trust them. It was time for me to go. But before I did, I had to face them one last time.

Dr. Deedle said you can't run away from your past or your family, but I had to. X was wrong when he said it was all Elenore's fault, and he was right when he said I was at the center of everything. He really was as intuitive as his sister. I was the catalyst that caused the destruction of two great families. I had to leave before I destroyed anything else and before they discovered the truth about Maddy.

There was a small part of me that was afraid X told them I murdered Maddy and a larger part of me that feared they may believe him. Vinney had already questioned my arrival in the States, back when I bumped into him at Brooklyn Keeps Cemetery after my run in with Damian Hurst. If Vinney really looked into it, he would discover I came home earlier than I had let on to Elenore. I knew I shouldn't have said anything to X, but in the heat of the moment, I wanted to hurt him, like he planned on hurting me. Going to jail for killing the wrong person would be worse than death for someone as smart as X. In the end, my anger got the best of me, but it was like X said, it was nice to talk to someone, even if the conversation was one sided.

I needed someone to know. I had to tell someone. It had been boiling up in me, ready to spill over. Now the pressure was off. I felt somewhat normal, if that's even a thing after committing murder. I was glad my confidant was X. In the end, I ended up liking him, even though he did kill Elenore. X, like me, had his reasons. We were the same, we were kin in blood. The difference is he got caught.

The front door to the Elenore Fielding House opened and there Chamberlin Fielding was. He stood as beautiful as a real angel with his golden hair, his heavenly blue eyes, his high cheekbones, and his soft mouth. He was perfect, truly perfect. He was wearing a white T-shirt and blue jeans. His casualness made him look more like he was wearing a disguise than ever. I wondered where he hid his wings.

"Come in," he said, his cheeks coloring to a deep pink. I knew mine must have been tomato red. I felt the heat rush to my face as if I was walking into a sauna, not a place I called home just a few short days ago.

"Trinity—"

I cut him off. I had to speak first before I lost my nerve. "Chamberlin, I'm sorry. I'm so sorry I ever thought you could murder anyone, especially Elenore. I'm ashamed."

He wrapped his arms around me. I smelled Gain detergent and then there was that hint of him, that boy from my childhood and my dreams, that brought me to tears.

"It's okay, Trinity," he said in a kind voice. "I don't blame you. I know how it looked. It looked awful. I tried to explain, and I wanted to try again. I'm just glad you know the truth now. I told the truth about why I went downstairs and why my towel was dry."

"I know," I said, stifling my tears in his shirt.

His hand ran down my back. I missed his touch. I missed him. "I'm sorry for the confusion Trinity. I am."

"It's not your fault. I should never have doubted you."

Again, his hand ran down the length of my spine, but this time the little hairs on the nape of my neck bristled. It was a strange feeling, somewhere between yearning and fear. But what did I have to fear? Not Chamberlin . . .

He released me from his hug, giving space between us. My eyes settled directly on the wingless angel on the newel post. Her dark eyes, searching, piercing.

"I do have something to be sorry about," Chamberlin said, bowing his head. Everything seemed darker with his eyes in shadows. "I kept a huge secret from you half our lives. I'm sorry for not telling you the truth behind your father's death. Elenore and I decided together not to tell you. Maddy had no say, she was too young, but we figured no good would come from you knowing the truth. You would end up hating us and be left with no one. At least how it stood, you had us as siblings."

"Elenore's always right," I said, dragging my thumb under my eyes, removing my smudged eyeliner.

He laughed in a quick burst. "She really was."

"I'm gonna miss her. I'm going to miss everyone."

"You don't have to leave. Vinney and I want you to stay. This is your home."

I avoided making a comment on the subject. Chamberlin would never understand all the reasons I had to leave. Only X would understand. It was like X said, if Chamberlin had been the one murdered, then, and only then, could Tilly understand why he killed Elenore. Maybe if Chamberlin *had* been the one to murder Elenore, maybe then, one day, I'd be able to tell him the truth and we could be as one, but that wasn't the reality. I was the only murderer amongst the two of us.

Not knowing what to do with my hands now that I didn't have Chamberlin to wrap my arms around, I stuck them in my jean pockets. "Vinney and you are okay after the mess I caused?" I asked in a low voice. "I figured you'd hate him and me."

He softly brushed my hair away from my face and smiled. "It's me. I pouted all the way home to make Vinney feel extra bad and gave him a long lecture about not trusting me and not honoring Elenore, which really got to him. Then we buried the hatchet over a pizza and wings."

I faked a smiled. If only a pizza and wings could fix what happened between us.

"I'm glad he decided to still move in, I'd be lonely all by myself," Chamberlin said. "Vinney and I have had lots of ups and downs and I'm sure we'll have more, but we don't hold grudges when it comes to each other. In a way, he's like a second father." Mimicking me, he put his hands in his pockets. "Besides, Vinney was doing what he thought was right. He thought he was protecting you. I can't hate him for that. Just like I can't hate you for protecting yourself." He drew a long breath and murmured, "I just wish you didn't feel you had to protect yourself *from* me."

"Oh Chamberlin, I'm so sorry," I said, biting back new tears.

He bowed his head, falling back into his favorite stance with ease. "I think that was the worst part of it. The knowing you were scared of me. It really woke me up. I wouldn't change how things went down even if I could. It helped me see what was right in front of me."

"Tilly," I said.

He nodded, lifting his eyes to mine. "I love her Trinity. I can't believe I didn't see it before. But at that moment, in my dad's room, when no one believed me but her, it was like this light turned on in my head. I realized I was going to spend my life behind bars locked away from her. And now that I knew I loved her, I could never tell her, I could never hurt her like that."

He swept his bangs out of his eyes, his voice dropping to a whisper. "I'm sorry Trinity. I don't think there's much to salvage between us. But everything I felt for you was real. It was my boyhood fantasy come true, but I'm not a boy anymore."

My heart sank. I knew we were through; I did that to us. Chamberlin was right, there was nothing to salvage after I sent him to rot in prison for a crime he didn't commit, but to hear it said out loud deepened the wound.

"I'm very different from the boy you once loved and you're different too," he told me in a kind voice. "I think deep down we both knew that but had to try because that life was stolen from us. I don't want to hurt you, Trinity. I still love you. I just love you more like a sister."

It took all of my strength to smile, and I did. "Sister Fielding it is."

He kissed my forehead. "Sister Fielding it is."

"It would make Elenore very happy to know her stupid nickname endured," I said, playing off my heartache.

He hugged me again. This hug was different. We cleared the air. I would be heading to London under different circumstances this time. I broke from him and genuinely smiled. I would always love Chamberlin and I was okay with being his sister. I embraced Tilly's attitude. I was happy with my lot in life as long as Chamberlin was in it. That's intellect for you.

"Hey there," Vinney said, coming in with coffees. He handed me one from the cardboard carrier.

"You should have gone with slushies," I said.

He chuckled. "Maybe. I was going to give coffee up, but the Dunkin god called my name. Cops and coffee are like nerds and Dungeons and Dragons."

"Peas and carrots," I said.

Tilly strolled into the house wearing her Plant Haven uniform. "Don't forget creepy and the Fieldings."

Chamberlin took her hand. "I was going to say like Chamberlin and Tilly." He pulled her to him, giving her a quick peck on the cheek.

Chamberlin and Tilly it was. They really were perfect together. The great love Tilly predicted in Chamberlin's readings was not for Chamberlin and me but for them.

I couldn't hate Tilly even if I wanted to. She saved me. She put me before her brother. I could do the same for her. She deserved Chamberlin—not me.

Tilly hugged me hello. "Did Chain convince you to stay?"

I dodged the question. "How's your head?" I asked, noticing the Scooby-doo Band-Aid on her temple. It was a very fitting Band-Aid for the Elenore Fielding House.

She held up seven fingers, her nails freshly painted black. "Lucky seven. Seven stitches. I may have a little scar but with all my freckles it won't be noticeable."

"And you had a concussion," Chamberlin said.

"Yeah. I felt nauseous for like two days, but I'm all better now."

I didn't want to tempt fate, but I genuinely wanted to know, and I didn't get much information from Chamberlin and Vinney's text messages. After all, I'd thought I had killed him. "How's X?"

"He's good," Tilly told me. "Chain and I are visiting him after we see you off. Big B got him the very best lawyer and luckily, he's only seventeen so he's being charged as a minor. My dad and the lawyer decided to claim temporary insanity. It won't be that hard to prove. I mean I was there, like you, he was really insane, plus we have a family history of insanity."

I knew all about the Deedle's family history. Even with X knowing his past and his family, and with his father's guidance, he still couldn't escape his fate. That realization shook me. My knees felt weak.

Tilly, as always, was in high spirits. "It's the best bet to keep X out of jail and get him into a facility where he can get the help he needs. There's a really good clinic right outside of the city my dad's affiliated with, we're trying to get him in there."

"Isn't that career suicide for your dad?" I asked. I didn't mean to be insensitive, but I was surprised Dr. Deedle would sacrifice his career. He seemed so career oriented. If Dr. Deedle was embarrassed for just saying he liked Chamberlin before he was arrested, I couldn't imagine how he felt about his son being a murderer and claiming temporary insanity.

"Family first," Chamberlin said, taking Tilly's hand again.

That said it all, why I had no family. I always put myself first. I should know that by now. I wished I could get that into *my* thick skull. I was as bad as Maddy. How many times did I have to be told?

Tilly blushed, but her limbs resisted contortion. "Yeah, Big B doesn't care. He's gonna make sure we get X back as soon as we can. It helps a lot Chamberlin and you didn't press charges. Thanks again for that."

I nodded. That was right. Dr. Deedle wasn't career driven, he became a doctor to help people like his father and sister, and like X.

"It's not too bad," Tilly went on to say. "We only have to worry about the state charges." She glanced at Vinney, her flush deepening, the freckles connecting one at a time. "X is really sorry about Elenore. The guy who killed her wasn't my brother. I know that doesn't bring her back, but he wanted me to tell you he's sorry."

Vinney hugged her. "I know kiddo. Chamberlin and I have had a long talk about it. X is family too. I want to see him get the help he needs and get him back on his feet. Hopefully without the dog collar."

We all laughed. But there was a sadness in Tilly's.

"Well, should we do this thing?" Vinney said. "We don't want Trinity to miss her flight."

"I'll get the duct tape," Chamberlin volunteered.

"Where are we doing it at?" I asked, while Chamberlin rummaged through the junk drawer.

He shouted from the kitchen, "Dining room."

"The most boring room on the tour," I said.

"Not any longer," Chamberlin informed me, coming into the dining room with two rolls of white duct tape. "I thought Elenore would like the spotlight."

After being kidnapped and having my wrists and ankles duct taped together, I was hoping to never see duct tape again, but we owed it to Elenore to add her to the house's body count.

"Where should I lay?" I asked.

"On the table, half on half off," Chamberlin directed. "We're going with murder. A mysterious murder in the dining room that claimed one of the Fieldings' own. No motive. No suspect. Elenore Fielding was found strangled in a red dress, a red rose on the table next to her." Chamberlin scrunched his nose. "I'm still working out the tour details."

"You're not dead until everyone forgets you," I smiled, quoting one of the Fielding family's golden rules. "And now Elenore will never be. It's exactly the kind of story she liked."

"Never," Chamberlin said. "Elenore will never be forgotten."

Whether Elenore was part of the tour or not, I could never forget her. She, like Tilly, saved me. She murdered her own father to protect me. Elenore was the mother I never knew. I would always immortalize her.

"I added the part about the rose," Vinney told me proudly.

"Wow Vinney," I said with arched eyebrows, "you're really making yourself at home. It's very dark romance."

"I figured I'd help out where I can," he said. "Chamberlin has a lot on his shoulders now."

I took my place on the table, letting my legs dangle off to the side. Chamberlin and Tilly arranged my body as they saw fit.

"You're gonna run the house all by yourself?" I asked Chamberlin.

"Not by myself," he said. "I'm going to have a lot of help

from Tilly, and her dad is interested in being a tour guide."

"Dr. Deedle?" I said in shock.

"He wants to do it as Emmit Fielding," Tilly laughed. "He wants to dress up and everything. He says Chamberlin dresses up as a vampire with fangs so why can't he dress up, too."

I smiled. "That's cool."

Chamberlin nodded excitedly. "I think we're gonna book it as a tour with a historical flair: The Emmit Fielding Experience."

Elenore would have been proud; Chamberlin was all business. Her death and his arrest didn't thwart his dedication to his family.

"I'll have to come back to take that tour."

"I'm going to hold you to that," Chamberlin said, locking eyes with me.

"Of course, I'm gonna help when I'm free," Tilly said. "I'm not great at public speaking so I'm going to help out with administrative stuff and do tarot readings on the weekend."

"I guess, besides using my genius for tour stories, I'm security," Vinney said with a chuckle.

"It's a family affair then," I intoned in a soft voice, my eyes glassing over. I didn't blink. I knew if I did, tears would fall.

"Yep," Chamberlin said. "It's just like Elenore always wanted."

He handed a roll of duct tape to Tilly. She tore a piece off with her razor-sharp teeth. "And when X is better, he wants to help too. I think he'll make a really good tour guide."

I had a gut feeling he would.

* * *

After Elenore was officially added to the body count of the Elenore Fielding House, I said my final farewell to Vinney and the happy couple. With my business there done, I headed to the front door.

As I left the living room, I glanced back at Chamberlin and Tilly. Tilly was meant to be a Fielding. But if true love did breathe death, it wouldn't be executed for a while. I had a feeling one day they would have two girls and one boy with blond hair and blue eyes just like Chamberlin. History would repeat itself. Chamberlin's son, like him, would be the most beautiful boy in the world.

There was one last thing to do before I left. I snapped the wingless angel's hands off at the wrists and threw them in the gift shop wastebasket. I wouldn't need her torch light to guide me home again. I was never coming back.

Opening the stained-glass doors of the portico, I smelled the familiar scent of blood before I felt the cool glass strike my face. I was on my back now, the warm liquid of my dreams pooling around me like a red sea. The racing footfalls of Chamberlin, Tilly, and Vinney sounded like a stampede, each footstep reverberating under my head. My hands instinctively went to the source of the pain. An acute spike of agony cut through my lips and face. It was deep. It felt so deep—like my face was cut in half. Blood gurgled uncontrollably from my mouth, spilling over my hands. I had seen the future after all. I had glimpsed *my own* future; it was mirrored in Chamberlin's face because when I looked into his eyes, I saw myself. I was shown the open door of the house in my dreams, saw the blood on the stained-glass portico doors. I hadn't realized what the Dunn gift was trying to tell me and now it was too late. The gut feeling, that I was next to die, was dead on. But it wasn't Chamberlin who was going to murder me, it was the Elenore Fielding House.

Standing at my head, hovering over me with his cane was Elias Fielding. His smile continued to widen, twisting his face into a grotesque grin. "Tsk, tsk, tsk little Trinity Dunn," he said in a raspy voice that carried an echo. "There's a price to pay for murdering your sister. Trust me, I know a thing or two about that."

That was it, why I could see the house's ghosts after all the years of nothing. I killed Maddy, and they knew about it. And now there was hell to pay.

"Quick, call an ambulance!" Chamberlin shouted to Tilly. He sounded like he spoke to her through a windstorm, his voice wavering as it faded in and out. I was in his arms now. His white shirt—red. All was blood. All was red. All was death. His hands were on my face intertwined with mine.

"Stay with me," Chamberlin cried, his tears hitting my

cheeks. I felt each one. They felt cool on my feverish face. "Trinity, stay with me!"

He had asked me that in one of my dreams and now it came to pass, but I didn't have the choice to stay. I couldn't stay with him then and I couldn't stay with him now.

My eyes rolled back in my head at the sound of it. Polly was perched on the foyer chandelier, and she croaked out her name. "Poll-ee!"

I heard the sound of a baby crying. The sound grew and grew and with each wail of the infant's lungs they started to appear. A Spanish woman with dark hair dressed in a maid's uniform stood to the side of me with a crying baby in her arms. It was Angeles and Baby Ivette. Angeles looked uncannily like the carved angel she was said to have embodied in Fielding lore. Her eyes were dark—so dark—and full of anything but forgiveness. The only thing darker was the bruise on her neck.

Bethany appeared next to Angeles, her neck bulging off to the side. Emmit and Elenore appeared in nightgowns and nightcaps. They were all so clear to me it was as if they were amongst the living. William, Elias's son, appeared in his wheelchair. Mr. Fielding was there too. He looked how I remembered him, but on his shirt there was a red stain. He stood with his dark-eyed little sisters. There were so many faces I didn't know in the crowd. They inched closer to me, moving together in one big mass. Then I saw my father, his red hair and auburn eyes twins to my own. He held Mrs. Fielding's hand, as he did in death. His face was scratched as it had been when we found him at the bottom of the elevator. My father knelt on the side of me, placing his free hand on my shoulder. "Stay with me," he said.

Elenore appeared next to Elias, her head twisted at an unnatural angle. "You're a part of this family Sister. You belong here," Elenore said, repeating what she had said to me the night she died. "Better get the duct tape Linnie."

My eyes darted to Maddy. Damian Hurst was by her side. Blood weighed down his thick curls, his eyes not visible through his fogged glasses. Maddy placed her hand on my other shoulder. Dark crescents loomed under her soulless eyes. "Fieldings always take care of their own. Family first—it's the golden rule."

CHAPTER TWENTY-FIVE

A New Beginning

I woke up to my phone ringing. I felt for it on my nightstand, my fingers clumsy with sleep. My body was on autopilot. "Hello," I said groggily into the receiver, not checking who it was before I swiped on.

"Sister, it's Maddy." She was breathing heavily, like she had just finished a jog.

"Maddy?" I sat up, my hands going to my face, worried it would slide off like Chamberlin's had in my dream. I patted it up and down, giving it firm smacks with my palm. Just smooth skin— no cut, no blood. I scented the air—no trace of metallic iron, no blood. My hands too were free of the red liquid that had haunted my dreams—no blood. Dreams . . . Was it all a dream?

"Sister, you need to come home. We've been keeping a secret from you, and I can't keep it any longer. It's about your father's death. I have to tell you in person. Will you come?"

My heart pounded in my chest like it was too small to contain it. This already happened. I say yes and I go to Brooklyn to meet her. There, Maddy tells me her father murdered mine. In response to the startling news, I dump half of my bottle of sleeping pills into her soda while she's in the bathroom. Then she dies, then Damian Hurst dies, then Elenore dies, then I die. It wasn't a dream—no, it wasn't that. It was a glimpse into my future. It was generations of Dunn women protecting me. Family first.

I drew a deep breath, steadying my nerves before I spoke. "I know your father tampered with the tension wire to the elevator. I know he's responsible for the death of my father and your mother. I know about their affair. I know you caught them in the act in your father's room and told your dad after Chamberlin swore you to secrecy."

"Elenore told you!" Maddy said, sounding very frustrated. "I can't believe after everything, she told you." Her tone took on a whine. "It's just like her to tell me not to tell you and then go and beat me to the punch. She's been so mean. She took all of the money my dad left me. I was hoping if I told you the truth you could help me with her. Maybe talk to her. I don't want to live there any longer. I want out and I want my fair share."

My blood boiled. I understood how I could have killed her. Every fiber in my body wanted me to wrap my hands around her neck and squeeze. Madelin Fielding was beyond selfish and self-absorbed; I wanted to pop her like a pimple and see blood. She didn't even attempt to apologize for the part she played in getting my father killed. If it weren't for my dream, I would've gone to Brooklyn, and she would have dropped a bomb on me, and I would have exploded, murdering her. But given this second chance, I would not let her turn me into a murderer. I was better than Frank Fielding.

"Maddy, let me give you some advice," I said into the phone through gritted teeth. "Look past the thick glasses and see the real Damian."

"You know about Damian? Chamberlin told you, didn't he?! He's lying. There were no videos."

I closed my eyes and exhaled like I was crossed legged on a yoga mat. Think happy thoughts. I will not let her get to me. I will not kill her. I evoked Dorothy Fielding's prayer in my heart. It worked for Chamberlin, it would work for me. Dear Lord, please keep me the angel I know I am in my heart. Do not let the sins of my family turn me into a murderer.

"Chamberlin's not a liar," I told her, my voice coming out steady. "You're lucky to have him. Try his friend X, I think he likes you enough to kill for you. That has to be worth something and he's good for business. I heard him and Allison are getting really close. You better not miss your chance. That kid's going to be a brain surgeon or something."

X deserved better than Maddy, but he had to figure that out on his own. I gave him a shout out—we were kin in blood, after all. We were one in the same. I wasn't sure if that would help his love life but figured it couldn't hurt.

"So does that mean you're not going to help me with Elenore?" Maddy asked, her voice hitching.

I hung up. Vinney was wrong; there's no getting anything through her thick skull. This required divine intervention, and since I was just the recipient of such an intervention, I would pay it forward. I would act as a true Fielding and put my family first.

"Who was that?" Kris asked, craning his neck to kiss my shoulder.

"My sister Maddy telling me her father murdered mine," I said as I scrolled through my contacts looking for Vinney's number.

"What?!" he said, sitting up. "Are you being serious?"

"Yep, sure am. She's trying to get money out of me so she can move."

Kris's British accent came out extra thick. "Do we need to call the authorities?"

I didn't answer.

He planted another kiss, this one on my cheek. "Well, my little Tangerine?"

Finally, Vinney's number. I knew I saved it just in case. I texted him: Hi Vinney, this is Sister Fielding. I just wanted to tip you off. Maddy's boyfriend Damian Hurst stole the gun from Mikey's and he's planning to shoot Chamberlin. Don't give up on Elenore, she loves you.

I texted Elenore: Vinney loves you. He doesn't care that you killed your father. You can trust him with the truth, he won't turn you in. He will protect you and the family. He's good for business. And by the way, I'm coming home for good. But I don't want to stay in Frank's room. I know what's behind the wall. I'll stay in the rec room. One of the stained-glass panels in the portico doors is about to fall out, have Chamberlin fix it before someone gets hurt.

I texted Chamberlin: I know the truth about my father and I'm okay. I love you and I always will, but we're not meant to be together. You love the idea of me from your boyhood, not me. Real love is right in front of you in Tilly Deedle. Open your eyes. Don't worry about her dad not liking you. Tell him how you want to add American history to the tour, and he will be eating out of the palm of your hand.

I shut my phone off and got out of bed.

"Where are you going?" Kris asked.

I pulled my suitcase out of the closet. "Home."

"Home. . . ? You *are* home, Tangerine."

"Home to Brooklyn. Sorry Kris, things are not going to work out between us. I already have a nickname and it's not Tangerine. I was only with you because, well, because you remind me of my brother."

"Oh," he said, pushing his blond hair out of his blue eyes, "that's creepy."

"Yeah, it is," I admitted with a shrug. "What'd you expect? I'm a Fielding."

The End . . .

Want more Holly Knightley stories?

Find your next favorite story on my Amazon page now!

THANKS FOR READING!

If this book helped you escape, if only for a moment, please consider taking the time to leave a review or star rating on Amazon and all other platforms you use. It would warm the cockles of my little, black heart to hear from you.

Follow me on social media (I'm on all platforms under Holly Knightley). Sign up for my newsletter for the latest news, glimpse into my wacky process, and receive the occasional freebie. Stay spooky, and happy reading!